UNBRIDLED

Praise for D. Jackson Leigh

Blades of Bluegrass

"Both lead characters, Britt and Teddy, were well developed and likeable. I also really enjoyed the supporting characters, like E.B., and the warm, familiar atmosphere the author managed to create at Story Hill Farm."—*Melina Bickard, Librarian, Waterloo Library (UK)*

Ordinary Is Perfect

"There's something incredibly charming about this small town romance, which features a vet with PTSD and a workaholic marketing guru as a fish out of water in the quiet town. But it's the details of this novel that make it shine."—*Pink Heart Society*

Take a Chance

"I really enjoyed the character dynamic with this book of two very strong independent women who aren't looking for love but fall for the one they already love...The chemistry and dynamic between these two is fantastic and becomes even more intense when their sexual desires take over."—*Les Rêveur*

Dragon Horse War

"Leigh writes with an emotion that she in turn gives to the characters, allowing us insight into their personalities and their very souls. Filled with fantastic imagery and the down-to-earth flaws that are sometimes the characters' greatest strengths, this first *Dragon Horse War* is a story not to be missed. The writing is flawless, the story, breath-taking—and this is only the beginning."—*Lambda Literary Review*

"The premise is original, the fantasy element is gripping but relevant to our times, the characters come to life, and the writing is phenomenal. It's the author's best work to date and I could not put it down."—*Melina Bickard, Librarian, Waterloo Library (UK)*

"Already an accomplished author of many romances, Leigh takes on fantasy and comes up aces...So, even if fantasy isn't quite your thing, you should give this a try. Leigh's backdrop is a world you already recognize with some slight differences, and the characters are marvelous. There's a villain, a love story, and…ah yes, 'thar be dragons.'"—*Out in Print: Queer Book Reviews*

Swelter

"I don't think there is a single book D. Jackson Leigh has written that I don't like…I recommend this book if you want a nice romance mixed with a little suspense."—*Kris Johnson, Texas Library Association*

"This book is a great mix of romance, action, angst, and emotional drama…The first half of the book focuses on the budding relationship between the two women, and the gradual revealing of secrets. The second half ramps up the action side of things…There were some good sexy scenes, and also an appropriate amount of angst and introspection by both women as feelings more than just the physical started to surface."—*Rainbow Book Reviews*

Call Me Softly

"*Call Me Softly* is a thrilling and enthralling novel of love, lies, intrigue, and Southern charm."—*Bibliophilic Book Blog*

Touch Me Gently

"D. Jackson Leigh understands the value of branding, and delivers more of the familiar and welcome story elements that set her novels apart from other authors in the romance genre."—*Rainbow Reader*

Every Second Counts

"Her prose is clean, lean, and mean—elegantly descriptive."—*Out in Print: Queer Book Reviews*

Riding Passion

"The sex was always hot and the relationships were realistic, each with their difficulties. The technical writing style was impeccable, ranging from poetic to more straightforward and simple. The entire anthology was a demonstration of Leigh's considerable abilities."—*2015 Rainbow Awards*

By the Author

Romance

Call Me Softly

Touch Me Gently

Hold Me Forever

Swelter

Take a Chance

Ordinary Is Perfect

Blades of Bluegrass

Unbridled

Cherokee Falls Series

Bareback

Long Shot

Every Second Counts

Dragon Horse War Trilogy

The Calling

Tracker and the Spy

Seer and the Shield

Short Story Collection

Riding Passion

UNBRIDLED

by

D. Jackson Leigh

2021

ISBN 13: 978-1-63555-847-0

This Trade Paperback Original Is Published By
Bold Strokes Books, Inc.
P.O. Box 249
Valley Falls, NY 12185

First Edition: July 2021

Credits
Editor: Shelley Thrasher
Production Design: Stacia Seaman
Cover Design by Tammy Seidick

Acknowledgments

When questioned about another record-breaking milestone in her career, Stanford University Hall of Fame women's basketball coach Tara VanDerveer quoted her late father, who said, "You don't win the Kentucky Derby on donkeys."

I'm always conscious that my success as an author rides on the Thoroughbreds that surround and support me.

Dr. Shelley Thrasher has edited all but the first of the fifteen books I've published with Bold Strokes Books, I completely trust her gentle but incisive edits. She has become my teacher, my coach, and my friend. Thanks, Shelley, for being understanding when I needed more time, and so patient with my first attempt at writing a full-length novel in first person.

Also, I have to give a shout out to my writing sister, VK Powell. She's my brainstorming buddy and my go-to person when I'm stuck and can't see where to take the story next. Best of all, she never flinches when I ask her to beta-read a manuscript in two days. I hope I do the same for her.

Finally, I'll be forever grateful to Radclyffe for going after her dream of establishing a publishing house for LGBTQIA writers, and to BSB senior editor Sandy Lowe for her incredible organizational skills and hard work that keep the herd of BSB authors on track. Bold Strokes is about improving our craft, telling great stories, and being a big supportive family.

I love all of you guys.

For all the sexy ladies still searching for someone they can trust with their most secret, whispered desires.

CHAPTER ONE

I'm sure everyone tells you this, but I love this book. My entire book club loved it." The twenty-something woman's slender shoulders move gracefully under a thin V-neck sweater as she bends forward to place a newly purchased hardback of my latest mystery novel on the table for me to sign. While some lesbians, like men, are attracted to breasts, I drool over well-formed shoulders. I don't have a specific preference for thin, broad, slender, or muscular. But something makes me want to rub my cheek along some collarbones, nip some earlobes, lick some necks, and bite the trapezius—the muscle that runs from the neck along the top of the shoulder—of some women.

"Thank you." I give her my warmest smile, not the polite one I'd presented to the hundred or so people before her. She nervously tucks a few silky, blond strands behind one ear as I hold her gaze captive. "I'm delighted you enjoyed it. Should I sign this copy to someone or just write my name? Some people only want my signature so they can resell the book later on an internet marketplace." Pen hovering over the page, I'm pleased that her face transforms into genuine shock.

"Oh, no. I would never sell a signed copy of your books." The young woman flushes pink. "I mean, I have it already on my eReader, but I also collect hardbacks of my favorite authors...especially if I'm able to get them autographed."

I tilt my head, lift one eyebrow, and give her my flirty smile—stolen from a flirty Brit who once seduced me and perfected in my bathroom mirror. "I'm one of your favorites, then?"

"Yes." As if realizing she's gone all fangirl on me, she drops her chin and shakes her head. "Yes, you're one of my favorite authors. I love mystery stories, but I enjoy yours more because you write strong women characters instead of handsome male characters who have women throwing themselves at them or crusty old guys who look at women like pieces of meat on a rotisserie. Plus, some of your clues are so small that I miss them until they're revealed later in the book. So, when my club reads a new book of yours, we all try to pick out clues and write them down as we read, then compare who found the most when we all finish."

A new marketing idea was already forming in my mind. For now, though, I'd just use that idea as a reason to write off the expense of an even better idea—her, me, wine, dinner, and maybe some after-dinner delight. "Well, that sounds like the kind of book club I'd like to visit, Ms..." I let the sentence dangle for her to complete.

"Anna. I'm Anna Pierson." She holds out her hand, and I lay my pen down to take it in mine. Her fingers are warm but not damp, as I expect, considering her initial nervousness. "And you can sign the book to me."

I give her hand a slight squeeze before releasing it to take up my pen again. I pause a long second, then scribble with a flourish.

> *Anna, it was so lovely to meet you. I'm hoping to uncover more mysteries with you. Have dinner with me tonight?*
> *Your favorite author,*
> *Lauren Everhart*

I'm about to hand the book back to Anna, open so she'll hopefully read what I've written, when the store clerk who is assigned to assist me begins to noisily remove the display of books from my table. I lean to one side to peer around Anna, surprised that the line behind her has moved to the register. I look at Anna, who shrugs and stares pointedly at the store clerk.

Keeping possession of Anna's book to ensure she won't leave, I squint at the clerk's name tag and clear my throat. "Uh, Justin, is it? I really could use that mug of Earl Grey, two teaspoons of honey, please, that I requested earlier."

He frowns. "I'm not sure we have any, and I'm afraid it's too late because we're closing the store."

Anna reaches for her book. "I should go before I get locked in."

I place it on the table, then hold up one finger for Anna to wait before turning back to Justin. "I'm sure you do have tea and honey, because it's in my contract. My agent, not to mention this store's owner, will be very upset if they find out you haven't honored that agreement."

Justin slaps his hands against his hips and rolls his eyes in typical juvenile fashion. "It's a mug of tea." He reaches for his wallet and digs out a fiver that he holds out to me. "Starbucks is to the left, two doors down. Please, have a venti tea on me."

My thumb is hitting speed dial as I stand up from my chair and tower at least three inches over him. I switch to speaker when the call connects and a disembodied woman's voice begins talking.

"Hey, I'm ten minutes away. You ready for dinner?"

I clear my dry throat again. I really am hoarse. "I'm hungry, but my throat's pretty dry and sore from selling books all afternoon. Justin doesn't think you have any tea and honey."

"What? That little…"

I quickly tap the phone to take it off speaker. I love the person behind that voice, but she suffers from potty mouth when she's angry, and Justin is turning pale. "Did I forget to mention that the store's owner, your aunt, and I are old friends?"

"I'll go get that tea for you." Justin darts past Anna and runs for the staff room at the back of the store.

I turn to Anna, who is covering a smile with her hand, and speak into the phone. "Sal, honey, calm down. Yes, I know he's your nephew. I'm sure you'll explain to him about contracts and consequences. Don't fire him. If you don't teach him to respect women and men equally, who will? He at least offered to pay when he told me to go next door to Starbucks to get my own tea." I immediately hold the phone away from my head so Sal's response won't scorch my ear. "See you in ten," I say, then end the call while Sal's diatribe is still at full volume. "Sorry. I just don't have much patience with arrogant males, especially those half my age. So, I couldn't resist having a little fun."

I sink back into my chair and notice Anna has retrieved her book. Her long-fingered hands with manicured nails clutch it to her chest. Mmm, mmm, mmm. I should tell Justin to stir a shot of Fireball in that tea instead of honey. Then maybe I can persuade Anna to put down that book and clutch me to her chest instead.

I'm about to ask if she read the inscription I wrote when a high cackle comes from the checkout counter at the front of the store, where an older lady is ringing out the day's sales. "LaSalle is going to take that boy to the woodshed for sure." Another cackle of laughter. "His face when her voice came from your phone...I thought he was going to wet his nappies. I think I *have* wet mine a little from laughing so hard."

Okay. That's more information than we need, but Anna's chuckling along with her. "I can't believe the little shit offered *you* money to go get your own tea. He's nobody, and you're best-selling author Lauren Everhart," she said.

Anna is a lot more relaxed than she was twenty minutes ago, but I need to make myself a little less godlike in her eyes if I want the evening to go forward as I hope. I want her naked skin against mine before the night ends, but only if she truly desires me. Not because of my minor fame.

"Best-selling is a term with a lot of qualifiers," I say. "It has little meaning if you're talking about Amazon, which is totally skewed by Amazon Unlimited. And it's measured differently depending if you're talking about the *New York Times* list or the *USA Today* list or *Publishers Weekly*. And you can't count just books sold, or else the best-sellers list would consist of nothing but the top-selling romances, because that genre sells way more than any other. But that's a long discussion for another time."

Justin appears with a tray that holds a steaming mug of tea, several napkins, a spoon, and a squeeze bottle of honey. "I stirred in two spoons of honey but brought the bottle in case you wanted more. Is there anything else?"

I look to Anna. "Are you in a hurry? Can you chat for a few minutes?"

An expression of delight illuminates her lovely features. Okay. She obviously hasn't read my question in the inscription. "Yes. I mean no." She shakes her head. "I'm not in a hurry, and I'd love to chat."

"Justin, can you find a chair for Anna?"

For a second, I think he's going to bow as he backs away, but he nods and trots back to the employees' break room.

"I love the chance to talk to readers to find out what in my books speaks to them. What compels them to like my characters and my stories." I pause when Justin reappears with a chair.

"Thank you," Anna says softly.

"I need to run the vacuum...so I'll be back there if you need anything else." He points to the very rear corner of the store.

"Thank you, Justin. That's a good idea," I say. "Because I'm very hungry, I'm going to run interference so Sal doesn't chew you to pieces right away and delay my dinner."

He nods. "Great. Thanks. I'm sorry. Really. I was an ass, Ms. Everhart."

"Yes, you were. Now go vacuum."

We watch him disappear and wave good night to the cashier with the confessed soggy underwear. Hopefully, she's wearing special panties to absorb those little accidents that plague women as they grow older.

"So, I'm interested in how many of your book-club members had the plot figured out before the end of my whodunit." I lay my forearms on the table to shorten the distance between us and lower my voice. Justin starts the vacuum cleaner, and she moves closer to hear me over the noise. Thank you, Justin. I have to make hay while I can because Sal will arrive at any minute.

Anna purses her lush lips, then wrinkles her nose. "Before we get into that, can I ask you something personal?"

Ah. She's feeling the attraction, too. I smile and nod. "You can ask me anything."

She points to my hands. "Do you have a problem with your right hand?"

I stare at her. I'm not expecting that question. "My hand?"

Uncertainty flashes across her face, and then her jaw sets and her shoulders straighten. "Yes. You're probably not aware of it, but you've been rubbing it off and on since you signed the book for me."

She's right. My face heats with embarrassment, and I sit back in my chair. I type all my research notes and my manuscripts. The only time I handwrite anything is when I sign books. This Raleigh store is my last tour stop, and I've signed nearly two hundred today. A hundred for people this afternoon, and a hundred this morning in my hotel room for Sal to shelve in her other two North Carolina stores after I go home. My hand is killing me, but I'm not about to confess sore joints to a woman likely ten years my junior. A woman I'm hoping will warm my sore hand later in the warm, wet heat of her sex while I bring her to a second and third climax.

I shrug. "Like most writers, I don't actually write much. I type everything—research notes, manuscripts, edits. I've been on this promotional tour for the past five weeks, signing hundreds of books three or four days each week. I guess I've been working a different set of muscles in my hand."

Her eyes widen. "Your agent must be a slave driver."

I laugh. "She is. But I also have a hard time saying no when one of the few remaining independent bookstores asks to be wedged into my schedule. I earn more on ebooks, but I hate to see the demise of neighborhood bookstores."

Anna's gaze drops to my hand again, and I realize I'm rubbing my left thumb into the palm of my sore right hand. I drop my hands to my lap, out of sight below the table where I've been signing books, and feign nonchalance. "My aunt owned a bookstore when I was a kid, and I loved spending the afternoon there among the boxes and shelves of books."

"That must have been wonderful. When I was in high school, I decided I wanted to be a librarian."

I smile and prop my elbow on the table to rest my chin in my left hand, giving her my full attention while leaving the distracting right hand out of sight. "So, that's what you do when you're not running a book club?"

Anna holds out her hands, cupping them together. "May I see your hand?" She is clearly asking for the hand I'm hiding. I hesitate at the shift in dynamic. I'm running this encounter. I initiated the flirt and set the pace. I will carry it to a pleasurable end, or maybe I'll stop it right now. I sit back in my chair.

An attractive blush creeps across her cheeks, and she relaxes her hands, palms up, and lowers her gaze to the table. "Sorry. I was only trying to answer your question. When I'm not in charge of a book club, I work as a physical therapist," she says, her glance darting up to mine . "I do a lot of work with hands and thought some light massage and pressure treatment could help. I apologize if I overstepped."

I relax but let her apology hang in the air for an uncomfortable minute, then lay my hand on the table—literally. "I would appreciate your expert assistance, but only if you answer yes to the inscription I wrote in your book."

Her smile is shy as her warm fingers gently probe my wrist, palm, and fingers. "I haven't read it yet."

I pick it up from the table where she laid it to take up my hand massage and open it to the inscription with my left hand, then push the book close enough for her to read. Her massage slows as she scrutinizes it and stops when she looks up. I hold her startled gaze.

"I...I...yes. I would love to have dinner with you, but isn't your friend expecting to eat with you?

I shrug, then grimace when she finds a partic"ularly sore tendon in my palm. She clamps down on a pressure point in my wrist that instantly numbs the spot as she continues to massage. I relax again and smile. "Let me worry about that."

At that moment, keys rattle in the front-door lock, and LaSalle de Blanc barrels in. She's a large woman—like a retired pro-football linebacker rather than buxom and curvy—with the soul of a poet and a mouth like the toilet on a dysentery ward. "Where is the goddamn little arrogant twerp? I don't care if I did promise my sister, this little motherfucker has to get over himself. I'm stuck with him all summer, but I can easily make him clean shitters and mow grass instead of learn the book business."

I reluctantly withdraw my hand from Anna's and catch LaSalle by the arm when she turns and homes in on the vacuum noise. "Hold up a minute, pal."

"Don't defend him, Lauren. You know how hard it is to get big-time authors to do signings in small bookstores. I'm lucky it was you, and not some other writer who'd post on social media the little shit's insulting offer to pay for you to get your own tea. It'd yank my stores from the A-list and put them on the blacklist of every publicist in the business."

I guide her to sit in my chair, and Anna stands up and pushes her chair over so I can sit facing LaSalle. Her fear is real. Independent bookstores are hanging on by a cobweb, trying to find new ways to draw customers away from the convenient internet and into their stores. "Listen, don't you think it'd be better if you took him to dinner and explained the impact his mistake could have had on your business if it hadn't been me?"

She scowls. "Dinner sounds like a reward. I'd rather give him a goddamn kick in the pants."

"He apparently has plans with friends. Keeping him from that to have dinner and a lecture from you will be punishment enough. And, hopefully, you'll stay calm enough to teach him something about the book business."

Her scowl deepens.

"You know he wants to be a writer. He'll need to understand the industry to be successful, whether he proves to be a great writer or works as a publisher or agent. Make this a teaching moment."

LaSalle blinks at me, and then she looks at Anna, who is nodding in agreement behind me. "Hello?" She stands because, while her personality is rough around the edges, LaSalle's innate chivalry will never let her sit while a lady stands.

I jump from my chair to make the introductions. "LaSalle, this is Anna Pierson. She's the organizer of a local mystery book club, and they've been reading my latest. She's agreed to accompany me to dinner so you can take care of your Justin problem."

LaSalle cuts me a "you dog" glance before politely taking Anna's hand in hers to give it a delicate shake. "That's so very nice of you, Ms. Pierson." Then her sweet tone turns sarcastic. "Lauren and I can catch up some other time." This isn't the first time since we became friends in our youth that one of us has blown off the other for the opportunity of female recreation—uh—company. But I have a bone to throw. A big, juicy bone.

"Lauren also is a physical therapist and just finished an amazing massage on my hand." I hold it up and flex the fingers. "So, I thought I could stay over another couple of days and sign some books at your Chapel Hill store. That'll give me time to talk to you about a fantastic marketing idea that came to me while Lauren was telling me about her book club."

LaSalle's eyes light up. "Check out of that airport hotel and stay at my house. Justin's living in the apartment over the garage, so he won't be in our hair."

"I'll do that first thing tomorrow. Tell Dorine I'll be there for lunch." I pause. "You haven't run her off, have you?" Dorine is LaSalle's longtime domestic manager who threatens to quit at least twice a month.

LaSalle slaps me on the shoulder. "As if. She'll be ecstatic to see you. Don't be late. You know she hates that."

I grab my leather messenger bag and guide Anna toward the door. "Don't worry. I'll be early."

Chapter Two

"I can't. Lauren, I can't."

"You can. Relax and just let it happen." I slick my fingers with lube to sooth the sensitive tissues of her overworked sex, raw from the continuous fucking I've been giving her for the past three hours with little respite.

"I want a chance to please you." Anna groans, and her sex tightens around my three fingers as I rake them across her G-spot each time I push into her and pull out to thrust again.

"You *are* pleasing me. You look so beautiful, giving yourself to me like this." I stare down at her long, perfect back and the muscles of her buttocks flexing as I rock her with each aggressive thrust of my hips against hers, my painfully turgid clit rubbing against her ass. I press the tip of my lubricated thumb against her puckered anus and bend to brush my hardened nipples against her back when she raises her head at this new intrusion. "Oh, baby, you feel so good, so tight around my fingers." I tighten my thighs to support my weight, glad now for the running habit that keeps my legs strong, then find her clit with my other hand. She hardens under my light massage, her breath coming in short pants now. She's near climax again, but mine is still elusive. Always just beyond reach unless...

"Give me your hand," I say, guiding her fingers to the spot that will make my clit explode and using them in my desperate quest for satisfaction. I rut against her with my whole body, our sweat-slicked skin sliding as easily as my fingers invading her, taking her again and again.

"Oh, Lauren. Oh, God. Oh." Anna shudders, then goes taut in the vise of orgasm.

Damn. I know this will be the last I'll be able to draw out of this poor young woman, and still I hang on the edge. I need my own release to cleanse, to purify myself of stress and frustration.

When Anna cries out and her cum pours onto my hand, I close my eyes. In my mind, I'm the one on my belly with a strong, long-fingered hand filling me from behind, thrusting in and out, in and out as it inches me up the mountain of pleasure. At last, I can feel the orgasm coalescing in my groin. My thrusts turn erratic because I'm frantic to hold on to the mounting sensation. Yes. Yes! I give voice to my ecstasy, claiming the victory. I stroke myself against Anna's hand, milking the spasms of pleasure and painting my cum on Anna's ass.

"Enough, please."

I'm done, too, and roll to my side at Anna's pleading. I fling an arm over my eyes. I hate the old, submissive Lauren. Finally stepping up and taking control of my life after years of therapy has freed me, then fueled my success in every other aspect of my life. So why do I still desire submission in my sex life?

❖

I stroll into LaSalle's mansion—er—home promptly at half past noon. Lunch is always at a respectable one o'clock. LaSalle would like to eat earlier, but Dorine—the de Blanc domestic manager descended from a family of executive housekeepers, or managers as they prefer to be called now—insists that noontime lunch is for secretaries and factory workers. So, as long as Dorine reigns in the de Blanc household, lunch is served promptly at one o'clock.

I sneak quietly into the luxurious chef-quality kitchen, intent on swiping one of the fabulous red-velvet cupcake bites from the platter on the island while Dorine is hunched over the sink, back turned to me and water running as she scrubs away at a broiling pan.

"Only one before lunch. You're not too big I can't still take a switch to you and that big moose that lives here."

LaSalle and I were convinced as children that Dorine has eyes in the back of her head. LaSalle's parents were always busy but great. My parents, not so much. Dorine doctored our scrapes, drove us to after-school activities or dentist appointments. She also had carte blanche to discipline us—from standing us in a corner, to house arrest, or even to cut a switch and apply it to our legs when we'd been deliberately bad. The switch was almost always wielded on LaSalle because she would boldly go where and do what no sensible child dared.

I grab a mini-cupcake and bend to kiss Dorine's weathered cheek. "Where is the big moose?"

She waves a soapy hand toward the French doors. "Outside, mixing mimosas and pretending she's lord of the manor."

I laugh and pop the moist red morsel into my mouth, savoring the cream-cheese icing. "Oh my God. This is so good." I wrap my arm around her shoulders and rest my head against her soft, tight curls. "Divorce William and marry me?"

She chuckles and dries her hands. "My answer is still no. I love William, and you lack a certain piece of anatomy that I have a fondness for." She wraps her arm around my waist and hugs me back. Her brown eyes soften when she steps back to inspect me. "You're looking good, baby girl. Getting out from under your daddy has let you blossom into a beautiful woman."

"Thanks, Dorine. It's been a long, hard road but worth every therapy session and every dollar of that trust fund I had to give up. God bless Grandmother for leaving me the means to buy my freedom."

"You would have eventually earned it on your own."

I think about that possibility for a fleeting second, then shrug. "Maybe not. It's my new editor who helped me grow the wings to really fly. She's the best."

Dorine flicks her hand towel at me. "Go on now, or LaSalle will be in here underfoot looking for you. I need to finish getting lunch together." She goes to the refrigerator, dismissing me like I'm still the kid she knew years ago. I smile and head for the veranda, snaking out a hand as I pass the kitchen island.

"I said only one before lunch." Her back still turned, Dorine's stern admonishment makes me snatch my hand back empty of the intended second cupcake.

"Damn." I swear under my breath.

"Language, missy. Don't make me pick a switch."

❖

LaSalle laughs and holds out a mimosa to me as Dorine's empty threat drifts through the French doors to the expansive veranda overlooking the manicured lawn bordering the neighborhood's golf course.

"Tried for that second cupcake, huh?"

I grin. "They are so good."

"She'll guard them like a pit bull until you do justice to whatever she's prepared for lunch. I keep telling her that I'm not six years old anymore and I can damn well eat all the cupcakes I want."

"And how's that working out for you?"

LaSalle adds more champagne to her own mimosa and shrugs. "She took her apron off and told me I could also bake my own cupcakes in the future because she was too old to work for an uppity woman-child."

"You can't boil water without catching the kitchen on fire."

Lasalle's grin is so wide I wonder how many mimosas she's consumed before my arrival. "I know, right? But I'm world-class at begging, so I dropped to one knee and held out her apron like a knight swearing her sword and loyalty." LaSalle slides from her chair onto one knee and lifts a linen napkin in reenactment of the moment. "Please, Ms. Dorine, I'll shatter if you leave and starve if left to my own cooking. There's no chef in the Southern states who can compare to you."

I laugh heartily at her antics. She should be on a stage somewhere, but Hollywood likes women skinny and pretty, rather than handsome and athletic like LaSalle. And I'm selfishly glad that her bad knees cut short her stint in the women's professional football league, and she created a new career from her second love—reading. That thought draws me back to my purpose for sharing lunch... other than to spend time with my closest friend. I drain the rest of my drink and hold out the empty glass for LaSalle to refill.

"So, my new friend last night gave me an idea I think will promote my books and your stores."

"Do tell." LaSalle raises an eyebrow as she hands over my freshened drink. "I'm interested in anything that will bring people into the store instead of have them shop online."

"Have you heard about these places where they lock a group of people in a room for an hour, and they have to look for clues and solve a mystery to unlock the door before their time is up?"

"Sure. We have a few of those around here. I've been meaning to get a group together and try one out. It sounds like fun."

"What if we work with one of those local businesses and set a series of scenes up in your stores? Each scene will have clues that solve an immediate mystery and contribute to solving a bigger mystery at the end of the series. We can run it locally but also set it up virtually. As the exercise progresses, readers will be asked to submit their ideas about the clues and extrapolate their suspicion of who-done-it. I can incorporate some of their ideas in my next novel, your stores will get a ton of publicity, and so will the local business we choose to help us set it up."

LaSalle's face lights up. "It's brilliant." Then her expression morphs into a grimace. "I can't imagine the ton of legal paperwork involved to make that happen."

"If I can get my publishing house to bite on it, they'll handle any contracts we need."

"How will we decide who gets to physically participate?"

"Hmm. How about we take applications from groups of three? They have to be avid mystery readers, not just anyone interested. Each group can email in their background and why they read mysteries.

We'll narrow it down to a group of finalists, then interview them to make sure they really are readers before we pick three top groups. Others can play along virtually."

LaSalle taps her fingers against the glass-topped table as she mulls this suggestion over. "Just to make it interesting, what if I contact our local cops and see if they want to put a fourth team together and test their skills against the mystery readers?"

"Excellent idea! Community involvement. And when the book is written, I can dedicate a portion of the proceeds to some worthy local cause."

LaSalle holds up her drink, inviting me to clink my glass against hers in an adult version of pinkie swear. "For the love of intrigue."

"For local bookstores," I respond. "Long may they survive."

LaSalle agrees with another clink of glasses as Dorine emerges with our lunch.

CHAPTER THREE

Marsh Langston paces in a small oval with the grace of a mountain puma, ringmaster to the circus of children trotting their ponies around her.

"Don't hunch over, Jillie. Straighten your back. Yes, like that. Robby, let up on the reins. You can't try to make him trot with your legs and tell him to stop with your hands."

I drink her in, the same as I have during all the lessons my niece has taken from her over the summer. She's wearing the same dusty, scuffed, knee-length brown riding boots—ruggedly elegant. No jeans today. Russet riding breeches hug her long, well-developed thighs and deliciously muscled ass like a second skin. My hands itch to close around her trim waist and draw her to me. Her short-sleeved green polo stretches tight across her broad yet slender shoulders and snug around sinewy biceps as she gestures instructions. Her blond hair, cut short to feather against her neck, is dark with perspiration below the ball cap that shields her head and face from the sun. I despair that dark sunglasses hide her azure eyes from me, then sigh at my dramatic thoughts.

The longer I watch, the greater the dampness between my thighs grows. I smile to myself. Observing these riding lessons—or rather the instructor—has become my favorite pastime of the break I'm taking between novels.

Okay. It's more like a block than a break.

My find-the-clues, solve-a-mystery idea caught on and burned through the mystery-intrigue literary world like a California wildfire. I've finally made a few best-seller lists with the book I wrote from the exercise, and even appeared several times on the daytime talk-show circuit. Now I'm at a loss for an idea to top that. Am I washed up already? Have I used up all my allotted creativity too early in life? Am I a flame-out at thirty-four?

My sister, Katelynn, knew I needed a distraction from the hole I was digging in my self-confidence when she called to ask if my niece, Amy, could stay with me for six weeks while she and her physician hubby went on a medical mission-slash-research trip this summer. I'd been at a loss. I do enjoy my niece's company. I'd just never had to entertain a ten-year-old for such a long period.

When I bemoaned the kid-duty to a friend over coffee the next day, her eyes lit up. I could enroll Amy to take riding lessons with her daughter, who's the same age. I later came to suspect she just needed someone to drive the girls to the lessons twice a week, but I instantly forgave her when I met the instructor.

Marsh Langston is worth every minute I sit in the sun, shaded only by the broad brim of my floppy straw hat, and fan away the heat. She is a bottle of sparkling water in my current desert, and I salivate over her.

I was aghast the first week when I wore light-blue cotton trousers that clearly showed the dampness between my thighs caused by imagining her tall, strong body against mine, her long, sure fingers touching me. Since then, I make sure to wear an absorbent panty-liner to keep my clothes clean, though my thoughts are increasingly filthy as I watch her move about the ring.

I bring my folding camp chair and stay for every lesson, despite the unrelenting sun and dust from the riding ring. Still, I've yet to make any headway with her. I've approached her several times, after my niece's lesson, with small talk. Marsh is polite and friendly enough, but distracted by the children asking questions as they unsaddle their lesson ponies and groom them for turnout. Still, I've glimpsed that hungry look in her eyes before they lose focus as though she's been looking past me all along. And I've felt her gaze burning down my back and lingering on my ass. Each time, it pebbles my skin and tightens my belly.

Today is Amy's final lesson and my last chance. I'm one of those women as comfortable in a dress as in hiking gear, so I've tried a variety of summer outfits over the weeks to see which draws the longest looks from her. I've decided she prefers sporty women—not too femme, but not too butch. So, today I settled on khaki shorts and a sleeveless oxford to display my well-toned limbs, and my favorite Nikes, the kind only serious runners wear. I'm also wearing my collar jauntily turned up—yes, I know that went out in the eighties, but I'm convinced the style will return—and my favorite floppy-brimmed hat for a more feminine flair.

When the lesson comes to an end, I stand and fold my chair. I lay awake most of last night, mustering my courage and practicing the right words. God, I haven't been this nervous over a woman since my college days. I pull my bandanna from my pocket and pat my neck and face dry of perspiration and wait. When she finally holds the gate for the last child to exit, I approach.

"Marsh, do you have a minute?"

She glances over her shoulder at me while closing the gate, then casually turns to face me. Her mouth curves into a faint smile. "Sure."

My heart stutters as she removes the dark shades to expose eyes more brilliant than a Montana sky. Fat beads of sweat gather where her sunglasses had molded to her high cheekbones, and she moves to wipe them against her shoulder. I automatically hold out my small bandanna. She stares at the sporty pattern and "On the Move" logo.

"To wipe your face and neck if you want," I say. "I run and bike, so I always have one with me. It's absorbent, like those towels they advertise to wipe your car dry. A friend owns the company that makes these for sports enthusiasts. They're lightweight enough to tie around your neck or fold up small enough to put in your pocket." I'm babbling and totally off course from what I've rehearsed, but she takes the offered cloth.

"Thanks," she says, wiping her face and neck. She looks at the cloth, examining its texture. "Nice."

"Keep it," I say. "I have a box of them." I want her to have something of mine.

"Thanks." She stares at me for a long moment and then smiles again. "You wanted to talk to me?"

"Oh, right." I flush with embarrassment, realizing she's waiting for me to speak while I stand there like a starstruck schoolgirl. I nervously pull my hat off and comb my shoulder-length hair back with my fingers. "Sorry. I think the heat's getting to me."

I'm being silly. I'm a successful novelist and still attractive in my middle thirties. How has she taken control of this interaction? I internally scold myself. Nobody controls me any longer. Not in my business life and not in my personal life. I lift my chin, square my shoulders, and plunge in.

"Today is Amy's last lesson. Her parents will be returning from their trip this weekend and taking her back to Raleigh."

"I'm sorry to hear that. Amy's been one of the best students in this class. She's a natural rider. I can recommend a good instructor in the Raleigh area if she wants to continue." She gestures to the barn. "I have the information in my office."

"That would be wonderful. This class is all Amy's talked about this summer. I'm sure she'd like to continue."

I'm a respectable five feet, eight inches tall and leggy, but Marsh still bests me by four or more inches. My confidence swells when I notice she's politely shortened her long stride to match mine as we walk to the sprawling stables.

A continuous traffic of adults, children, and horses fills the wide aisles of the T-shaped facility. My niece and her friend have their lesson ponies in line at the wash stalls, so I'm satisfied they'll be occupied for at least another thirty minutes. I step through the office door Marsh holds open, and she closes it behind her, shutting out the noisy chatter, occasional whinny, and the clop of hooves on hard-packed clay.

Light from a single window glints off the glass of a tall trophy case that takes up half of the opposite wall. Framed action photos of horses jumping obstacles or prancing through a dressage routine cover the other half. A blanket and pillow are bunched at the end of a large, worn sofa along the wall at my left, and a half-opened door on my right appears to lead to a private bathroom. The scarred hardwood floor is partially covered with a braided rug. The desk centered in the middle of the room and other sparse pieces of furniture are a bit battered, but clean. The room smells of wood polish, leather, and... fresh-cut hay? My eyes fall on a tight bale shoved against the wall near the door.

Marsh follows my gaze. "Oh, a new vendor brought that sample by yesterday." She sits at the desk and begins to rummage through a drawer.

"It smells wonderful in here," I say.

She looks up at me, as if she's really seeing me for the first time, and smiles. "I have to confess that's why I haven't already taken that bale to the feed room. I love the scent."

She holds my gaze a moment longer before returning to her task. I move to the back wall and peer at the photos. After a moment, I gasp. "Are all these photos of you?"

"Those are photos of champion horses I've ridden." She extracts a business card from the drawer and begins to copy the information from it onto a notepad. "I hired out as a professional rider until I got tired of the constant travel, so I just happen to be in those photos with the horses."

That also explains the trophy case. I'm amused to see the prime shelf is dedicated to trophies awarded to her by several local groups for her involvement in a therapeutic riding program, Special Olympics, and a program for disadvantaged youths.

"I've written the name of a former colleague who teaches in the Raleigh area now, along with the name of her riding stable, address, and phone." She holds out a slip of paper. "She has a program pretty much like the one here. They provide schooling horses, like we do, or will board a horse if your sister decides to lease one or buy one for Amy to ride. Jodie, my friend, could help them find the best horse within their budget if they want to do that."

I step close and take the paper, letting my fingers trail across her palm while I hold her gaze. "So, Jodie is a close friend?"

Marsh raises an inquiring eyebrow but doesn't answer. My confidence stutter-steps.

"I mean, well, you know her well enough that I can trust her with my niece's safety?"

"Amy will be safe with her. All the kids love Jodie and her husband, John."

"Then I'll trust your judgment. Thank you, Marsh. I'm indebted to you."

"It's no trouble," she says, her voice an octave lower than it was a moment ago.

"But I wanted to ask about something else," I say, also lowering my timbre.

"What else can I do for you?" she asks, those summer eyes turning to blue flame.

What else, indeed. Lock that door. Rip my clothes off. Thrust your tongue into my mouth, fill me with your fingers, and claim me right here on this sofa. I tamp down my lascivious thoughts.

"I'd like to take riding lessons."

"You?" She blinks, then turns away and removes her ball cap as she strides into the bathroom. She returns, rubbing a towel over her sweaty hair to dry it, but lingers near the doorway.

I frown, instantly hating this new distance she's put between us. "Am I too old?"

She drops her hands, her face no longer hidden by the towel. Damn. She's even sexier with her hair in complete disarray. "Of course not. We have two adult groups that meet twice a week—one morning group and one evening group. We also have one that meets once a week on Saturday mornings."

I close a bit of the distance and casually prop my rear against her desk. "I was hoping to arrange private lessons."

"Private lessons?" She sounds as though she's tasting the words rather than asking for confirmation.

"Yes," I say, almost cringing at the eagerness in my voice.

"I'll need to check the schedule," she says slowly.

I pick up the pen and notepad she used earlier and neatly print my name and phone number. "Call me when you do. My schedule is very flexible, and I'd like my first lesson to be very soon." I tear off the paper and fold it. Rather than leave it on the desk, I tuck it into her hand, giving it a lingering squeeze before I go to the door and pause. "Hope to hear from you soon."

❖

I'm deliciously breathless from a self-induced, Marsh-inspired orgasm when my cell phone chirps two days later.

"Hello."

"Is this Lauren?"

"Yes. Marsh?" I close my eyes and savor her smooth alto a million times sexier than I conjured in my fevered fantasy only moments before. God, I might come again just talking to her.

"I called to schedule the lessons you requested."

My fingers twitch where they still lie against my slick, tender clit. "I could come now." The sound of shuffling papers at her end of the line stops, and I suppress the impulse to giggle at my double entendre.

"I have some questions before you mount up the first time," she says. The paper-shuffling resumes.

I swallow a moan, instantly snatched back into my earlier fantasy. I'm bent over the desk in her office, and she's mounted me.

"Have you ridden before?"

"Once or twice." My clit swells, and my fingers stroke with renewed purpose. "It's been a very long time."

"I'll make sure to hit all the important basics in the first lesson, then."

I thrust my fingers into myself and imagine they are hers pounding into me, hitting all the pleasure spots that make me want to scream. In and out, in and out, then back to my clit.

"Of course. You're in charge. After all, you're the one with the riding crop." I make no effort to conceal the quickening of my breath. A few seconds of nothing but my breathing and her silence take over.

"Lauren?"

"Yes?" My voice is tight like my belly because I'm struggling now to hold back my impending orgasm.

"I wouldn't allow a crop during your first lessons. That's reserved for more advanced lessons. If you want private lessons from me, you'll have to do only what I tell you and exactly as I instruct."

I still my fingers, denying my climax. Somehow, I know we're talking about something different now. "I understand." I remove my hand from between my legs and blow out a breath.

"As long as we're clear."

"Perfectly." My breathing returns to normal.

"Good. Tomorrow morning? Eight o'clock?"

"I'll be there."

❖

I climb out of my Volvo SUV at eight o'clock the next morning, a bit sleepy-eyed despite my anticipation. I'm not a morning person, but if Marsh is, well, I can rise to the occasion.

The stable is already busy. Boarded horses are being turned out after a night's sleep and breakfast in their assigned stalls. Schooling horses are being led in to begin another day of work after spending their night in the freedom of large paddocks and open run-in sheds. I skid to a stop just in time to avoid a rake full of fresh manure tossed toward the cart parked in the middle of the wide corridor. A lanky teen sticks his head out and looks sheepish.

"Sorry, ma'am." He emerges from the stall and repositions the cart to just outside the stall he's mucking.

"I'm looking for Marsh. Have you seen her?"

"She was in her office at six this morning." He scowls. "I know because I overslept a little, and she had me in there chewing my ass." He forks another pile of manure and tosses it into the cart. "It's not like this shit's going anywhere if I'm thirty minutes late."

I smile. "Thank you. I'll check her office."

The door is partially open, and I can hear someone moving about inside. My heart pounds as I knock politely and push the door slowly open. Then my heart slows. A handsome man in jeans and a polo that stretches tight over his broad chest and thick biceps turns toward me. I've seen him around, teaching other classes.

"Hey, you must be Lauren."

I pause a beat, looking around the office and pointedly toward the open bathroom door. Something is amiss. "Yes. I'm scheduled for a private lesson with Marsh."

He rests his hip on the desk and regards me. "Marsh rarely gives private lessons anymore. When she does, she never takes on a beginner. She only instructs advanced students." His tone is gentle. "And occasionally an intermediate student she feels has real promise."

I narrow my eyes at his presumptuous assessment of my skills. "I'm sorry. Who are you?" I have verbally eviscerated many pompous critics of the popular fiction I write, so this horseman is hardly a challenge compared to those wordsmiths.

"I'm going to kill her," he mutters under his breath before he stands and holds out his hand. "I'm Alex."

I glare at him and ignore his attempt to defuse my building temper. I shove my hands into the pockets of the doe-colored riding tights I've carefully paired with a pastel-green polo shirt to entice Marsh.

"Okay." He withdraws his hand cautiously, as though I might lunge and bite it off. "I'll teach you the basics, caring for your horse and equipment, tacking up your horse correctly, ground handling, and then basic riding. Each lesson will last an hour. How many lessons it requires to master the skills depends on the speed of your progress."

I do not like being handled by this man. I was handled by my father, then by male teachers, agents, and publishers until I declared my sexual orientation and achieved enough wealth and following to tell those men to stuff their advice up their asses. Then I hired a cutthroat female agent and demanded a female editor. I will not settle now for anyone except the woman who's been riding my dreams for the past weeks.

"I'm sure you're capable, Alex, but there seems to be a misunderstanding. I arranged to have private lessons with Marsh Langston, not you."

"It's what I'd like you to do."

I freeze as Marsh's warm breath washes over my neck. She steps around me and holds my gaze. My resistance is melting with every second that ticks past. "But—"

"I thought we had an agreement. You would do exactly as I instruct."

Unless you're prepared to repay me for your four years at Wellesley and you live under my roof, you will do exactly as I tell you.

My father's words crack like a whip in my brain. Bastard. Nobody will ever control me again.

Marsh tilts her head, her expression curious. "I can recommend another excellent riding instructor if you aren't comfortable with my terms." She waits a few beats. "It's completely your choice, Lauren. I will never force you to do something you don't want."

I realize she's asking me—not telling me—to allow her control. No one has done that before—ask me for control. It feels strange. I waver.

"I was looking forward to working with you," I said, lowering my eyes and voice at the admission. I regret it immediately because my gaze falls on her breasts, and my mouth waters at the sight of her nipples straining against the thin fabric of her shirt.

She places one long finger under my chin and forces my eyes up again. Her mouth twitches with only a hint of a smile, but amusement shines clearly in her eyes. "You will. I can learn more about your potential by watching as Alex instructs you."

"You'll be watching?"

"Yes. I will."

I glance over at Alex, who has suddenly found something

interesting in the paperwork on the desk. I lean close to Marsh, lowering my voice to a whisper even though Alex is close enough to still hear. "I don't...I mean, I prefer women...teachers... exclusively."

She raises an eyebrow, but I straighten my shoulders and raise my own eyebrow in challenge. We both know I'm not talking about equestrian lessons, and I'm not going to let her pretend otherwise.

She bends to place her mouth inches from my ear and stage-whispers. "Alex is my brother's husband. He prefers male... students...exclusively." This explanation draws a wide smile from Alex, who continues to pretend interest in his paperwork.

A hot flush suffuses my neck, traveling up my cheeks. I clear my throat to recover my voice and a bit of my dignity. "And after I've covered the basics with him?"

Her blue eyes glitter like sapphire shards. "Then we'll see if you've shown enough potential to advance further with me."

Marsh shadowed my lessons for the next two weeks. Alex was a very knowledgeable instructor, and I'd even begun to enjoy his company. Sometimes, the lesson would be nearly over before I would feel her eyes on me. When I'd turn to glance her way, I'd find her propped against a tree, her eyes following my every move. The sight of her heated my skin as I tried to concentrate on my lesson and fueled my dreams later that night.

I raced through the groundwork, hanging around the stables after my lesson to watch others being schooled and picking up more tips. I pored over equestrian books and studied every piece of equipment in the tack room until I was nearly an expert on saddles, bridles, and bits, and how to put them on a horse. But I faltered once I was astride a mount.

As a runner and a biker, I've learned to find my rhythm and adjust my pace. An equestrian must find the horse's rhythm and adjust to the horse's pace. It was like helping someone learn to lead when you dance. I was never any good at either leading or following.

"Keep your hands steady. Don't saw the rein back and forth if you want her to keep a steady gait."

"She keeps speeding up. That's why I'm pulling back. Then she goes too slow, so I'm lifting my hands and giving her rein to speed up."

"Your legs have to say the same thing your hands are saying."

I drop the rein, which thankfully isn't a split rein so it doesn't fall to the ground, and throw my hands up. My mare—better trained than me—slows to a stop. "I can't sit her trot without gripping with my knees, and she takes that as a signal to speed up. It's an endless cycle."

This is hopeless. I should just invite Marsh to dinner and shamelessly throw myself at her. Maybe if I dance on the table naked, she'll sleep with me. The mare and I both hang our heads at my inadequacy.

"I've got this, Alex. Do me a favor and go check the feed shipment they're unloading to make sure Hurley's isn't shorting us again."

I venture a glance at Alex, but my shame is too great to face the disappointment I expect from Marsh. He gives me a wink of encouragement and a smile. "Sure, Marsh."

I await judgment as Alex's footsteps fade, and the clang of the riding ring gate closing breaks the silence between us. I'm bouncing between quitting and walking away with a tiny bit of my dignity and begging for her to let me try again. I don't expect her hand, warm around mine, lifting and measuring my fingers against hers.

"Do you write your novels longhand, or do you type?"

She knows about my books? I relax a tiny bit. "I type everything."

"Are you thinking of each letter as you type? Or even each word?" Her fingers entwine with mine and gently squeeze.

"Uh, no. I, uh, just think of the sentences, and my fingers find the right keys. I've been typing for so many years I don't really have to think about it."

"Riding will eventually become the same way. Like shifting gears in a car. When you first begin driving, you have to think about which gear to use, but soon it becomes second nature. You push the clutch, shift the gear, let off the clutch, and press the gas, all without thinking of each individual move."

"I can drive a stick shift." I look into her beautiful eyes and want to believe her. Wanting, however, won't make it so. "But I've never really mastered dancing with a partner." Maybe it's a left-brain, right-brain thing.

"You've never danced with me."

I fight the overwhelming urge to close my eyes and immerse myself in this new vision…my hand in hers, her other hand pressing against my back to draw me closer as we glide and twirl in a slow, sexy, graceful pattern. Then I ruin it by stepping on her foot.

She releases my hand and trails hers down my thigh. I remind myself to breathe. "You simply have to get your legs in rhythm with your hands."

Oh, God. My brain instantly jumps to a new vision—my legs hooked behind her thighs and flexing to sync her thrusts with my hands as they massage her breasts.

She strokes my thigh, stoking the fire building in my belly. I worry that I'm leaving a wet spot on the saddle as she steps back. "Dismount and bring your mare over to the gate."

I swing my leg over and pull my foot from the stirrup to drop to the ground. Neither of us comments on my wobbly legs as Marsh steadies me for a moment. I follow her to the gate, where she replaces my mare's saddle and pad with a woolen pad with stirrups attached. She gives me a leg up to remount, then leads Fancy to the fence and vaults easily from the middle board to settle behind me on the mare's broad back.

Heat races through me as Marsh presses her long frame against my back and rests her hands on my thighs. Her faint scent of leather oil and spice envelopes me. "Okay. Start her off at a walk, counter-clockwise."

I lift my hands and the mare walks forward. As we move with the motion of the mare's gait, Marsh's hips push closer until I'm almost sitting in her lap. Her long legs come up so that her thighs press along the outside of mine, and I shudder. Even though morning holds a preview of autumn's chill, perspiration trickles along my jaw and down my neck.

"Nudge her into a fast walk with your knees, but don't keep up the pressure, and don't move your hands." Marsh's thighs gently tap against mine, indicating how I should signal the mare.

Our pace picks up, and when I instinctively tighten my grip on the reins, Marsh's hands are immediately on mine. "Relax. Don't tighten up." Her breath is hot on my neck, her voice smooth in my ear.

I close my eyes and imagine another place. We aren't on horseback, but in her office.

"Again. Signal her to trot."

I'm naked. She's naked.

"Don't keep squeezing. Keep your legs open and relaxed. Rest your weight on your hip bones as you sit tall, straight up and down, but not stiff."

I straighten to sit tall and smile when my aching crotch finds the mare's hard backbone under the thin wool pad. Legs open. I visualize her reaching between them. Marsh's fingers bite into my thighs. "No. Stop moving your hips. A sitting trot requires discipline. Let your weight help you match the motion of the horse. That's better." Her grip loosens. We go all the way around, then slow to a walk and turn back in the opposite direction to do it again.

Thirty minutes later, the seat and thighs of my riding tights are soaked from horse sweat and arousal. So are Marsh's jeans. I'm weak from wanting her, and my stomach muscles ache from the extra half hour of sitting-trot exercise.

I groan as I slide to the ground, and my leg muscles scream at having to bear my weight. Marsh takes the reins from me.

"I'll take care of Fancy for you. I want you to go home and have a good, long soak in the tub."

I start to protest. It's my responsibility to water, groom, and turn out the horse I've ridden. Her raised finger stops me before I can speak.

"That's not a request."

"But…"

She moves her finger closer to my face. I close my mouth and nod.

"Good. I also want you to drink plenty of water and eat some protein. Eggs and meat. Stay away from carbs. You don't want to carb-load after exercise. Bodybuilders do that to make their muscles swell." I might as well be naked under her hungry gaze. "You're already perfect. Carb-loading will make you stiff. You need to be flexible for your lesson day after tomorrow."

She opens the gate and leads Fancy through it. I trail after them, already feeling stiff and looking forward to a good soak. "Will you be my instructor from now on?"

Marsh stops and turns back to me. "No. Alex still has to teach you to post a trot."

Good grief. I watch her disappear into the stable and then hobble to my Volvo. Maybe it isn't too late to invite her to dinner and dance naked on the table.

CHAPTER FOUR

A long soak and generous doses of ibuprofen don't save me from the agony of sore muscles when I mount for my second hour-long lesson of how to correctly post a trot.

"Forget the sitting trot," Alex said over and over. "Posting a trot is entirely different."

That isn't going to happen. Marsh is noticeably absent, her white truck missing from its usual spot near the equipment building. All I can think about is our last time together, her breasts pressing against my back, my ass against her crotch, and her hand flat along my quivering belly as she encourages me to sit tall and straight in the saddle. I squirm with the memory of my sex, swollen and wet, bumping hard against the ridge of Fancy's backbone with each beat of her trot.

"Not up and down. The motion of your hips should be forward."

But this feels so much better.

"It's a two-beat motion. Rise to the outside diagonal. Sit back on the second beat."

Alex watches me struggle a while longer, then waves me to the center of the ring. His expression is uncharacteristically stern. "Should we even continue this lesson?"

I stare down at him from Fancy's back. I should apologize, but I am sexually and mentally frustrated by Marsh's absence. "I think my thighs and stomach are still too sore."

"If you posted the trot correctly, your calves would be taking all the strain."

"What's an outside diagonal? I don't really understand what you want me to do."

"Because you obviously aren't listening to anything I'm telling you." He runs his fingers through his hair and stares across the field for a long moment. "Lauren, if a little pain is an issue, then Marsh won't be a good fit for you." He sucks in a deep breath and lets out a heavy sigh. "She was hoping—" He shakes his head.

"Alex?" He evidently knows something of Marsh's plans, her feelings.

"Forget I said that." He looks up again, his smile forced. "Let's call it a day, shall we? Take the weekend to recover, and we'll try again on Monday, same time." He turns toward the gate.

Maybe if I'm honest, he'll be more forthcoming. "Alex, wait." I dismount, forgetting the soreness in my legs, and jog after him. I grab his arm. "Okay. I am a little sore, but that's not the problem. I'm distracted because Marsh isn't here and all I can think about was the last lesson when she took over." I brush back a stray strand that's freed itself from my French braid. "Hell. I'm only taking these lessons because of her."

"You're not really interested in riding?"

I shrug, but heat crawls up my neck as the image forms in my head. I am, but not the equestrian kind. "I am. But, honestly, I'm more interested in her."

He studies me, his brow furrowing. "Why didn't you just ask her out?"

"It certainly would be easier, wouldn't it?" I hold his gaze. "But I want her respect. I don't want to be just a fling."

He hesitates before he speaks, and when he does, he seems cautious. "Marsh doesn't really date…not in the traditional sense."

"Good, because I really hate the dinner-and-a-movie thing."

His smile is slow and lights his eyes. "She's in Germany, looking at a stallion she might buy a share in. She should be back early next week, but she hasn't booked her flight yet."

My heart soars. I have a local book-signing engagement on

Saturday. That will help pass the weekend. "Monday morning. I promise you'll have my full attention. I'm going to get this right so I can show Marsh when she gets back.'"

❖

I stand and push my chair under the table, edging away from the middle-aged billboard for designer clothing who is chattering excitedly about my latest novel I've just autographed for her. All I want is a strong drink and quiet. I've been signing books for hours, and my hand aches. I wasn't prepared for the crowd waiting for me inside and the line snaking deep into the parking lot of the Barnes & Noble bookstore.

After nine increasingly successful mid-market novels, this book is a blockbuster hit. I'd thought it risky and almost didn't let my agent have it. Fuming over a malodorous reviewer who said he could only tolerate my bland characters because of my thrilling plots, I made this heroine a bisexual detective with dominatrix tendencies. I had no idea of the reception it would generate.

"I'm so glad you enjoyed it," I say again. I look helplessly at the store manager, who hovers nearby. She immediately takes the woman by the arm, steps in front of the table, and raises her voice.

"I want to thank everybody for coming today and Ms. Everhart for so patiently signing books way past the time she agreed to be here. For those of you who arrived too late, we have some copies that Ms. Everhart signed earlier at the cash register."

I smile and give a little wave as members of the crowd applaud, then race to the cash-register line. I bend to grab my ever-present messenger bag in hope of a quick exit, but one last book slides under my nose.

"You can sign one more, can't you?"

I rise slowly, pheromones instantly recharging my batteries, and dive into those pools of blue. "Marsh. I'm so glad you're back. Was your trip successful?"

"Yes. It was." She smiles, her gaze roving over my face. "I went to buy a share in a horse but ended up buying another stallion entirely. He'll ship to the States as soon as his paperwork clears. It was a better deal."

"Wonderful." I pick up the book. "You shouldn't have bought this. I'd have given you one if I knew you wanted to read it."

"Oh, I've already read your book. Alex bought it the day it released. I read his copy."

"But—"

She gestures to a tall boy standing at the end of one row of books, and he walks hesitantly forward. As he draws closer, I realize I'm not certain he's a boy at all. Nor am I certain he's a she.

"This is Jules Ransom, a fan of yours and a former student of mine. I sort of promised to use my influence to get your autograph to repay a favor."

"Of course." I smile at Jules, searching the clean facial lines and lean body angles for some clue. My writer brain is cataloging each nuance. I've found my next character.

"Thank you," Jules says, the voice also gender-ambiguous.

"I guess Marsh told you I'm taking lessons from her, too."

Jules glances at Marsh, who nods. "Yes, she did mention it." Amusement flickers in Jules's eyes. "She's mentioned it several times."

"You've got your book," Marsh said. "Off with you."

Jules smiles for the first time and holds up the book. "Thanks for the autograph. Can't wait to read it."

I shoulder my messenger bag, and we also head for the front of the store. It's still early, and I'm not ready to let Marsh go. She must be tired from the time change, but she's gone to the trouble of finding out when and where I was signing books, then flying back soon enough to catch me here. That realization erases the last of my fatigue. I'm about to ask her to have a drink with me when I step awkwardly off the curb and groan when it pulls at my sore muscles. Her hand is instantly around my arm, steadying me.

"Are you okay?"

"I'm fine." I feel foolish and clumsy. "I pulled something the other day and stepped wrong just now."

Marsh frowns. "Alex said he stopped your lesson yesterday because you were too sore."

"You know how men exaggerate." I wave my hand dismissively, hoping he hadn't told her what a pouty bitch I'd been. "I'm fine."

"Some hydrotherapy and a massage would help."

"I'm okay."

"I have a treatment room attached to my cottage."

"Treatment room?" My writer's imagination and my heart rate kick into overdrive.

"I got banged up a lot when I rode professionally, so I installed my own equipment." We stop at her truck, and she props her hip against it, resting her arm along its side.

"You did?" I turn to rest my shoulders against the truck, just below her arm, and look up at her with an expression I hope is playful and flirty.

"I'd had enough of doctors and therapists," Marsh said. "I know my body well enough to be aware of what I need."

I make a show of looking down her long frame and back up, practically licking my lips. "Do tell."

"Yes." She captures me, holding me prisoner with those eyes. Her words are low and husky. "I know what you need, too."

WARNING, WARNING. My fantasy of being a starship captain rolls through my head. *Raise shields, Commander Seven.*

I tear my gaze from hers and suck in a deep breath, hoping the flare of my nostrils doesn't give away that she's spoken my worst trigger phrase. Only she knows what her body needs, but I don't know what mine needs? I've worked hard to take charge of my life, to overcome the submissive Lauren emotionally neglected by my mother and verbally beaten down by my father. Her showing up today made me feel a small bit of control in what seems to be developing between us. Now I feel like I've stepped into a steel-jawed trap. Before I can lash out or chew my leg off in a panic to escape—figuratively, of course—she steps back from her slouch against the truck, easing out of my personal space.

"But I'm sure you've had a long day. Maybe you'd rather go

home to have a long soak." She takes another step back. "I can recommend several stretches after your bath." Then she stops, and her gaze reaches for me as sure as an outstretched hand. "I had hoped to share a special reserve Jägermeister I brought back with you. My brother Harrison and Alex have no taste for anything but beer." She tilts her head as though considering something. "I imagine your palate is quite refined."

She's walking backward toward the rear of her truck to circle around to the driver's side, and my defenses melt a little more with every step.

Marsh smiles. "I'll see you Monday." She turns away, and an altogether different panic engulfs me.

"Wait." I limp a few cautious steps, then stop. I don't trust myself to be within touching distance.

Marsh faces me again, a spark of...something...lighting her eyes before her expression morphs into a well-schooled question.

"I was..." I'm nearly choking on the rush of words trying to burst from my mouth, so I clear my throat and begin again. "Actually, before I performed that graceful stumble off the curb, I was about to ask if you'd like to have a drink with me so I can wind down." I'm beginning to feel more like the best-selling writer and less like the inept equestrian. "My go-to drink after a long day of talking and signing books is Fireball, so Jägermeister sounds perfect." To her credit, Marsh doesn't point out that I'm inappropriately comparing a sow's ear to a silk purse.

"And?"

A hesitant limp closer. She is a magnet that gently tugs at my iron will. "I think I pulled something in my groin." Her gaze drops to where my fingers play along the juncture of my hip and thigh, and my crotch heats. "I'm not sure what would be good for that type of injury."

Her cheek twitches, her eyes never leaving my hand as I massage closer to the apex of my thighs. "Should I try to stretch out or just massage? Should I use ice or heat?" God, I'm wet. I don't know who might break first.

"Do you trust that I *do* know what you need?" Her words feel like an invitation this time, not a trigger.

"I do," I say as her gaze moves up to hold mine.

We stare at each other for a long moment, and then she smiles and dips her chin in acceptance of my admission. "Then I'll see you at the farm. Follow the drive that goes past the stables and up the hillside. My cottage is the one on the right. Parking is in the rear. I rarely use the front entrance."

I nod without hesitation and limp backward a few steps. "I'm right behind you," I say, but she's already climbing into her truck. Pain shoots down my leg when I spin to jump in my Volvo and follow. Crap. I can hardly walk. And it sure as hell isn't because my leg is sore.

CHAPTER FIVE

Marsh's cottage is everything I've imagined—immaculate, leather and wood—and lots of things I hadn't—exquisite modern and abstract paintings that hint of sunsets, horses, and Southwest scenes. Her home is much larger than it appears from the outside. It's hardly a cottage. More like a chalet—larger and better appointed than a simple cottage. Built-in shelves run from the hardwood floor to the cathedral ceiling, and between pieces of pottery and wood carvings are books and more books. Possibly more than a thousand books.

She moves behind the bar of the open kitchen and brings out some glasses while I turn in a slow circle, taking in the space. She disappears into an adjacent room, and I glimpse her open suitcase on a large bed covered in a summer-weight down quilt of brown and green. The brief glance doesn't allow me to decipher the pattern of it. When she emerges with the bottle of Jäger in hand, I look up and pretend I'm taking in the exposed beams overhead.

"Your home is beautiful," I say.

"Thank you." She places two delicate cut-glass tumblers on the counter and pours a scant quarter inch of the dark liquor in each, then sets one on the bar next to where I stand. Figuring it to be mine, I take the drink and inhale its pungent aroma of licorice and spices while Marsh continues preparing two more drinks in two taller highball glasses.

"I didn't realize you were such an avid reader," I say. I scan the titles for some insight to this woman who has so fully captured my attention. And why has she?

One of the pitfalls of being a writer is that you constantly dissect life as you pass through it—people, phrases, facial expressions, situations, etcetera—and catalog them in your head or in a notebook like parts of a puzzle you'll piece together in a story later. Why I'm so drawn to Marsh, however, isn't something I'm ready to dig into yet. Much less something that will ever find its way into one of my books.

I mentally scold myself for drifting into my own head and refocus on the books. But I find few clues to my host because the titles range from mystery to classics to pulp fiction. I scan down the eye-level shelf, moving slowly, then nearly stumble when I spot several full shelves of books about sex—the history of sex, sex manuals, sex in literature, the psychology of sex, and erotica. Several of the books are obviously very old, while others appear new. Some of the erotica is lesbian and very current. I recognize a few of the titles, and heat flashes through me like I'm experiencing early menopause. God, what I'd give for something to fan myself with right now. Better yet, a walk-in freezer. I close my eyes and try to calm my runaway libido.

I don't have to see her. I can feel her moving behind me, almost touching me. The sweet breath on my neck is no longer a memory from the barn office. It's real, and I've been caught perusing her erotica titles. Without thinking, I toss back the glass of Jägermeister in my hand. Its blend of licorice and spices is smooth and warm on my tongue, then sharp and hot. My throat tightens around the burn, and my eyes water. My effort to suck in a cooling breath produces a series of weak "hic" without the "up." I cough, then wheeze a scant breath into my lungs.

"Jesus. You don't drink Jägermeister like Fireball." Her arms come around me, and her hands press against my upper abdomen. "Close your eyes and breathe through your nose."

I fight down my panic at not being able to draw a full breath and close my eyes to concentrate on Marsh's hands pressing just below my breasts.

"That's right. Your diaphragm has to relax."

I draw in a breath, but my chest tightens again when I realize I'm bent over with Marsh plastered against my back, her hips snug against mine as she loosens her arms and begins to gently massage my upper abdomen. My breathing hitches again, but it isn't because of my paralyzed diaphragm this time. I will her hands to drop lower. Damn. This woman is administering first aid, and I'm thinking about jumping her bones.

"You can't toss back Jäger Reserve unless you are conditioned for it," she says, releasing me and stepping back.

I realize she's already snatched the glass from me and placed the taller glass in my hand. Then she takes my other hand in hers. Her fingers are long and her hand cool from handling the ice she put in the taller glasses. I want to shove that hand down my pants where I burn from desire rather than liqueur.

"Sip that." Marsh touches the glass she's placed in my hand.

Still unable to speak, I shake my head. Another gasp of air and I croak out the necessary words. "No more."

One corner of her mouth twitches with what I interpret as a smile, or maybe a smirk she's holding back. Is she laughing at me? I want to be furious, but I can't. The rosy tint of her neck and perfect ears gives her away. Our inadvertent, rather intimate position has affected her, too.

"It's only ice water," she says, leading me to sit on the butter-soft leather sofa that faces the large fireplace.

I groan when I sit as my thighs protest rather loudly to my brain. I forgot about those horse-sore muscles.

"Okay. That's it. Let's get you into the treatment room."

"No-o-o. I just sat down. Don't make me stand up so soon." I offer my best pout to persuade her. "I'm comfortable here. Just for a few minutes."

She laughs, no longer holding back her amusement at my predicament...well, more antics than actual injury. "You'll stiffen up if you sit there."

"I have to sit here. I can't get up just yet." I tug at her hand, encouraging her to sit with me. I maybe—but refuse to admit—bat my lashes a few times.

Marsh's eyes narrow and her expression turns hungry, then stern. She kneels next to my knees, her face close to mine. "We agreed that you would do exactly as I instruct. Are you changing your mind about our arrangement?" Her breath smells sweet from Jägermeister, and her blue eyes drill into mine.

"No. I haven't changed my mind." I sway toward her. Another couple of inches and my lips will be on hers. I want so badly to taste them, to feel her tongue against mine.

"Good. Because I have a waiting list of students requesting private lessons with me."

Really? I thought we were connecting...silently admitting a mutual attraction, and she's getting all bossy on me again. I edge back. She's kneeling too close for me to stand without pushing her away, so I scoot to the side a bit and steel myself. If I stand quickly, it shouldn't hurt as much.

"Marsh!" Is that me squealing? I would never. Shriek maybe. Before I can gather my courage to stand, Marsh slips one arm under my knees and the other behind my back, easily lifting me as she stands. I instinctively loop my arms around her neck and forget my intent to leave. She is so strong.

Marsh carries me through a doorway opposite her bedroom. The therapy room is more like a sunroom adjacent to the deck that spans the rest of the home's backside. Three of the walls are glass. Late afternoon is giving way to dusk.

"Ingrid, attend."

Ingrid? Housekeeper? Girlfriend? Sex slave? A disembodied voice speaks in German, flowing over us from surround-sound speakers mounted in the corners of the room. I have a penchant for languages and speak Spanish, French, Italian, German, and a little Russian.

"Good evening, Marsh. What do you desire?"

Marsh replies in German. "Initiate privacy settings, and bring lights to eighty percent."

The glass walls turn opaque, while the interior lights embedded in the ceiling come on but stay dim. I open my mouth to demand Marsh put me down. I'm getting the hell out of here because I'm not into threesomes. Wait. I stop trying to wiggle out of her arms. I'm dizzy from ping-ponging back and forth between indignation and swoon. I steady my rattled brain and review Marsh's tone and words. *Initiate privacy settings.*

"Tell me that's a computer and not some Fräulein you have watching us from a security booth somewhere."

She raises an eyebrow and lowers my legs so I can regain my feet. "You speak German?" Her perfect German heats me in places already too warm.

"Ja." I reluctantly release my hold around her neck but don't step back. "I switched my major in college when I discovered I have an aptitude for languages"—I offer her my most cheeky smile—"and language professors." I sway toward her, and she doesn't move away. Our faces are inches apart, and her gaze drops to my lips. Yes. I want her to kiss me with that mouth that forms the Germanic guttural inflections so easily. "How about you?" She speaks English with a regional accent distinctive to parts of Virginia, so I doubt German is her native language.

Marsh steps back, her eyes shuttering, her expression going from hungry to…well, unreadable. "I have business interests in Germany." She points to the hot tub. "Twenty minutes of hydrotherapy." She points across the room to a padded table. "Then your massage."

I stare as she turns away and begins to program the controls of the hot tub. She obviously considers my question sufficiently answered. I open my mouth to ask, to say…what? My writer brain kicks in.

If character one said this, how would character two react? Okay. How do you want this scene to end? Both naked in the hot tub. What should character one say to restore their flirtation?

Marsh activates the program she's punched in, and my attention is drawn to the tub. I'm mesmerized by the roiling water that reflects my current mental machinations.

What kind of business interests? Horses? Or something else? Her reaction seems too intense for business. It must be something personal. Old girlfriend? An ex? Perhaps a tragic riding accident? Should character one say nothing at all and pretend she didn't notice character two's withdrawal?

"It's ready for you."

I am so far into my head, I'm startled by her low burr in my ear. I stammer a protest. "I don't have a bathing suit."

Her touch to my shoulder is light, her fingertips tracing down my arm to clasp my hand. She leads me to the teak bench beside the stairs to get into the tub. "You don't need a suit. You can leave your clothes on the bench."

I turn to face her. I don't have a problem with stripping to get in the whirlpool...not if she is, too. "Are you planning to join me?"

The blue of her eyes darkens, and hunger flashes across her face for an instant before she schools her expression into casual nonchalance again. "I'm going to get fresh towels and open a bottle of wine."

It isn't a direct answer but does sound promising. Still, I hesitate. Marsh hasn't moved. Is she waiting for me to undress? The idea thrills my submissive desires but challenges my hard-won sense of control. The two opposing emotions wrestle.

"Are you shy?"

"No." My answer is a bit louder, more emphatic than I intend.

Marsh moves back without taking her eyes from me. One step. Two steps, and then she stops. Her eyes say everything that hangs unspoken between us. She's going to watch. How very brazen. I can leave. Or...I can stay. My choice. I choose to toe off my shoes but demurely turn my back to release the button on my pants and slide the zipper down to step out of them.

I can feel her gaze like hands moving down my toned runner's legs and catch a glimpse over my shoulder of her flared nostrils and parted lips. I congratulate myself for being right.

Our heterosexual majority has conditioned women to believe that breasts are our greatest allure. But the weeks I've spent ringside during my niece's lessons have revealed, without fail, that my tennis shorts drew Marsh's glances like a horse to clover. Legs are her kryptonite.

I take my time folding my pants before unbuttoning my blouse, unhooking the front closure on my bra, and letting them both slide from my shoulders, almost to my hips. I'm angled away from her now so she can see my left breast in profile, but a peek confirms that her eyes are glued by anticipation to another part of my physique. The big reveal is still hidden by the long tail of my silk shirt. I mentally applaud my choice of underwear, especially since I had no idea Marsh would show up at the bookstore.

I thank the heavens for every mile I've run, then let the silk flow slowly, very slowly over the curve of my buttocks and black thong. No flat ass for me. Marsh's face is a stoic mask, but the flush that again reddens her neck and ears is her tell.

My sex throbs and slicks. I'm no longer sure who has the upper hand as we play out our scene. I bend to pick up my blouse and bra, then feign nonchalance as I face her to slowly lower my thong down my legs to step out of it and toss all the clothing carelessly onto the bench.

"You were going to open some wine?" I look from her to the door in an obvious but silent order for her to go do it.

Marsh doesn't move. "After I make sure you don't slip when you get into the hot tub." She moves to my side—closer than necessary—and holds out her hand to steady my foray into the steaming, swirling water. I accept her assistance, oddly turned on that she is fully clothed while I am completely naked. She waits until I settle. The water and the massaging jets feel wonderful. I intentionally moan as I sink into the liquid warmth, and Marsh's slow blink confirms the effect of my sensuous sound. The tub is spacious enough for four but equipped with only two seats. Each seat has a cushioned headrest. Perfect.

Marsh clears her throat. "Close your eyes and relax while I open the wine."

❖

I jerk awake. Damn. Disoriented for a moment, I tense and take in my unfamiliar surroundings, then relax when I see the glass of champagne and small plate of sushi on the ledge of the hot tub. That's right. Marsh, Jägermeister, the undressing game. It all floods back. But the water is still now. Maybe the jets cutting off woke me. The lights are down, and the soothing cadence of a classical string quartet plays softly through speakers I guess are hidden in the walls or ceiling.

Marsh is nowhere in sight. Maybe she put my plate down and went back to get one for herself. I stare at the sushi roll, realizing I haven't eaten since breakfast. I should wait for her, but I'm starving and pop a slice of the roll into my mouth. The savory flavors flow over my tongue.

My lecherous libido flashes an image of something else I'd like to put in my mouth. I hum, warmed at the thought. Where is she? I swallow the first bite and stuff a second into my mouth, then nearly choke on the champagne when movement in a far corner of the room draws my attention. I cough, then take a large swallow of the sparkling wine to wash down the rest of the food in my mouth.

The person hunched over a small desk looks up from a book they're reading. "You're awake. Good." They gesture to my food. "Go ahead and finish your snack. I'll get everything ready."

"Where's Marsh?" My tone is demanding, but damn it, I don't care. I'm naked, for God's sake, and this person is a stranger... mostly. When they face me to answer my question, I recognize the young, androgenous friend Marsh brought to the bookstore. I decide the person is, indeed, female. What's her name?

"One of the boarder horses is down with colic, and the vet thinks they should trailer him to a surgery center. Marsh has gone to talk to the vet, then call the horse's owner. She'll be tied up for a while, I'm afraid, so she asked me to stand in for her."

Stand in for her? What exactly does that mean? Have I come on so strong that she thinks I'll jump any woman? My appetite has fled, but I grab the bottle of champagne and refill my glass as I silently seethe. Granted, this young butch is extremely attractive. If I met her at an out-of-town book signing or a convention, I wouldn't hesitate to invite her to my hotel room and my bed. But I'm here for Marsh and incensed that she must think I'm so shallow any attractive woman will be sufficient. Fuck her. And fuck…what is her name?

The woman's phone pings while I work through my mental rant, and she picks it up. I drain my glass again and grab the large, thick towel Marsh must have left within reach. "Thanks, but I think I'll go."

Her thumbs dance over the face of her phone as she types a rapid answer to whatever she's received. I don't know how people do that. I still type on the tiny phone keyboards with one finger. She glances up at me when she finishes, then back to her phone when it pings again, presumably with an answer to her reply. I take advantage of her distraction and quickly climb out of the whirlpool to wrap the bath sheet around me. I gather my clothes and am about to ask for a bathroom where I can dress when she looks up and springs to her feet.

"No. Don't go."

"Where's the bathroom? I'd like to get dressed." I make no effort to hide my irritation.

She points to a door behind me and to my left. "Could you just wait a minute?" She starts toward me, but my glare stops her after a few steps. She holds her hands up, palms out in a placating gesture. Her dark bangs have fallen over one eye, and she sweeps them back. I absently note she has sort of an Elvis quality—long, dark eyelashes, smooth skin, and full lips. Her eyes, like Marsh's, remind me of blue jewels. Jules. Her name pops into my head. I meet so many people on book tours that I often use a crutch to remember names.

"Look. I think I know what you're thinking," she said. "I'm not a stand-in for whatever you have going with Marsh. She's not like that." She frowns. "I'm not like that."

Shit. Has she read my mind? I bite down on the automatic apology my Southern upbringing wants to offer.

"She said you need to work some soreness out before a lesson on Monday. In addition to hiring out as a rider, I happen to be a licensed, experienced masseuse. Marsh and I trade services. Wait. That's doesn't sound right, does it?" She chuckles. "What I mean is, she's my riding coach, and I pay her with massages and teach some beginner classes for her."

I'm sure my skepticism is evident, even as I take note of her well-muscled arms and shoulders. I can almost feel her hands working the muscles on my lower back. I shift my feet. The warmth of the whirlpool is fading, and my muscles are already tightening. She gestures toward a stainless-steel towel warmer. "I have stones warming. They'll feel really good."

I love hot-stone massages. I shift and wince. My thighs and calves are aching, and I can't blame Marsh for having an emergency at the barn. Still, I'm not ready to give up my peeve.

Jules's phone vibrates on the desk. She glances at the screen, then scoops it up and accepts the incoming call. "Hey…no, she says she's leaving. Okay." She takes a cautious step toward me and holds out the phone. "Marsh would like to speak with you."

I narrow my eyes as my writer brain analyzes the request. Not *Marsh wants to talk to you*, but *Marsh would like to speak with you*. The careful wording implies choice and consent. Is the word choice intentional? I put that possibility aside to ponder later and accept the phone. "Yes?"

Marsh's smooth voice fills my ear so completely that I can almost feel her breath on it, like before. "I'm sorry I had to leave, but Jules is as qualified to massage the soreness from your legs as I am."

I have a mental image of me lying on my back, eyes closed while Marsh's strong hands work their way up my calf, then the length of my thigh to where I need her desperately. I shift my stance again, this time to relieve the throbbing in my crotch. I turn my back to Jules, even though she's apparently pretending not to listen as she spreads warmed towels over the padded massage table. "I doubt that." A short silence follows my mumbled response.

"Lauren." Her voice drops an octave. "Monday's lesson will be a waste of my time, and your time, if you are too sore. You must do everything I ask if I'm going to invest my time with you. Let Jules help."

I start to put my fist on my hip and give her an earful Julia

Sugarbaker–style, but one hand is filled with my clothes I have yet to put on, and the other is holding the phone. Crap. I sigh. My deepest desire screams to give in to her, while my brain is yelling "oh, hell no" because nobody tells me what to do, and I need to puzzle out why Jules thinks I might see her as a sexual substitute since Marsh is now unavailable. Yellow caution lights blink all around that situation. "I don't know, Marsh."

"It's your choice, Lauren, but I'll be disappointed if you decide our agreement isn't what you want."

Our agreement. What exactly are we talking about? Private riding lessons? Things that sound dirty but aren't? Or what's happening between us outside the riding ring? There is something, isn't there? It can't be my imagination. Can it? My decision clicks into place like a domino laid. Do I want to keep playing when I'm not sure of the game?

"Lauren?" Her voice is honey, and I'm a fly willing to drown in it. I'll puzzle out the why and what we're doing later.

"My legs *are* sore."

Marsh correctly interprets my confession as concession. "Let Jules help, and then go home," she said. "No more alcohol. You need to hydrate those muscles, so drink plenty of water, take an anti-inflammatory, and stretch for about twenty minutes before getting into bed."

"Yes, Coach."

"Good."

I imagine her lips curling into a slight smile and shiver. "Should I come down to the barn before I leave?"

"No. We're loading the horse on a trailer now. I'm driving him to a veterinary surgery about ninety minutes from here and will probably stay overnight. The owner's out of the country this week."

I inwardly pout. I imagine stopping by the barn after my massage and finding Marsh standing on the edge of a pool of light coming from the poor patient's stall. I picture myself going to her and finally claiming, completing our earlier near kiss. Then Marsh sweeps me up into her arms and carries me into her office...

But I'm not going to see her again tonight. "Oh. Well, good luck. With the horse, I mean." I'm at a loss for what else to say. "I'll see you on Monday," Marsh says, ending the call and my fantasies for the evening.

I hand the phone back to Jules, who is leaning against the massage table, waiting for my decision. Hmm. Go home and sulk. Or climb onto that table draped in warm, thick towels and give my sore muscles over to Jules. I pour the last of the champagne into my glass, knock it back like a shot, and head for the massage table.

Chapter Six

No. You've had a break from writing for the past three months." My agent, Connie, shuffles some papers on her desk, mumbles something to someone offscreen, then makes a shooing motion. The woman is a multitasking queen.

I roll my eyes at her, hoping she sees me. I'm a drama queen, especially on these dreaded video conference calls. For some reason I feel like I'm on stage and need to talk louder and gesture more grandly.

"Flying all over the country to sign hundreds of books and getting up in the middle of the night to look awake and perky on all those early morning talk shows is not a break. It's more work than writing."

"Your readers are anticipating your next book, and they'll only wait so long before they'll forget your name and chase the next new author on the list."

Another window opens on my laptop screen. My editor, Edith, has joined our little meeting. Her mouth is moving, and she waves her reading glasses around as she talks, but we can't hear her.

"Unmute your mic," Connie shouts.

Edith and I both grimace at her volume.

"You don't have to yell," Edith says, her mic now unmuted. "I could hear you fine. You just couldn't hear me."

"Hi, Edith." I'm relieved she has joined in and distracted Connie from lecturing me—at least for a few minutes. I, rather my writing career, is ultimately the sole agenda item for today's video meeting.

"Hello, dear. How's everything?"

"Peachy. I know Connie works seven days a week, but why are you working on a Sunday?"

"Darling, I just got back from a four-day publishing conference in Miami. The beaches and ocean there are so amazing. I'm just trying to catch up a bit while I do laundry so tomorrow won't be so hectic when I go in to the office. Now, let's talk about you."

"I was telling Connie that I'm planning to take a break before I dive into another book."

"And I was telling her she needs to churn out another best seller right away," Connie says.

"You make it sound as easy as baking cookies. I can't throw a bunch of characters in a bowl, stir, and bake. Writing is a bit more complicated." My sarcasm isn't fair because Connie already knows this. It's also not swaying her to my cause. I need backup. "Tell her, Edith."

"I'm afraid I agree with Connie," Edith says. "Making the best-seller lists isn't the hardest part of being a successful writer. Writing the next book is the toughest thing you'll ever do."

Hearing that isn't helping my writer's block. "I sense a conspiracy. You two have been meeting in secret so you could gang up on me."

Edith has the good grace to look guilty, but Connie is unrepentant.

"Damn right, we have," Connie says. "Somebody needs to kick you in the butt. You've been back from your book tour for two months. Edith needs to get you on their publishing schedule, and I need to start arranging your next book tour."

"How can you book a tour when I haven't even written the book?" I know I'm being difficult. Planning your life so far in advance is the bane of being a writer. "What if I die before the book is finished? Accidents happen, you know."

"It's easier to cancel than to schedule late," Connie points out. "But you don't need me to say what you already know. What you do need is a kick in the butt to get you back to work." She slaps her hand down on her desk to punctuate her statement.

I sit back in my chair and cross my arms over my chest to glare at her.

"I know you, Lauren. You need to write like you need to breathe," Edith says, coaxing me. "What's hanging you up? Is there something we can do to help?"

This question makes me smile. Or I would smile if I wasn't pretending to be stubborn. Edith approaches life like she edits—cutting out unnecessary verbiage and digging down to the bones of the plot. Her question, though, is one I hoped wouldn't come up.

They both wait while I cover my face with my hands for a long minute. I finally mumble my answer into my fingers.

"What? We can't hear you." Connie's face fills her screen, as if she's leaning in to detect a whisper.

"Can you uncover your face and repeat that for us?" Edith, as usual, is precise in her instructions.

I obey like the child I'm being. "I said, I don't even have an idea for a book. I'm dry. Completely."

Connie stops shuffling papers and gives me her full attention. Edith rests her chin in her hand. They both stare at me. Their jobs are to fix, then sell my work. My job is to come up with story ideas, research, and write. I'm the cash cow lying down on the job.

"You always have ideas tucked away and usually complain that you wish you could work on more than one book at a time," Edith says. "Nothing in your idea file is sparking your imagination?"

I shrug, because I haven't read through the file. "I haven't had time, but I will. I need time to research some things."

Connie narrows her eyes. "What have you been doing for the past two months?"

Flashes of my many fantasies about Marsh fill my mind and heat my body. God, I hope the camera on my laptop isn't good enough to show my red cheeks and ears. I clear my throat. "I've been taking riding lessons."

"Riding lessons? Is that a euphemism for sex? Because I could understand that distraction."

Not yet, but I'm still working on that. I cut her off. "Horseback riding. It's great exercise but rather time-consuming, what with all the horse care that goes with it. Horses aren't like golf clubs you just toss into the trunk and forget about when you come off the course."

"What type of riding?" Edith asks.

"Horse riding." Connie's tone is incredulous. "Didn't you hear her?"

Edith makes a rude noise for Connie's benefit. "Are you intending to event a horse, join a hunt club, hang out at the racetracks, or just trail ride for pleasure? I took lessons when I was a child and competed in some local shows. It was great fun."

"I thought we were talking about work, not playing around." Connie is shuffling papers again and looking at her watch.

Edith ignores Connie's remark. "A lot of money and wealthy people are tied up in the horse business, and a lot of shady stuff goes on behind the scenes. It can be a great setting for a very intriguing novel, especially since this is Lauren's current interest."

She has a point, but my interest is focused on a certain riding instructor, not necessarily the business of equestrians. On the other hand, a little research into the business of horses could give me an excuse to see Marsh somewhere other than the stables. I could invite her to my house for dinner under the pretense of quizzing her about the show circuit.

"That's not bad," I say, warming to the idea. I nod to confirm my decision. "I think I'll do that. Give me a few weeks, and I'll give you a story summary."

"See? I knew you'd come through," Connie said. She looks at her watch again. "Gotta go, kids. I've got another conference call in five, and I need a bathroom and coffee before that." Her window blinks out before Edith and I have a chance to say good-bye. Typical of Connie, so we're used to it.

"Thanks for the suggestion, Edith. You're the best."

"That's why I get the best writers assigned to me." She smiles at our long-standing joke. "Good luck, and don't hesitate to call if you need to bounce ideas around."

"Will do. You take care."

"Always," she said. "Talk to you soon."

Her window blinks out, so I also hang up on the meeting. I stare out across the manicured lawn of my backyard to the mountains beyond. They're right about needing to get my next book out while my name and last book are still on the minds of the readers. The sun has shifted to glare off my screen, so I tuck my laptop under my arm and retreat indoors to start my research.

My research mostly turns up sex scandals—male trainers molesting and sexually assaulting young girls under their supervision. It's disgusting but unfortunately not unique to the equestrian world. While parents are constantly on guard against entrusting their daughter to a lesbian coach, they turn them over to male-predator coaches without precautions or second thought to their child's safety.

What would my upper-class parents have done if I'd been twelve years old, or even sixteen, and told them a successful male trainer had molested me? The thought sours my stomach, because deep down I believe my parents would side with him. They wouldn't want their friends to know their daughter was tainted by sexual assault, and they wouldn't rock their social boat by bringing charges against the offender.

So, no. No sex-scandal story written by me. I write mystery-slash-intrigue stories with strong women characters—women we all want to be, not the victims or human property that many women are.

My research isn't a total downer. I spend hours looking at and reading about hot female equestrians riding gorgeous, powerful horses. I consider writing something that involves wild horses and then am tempted to delve into the polo world. But I keep returning to the most elite among this elite sport—eventing. It's Olympic, extremely athletic jumping, cross-country jumping, and precision dressage, which is a sort of horse ballet. Combined, it's the truest test of equestrian skills and training. And it's what Marsh does. Hmm. I wonder…

I type "Marsh Langston" into my search engine, and a list of hits appears on my screen. Wow. I spend the next ninety minutes clicking on websites, drooling over photos, watching videos—mostly out-of-focus, amateur-filmed stuff—and reading about my sexy riding instructor.

She won a spot on the US Equestrian Team but missed the Olympic games because she was injured. Three years later, she was considered the top rider on the US team. Then nothing. About eight months before the 2016 games, she's no longer mentioned in any articles about the team. What happened?

I scour websites, try four different search engines, and subscribe to at least six equestrian publications to gain access to their archived stories. After some hesitation, I access my two subscriber services that search all public records, including police and court records, property, and business records.

According to her list of past addresses, she lived on the West Coast through her teens and most of her twenties. She made annual trips to Germany for about five years, staying several months each time, according to an interview she gave while on the US Equestrian Team. I sip coffee as I scan through the records data, then nearly spit it all over my laptop when the next page includes a criminal record. I grab my reading glasses I rarely use with my computer and squint to make sure I'm seeing the report clearly.

She was charged with drunk driving and underage drinking when she was eighteen. Eh. A youthful indiscretion. She also had a couple of traffic tickets, mostly speeding. But the year she disappeared from the equestrian-team news, she'd been charged with conspiracy to commit fraud, cruelty to animals, and destruction of private property in North Carolina. All three charges were later dismissed, but, like things posted on social media, they last forever on public records. Is that why she doesn't ride competitively anymore? Cruelty to animals? I just can't see it. Even the most cantankerous horse gentles under her hands. Barn cats lounge in her office, and Alex constantly complains that his terrier likes Marsh better than him.

So, what happened that year?

Chapter Seven

Monday dawns bright and cloudless. The early morning air is crisp even though the day is forecast to warm to a pleasant seventy-two degrees by afternoon. Autumn is right around the corner, and the weather people are predicting a colorful display as Virginia's hardwood forests transition for winter. I already see glimpses of bright red and yellow as I drive to my much-anticipated riding lesson with Marsh.

The rest of my internet searches the day before turned up nothing else, so I mentally gather all the questions in my head and tuck them away for later. Right now, all I want is to concentrate on my lesson so I can impress Marsh. Then I want to drag her someplace where we can be alone and kiss her until my lips are sore. I want to… I slam on the brakes of my Volvo SUV and whip the steering wheel sharply to the right, nearly taking the turn into Langston Farms on two wheels. God. I have to stop the sex daydreams. I park beside the huge oak where I sat most of the summer watching my niece take lessons. Or, rather, watching Marsh teach the lessons. The thought instantly conjures a vision of Marsh's ass in skin-tight riding breeches as she turns in circles to watch individual students. I grasp my crotch with my left hand and squeeze to discourage the throbbing in my sex.

I jump at the sharp rap on the hood of my vehicle. Alex, leading a schooling horse up from the pasture, peers at me through the windshield.

"You plan to sit in your car all morning? Fancy's waiting in her stall."

I unbuckle my seat belt and climb out of the SUV. "Is Marsh here?" I sound a bit too eager. "I was wondering if everything went okay Saturday…with the horse she had to take to a surgery center."

Alex nods but doesn't smile as we head to the barn. "Butter survived, but Marsh thinks the client needs to lease a different horse. It's his third colic, and each episode has been worse. He just isn't cut out for trailering all over the countryside to shows. Some horses aren't."

"That makes sense, doesn't it? I would think surgery will require several months of recuperation. They're going to miss the rest of the show season if the rider doesn't lease a different one."

"The rider is a fourteen-year-old girl, and she's gotten attached to Butter. She wants to buy him, but her father says if he buys Butter for her, then he won't be paying for a lease on another horse for her to show."

I remember being fourteen and filled with the confusing onslaught of puberty-induced hormones and emotions. I was also terrified of my father, who considered bullying an effective parenting tool.

"Is the girl any good as a rider?"

"Exceptional. Marsh says she could be Olympic material by the time she's eighteen if she stays focused."

Hmm. Rough spot for a teen. "Still, I'm sure it's hard to give up a horse you've come to love."

Alex shrugs. "The kid needs to toughen up, and her father needs to learn something about raising daughters. Marsh will work it out so everybody's happy. She almost always does."

Add diplomatic to her list of qualities—talented, sexy, commanding, devastatingly handsome, so sexy, and now this. Did I mention sexy? Because the word is screaming in my head as she walks Fancy toward where Alex and I are clipping his mount into the cross ties in the spacious corridor of the huge stables.

"Good morning," she says, clipping Fancy into another set of cross ties so she faces the horse Alex is saddling.

"Morning." Good God. If my voice gets any lower, I'll be purring. I clear my throat. "Alex is just catching me up on how everything turned out Saturday night. I understand the horse survived and will be fine."

"His show career is over, but he'll be okay."

Are we talking about a horse or about Marsh? I can't put my finger on what is different about her today, but her usual air of authority seems a bit deflated. Her eyes are a pale version of their normal brilliant blue. Still, she moves with the same fluid grace as she wordlessly begins saddling Fancy. Getting my horse ready for the lesson is my responsibility, but when I glance at Alex, he shakes his head and mouths *let her*. So, I do.

"You need to stretch," Marsh says.

"I'm good. I went for a short run early this morning before I showered, so I'm warmed up."

Marsh tightens the saddle's girth. "That was an instruction, not a request." She runs her fingers between the girth and the horse's barrel to make sure no skin is pinched. Her voice is calm for the horse's benefit, but the hard look she tosses at me carries a different message.

I snap my mouth shut on the retort forming in my head and step outside to use the hitching rail to perform my warm-up stretches.

I'm not sure what to make of her mood, and Alex appears similarly at a loss.

I watch them out of the corner of my eye while I stretch. Marsh seems to take extra care as she checks the fit of Fancy's bridle, feels along her legs for heat that would signal inflammation, then lifts each foot to double-check for anything like a rock or stick wedged in the metal shoe that could bruise Fancy's foot. I strain to hear the mumbled conversation between her and Alex, but without success. The sound that does carry is the distinctive ping of Marsh's phone. She takes it from her pocket and reads the screen, then heads toward me.

"Alex will get you started. I have to make a phone call or two, and then I'll be back to see how you're progressing."

I straighten, surprised she's delivered the message herself rather than just going in the office and leaving Alex to explain. Has our near encounter Saturday changed something between us? Maybe Marsh is having a weak moment. "Okay." My acknowledgment bounces off her back because she's already turned away and is striding toward the office.

Alex is watching her, too, his brow knitted. Then he unclips and leads his horse out into the sunshine. "Bring Fancy. We'll mount up here and ride to the training ring."

"Is Marsh okay, Alex? She looks tired and seems a bit, I don't know, off today."

"She's got to be tired. She stayed with Butter Saturday night, yesterday, and most of last night, I guess. When our alarm went off at four thirty this morning, we heard her truck pass our house on the way to hers." He shrugs. "Sometimes, she…" He stops, then shakes his head. "Marsh is very private. I shouldn't be talking about her."

Damn. He was about to give me some inside information, but I have to admire his restraint in keeping her confidences. Alex is a good guy, and I'm not going to goad him to say something he'd rather not. Besides, I want to discover everything about Marsh myself. I love the challenge of a good mystery, and Marsh Langston is the most intriguing puzzle I've ever encountered or dreamed up for a book.

❖

My lesson isn't very productive because I can think of nothing but Marsh, who doesn't reappear the entire hour I bounce around in the saddle. I'm convinced—and Fancy would have agreed if she could talk—there's no rhythm to be found between us. She waltzes smoothly around the riding ring while I tap-dance in the saddle. We both sigh in apparent relief when Alex calls a stop to it.

"Don't get discouraged," Alex says. "It'll kick in when you least expect it. You'll find that rhythm and wonder why it seemed so hard before."

I give him a skeptical look. He's ridden alongside me much of the lesson, trying to get me to match his movements as he demonstrates how to correctly post a trot. He can't deny my awkward efforts show no improvement.

To Alex's credit, he shrugs off my skepticism and laughs. "Really. It'll happen. You just need to relax and quit trying so hard." His phone chimes and he pulls it from his pocket, frowning as he reads the text. "God damn it."

"What's wrong?' I ask. I try not to gawk over his shoulder, but a glimpse before he begins typing a reply reveals the text is from Marsh. "Alex?"

He curses again under his breath as he types. Before he finishes his reply, Marsh strides out of the barn and toward her truck. At the same time, a Mercedes sedan emerges from the driveway and skids to a halt. A young teen throws open the passenger door and runs to Marsh.

"Ms. Langston, you've got to do something. Dad says the owner wants to put Butter down, and he can't do anything about it. You can't let them. You have to stop them."

The driver of the Mercedes gets out but props against the car's fender rather than approach. She looks young to be the mother of a fourteen-year-old and offers only a helpless shrug when Marsh glances her way. Maybe she's an older sister or a stepmother?

Marsh takes the girl by the shoulders and bends so they're eye to eye. "I just talked to your father, and I'm going back to the surgery right now to consult with the doctors. Then I'll call the owner. If I can do anything to save Butter, I will. I promise. But, Grace, you need to prepare yourself. He might be too sick, and we don't want him to suffer needlessly. *You* don't want that, do you?"

Grace shakes her head, but tears run down her cheeks. Marsh pulls a cloth from her pocket and offers it to her. I recognize the bandanna I gave her before, and despite the drama currently unfolding, I feel stupidly pleased Marsh not only kept it but has it in her pocket.

Grace wipes her face. She reminds me of a gangly colt, all legs and arms. Nevertheless, I can tell she's an athlete in the making. She's already tall for fourteen and moves with more coordination than a still-growing adolescent should. She stares at the ground, obviously trying hard to bring her emotions under control. "He's not going to be able to jump anymore, is he?"

"Maybe, but I think we need to face that Butter isn't cut out for going to shows every weekend. He tenses up and doesn't drink enough water. This is the third time, and the chance he won't survive increases with each colic. Even if he gets well this time, you're going to have to find another horse to show."

Grace's breath hitches, and she looks up at Marsh with watery eyes. "What will happen to him?"

Marsh surprises me by pulling Grace into a hug. "You let me worry about that, kiddo." She releases Grace and steps back but keeps her hands on the girl's shoulders. "Right now, I need to go to the surgery and decide the right thing to do. I'll call you after I've seen Butter and talked to the doctors, okay?"

Grace nods, then chokes out, "Tell him I love him."

"You bet." Marsh glances over to where Alex and I stand. "Alex is going to have to teach my classes today while I'm gone, so I bet he could use your help with the younger riders. He also has several horses that need exercising. Can you do that for me while I see about Butter?"

Marsh looks to the woman leaning against the car. The woman mouths *thank you* to Marsh and calls out to Grace. "You need to change your shoes if you're planning to stay. Aren't your boots still in the trunk?"

"I'll get them." Grace trots back to the car.

Alex hands his horse's reins to me and walks to Marsh. I'm not about to be left out of this, so I follow, horses in tow.

"You're dead on your feet," Alex insists, his voice low. "Have you slept at all in the past twenty-four hours?"

"I'll be fine," Marsh says.

"You push yourself too hard. You don't have to take care of the whole world, you know." Alex isn't backing down. "We can cancel the classes for today. I'll just turn all the horses out for exercise, and I'll bring them in tonight."

"Call Jules to see if she can help with a class or two. She was planning to train today anyway."

"Damn it, Marsh. Listen to me. If the owner has told the surgery to put the horse down, just let them do it. I know you don't want to hear it, but some things aren't up to you to control."

Marsh shoots him a look that would send any sane person running, but Alex stands his ground, glaring back. "I'm going to call Harrison. Maybe he can talk some sense into you."

"No." Marsh's answer is curt and final.

Fancy chooses that moment to head-butt me in the back, pushing me practically between the two as they quietly argue. She's probably impatient to be rid of her saddle and get some turnout time. Because, you know, she's a horse and couldn't possibly understand what's going on. Right?

"I can drive you," I offer. "You can catch a nap, and Alex won't have to worry about you falling asleep and running into a ditch somewhere."

Alex jumps at the offer. "You don't mind?"

"Maybe I mind." Marsh glares at Alex.

"Really, I have absolutely nothing else planned for today." I fish for a more convincing reason. "Besides, I'm thinking about making one of the main characters in my next book a veterinarian. I'd love to see the surgery and maybe talk to them about letting me come back another time and spend the day…you know, for research."

They both look at me for a long moment.

"Okay," Marsh finally says. "But you do exactly what I say when we get there. This trip may not have a happy ending."

"I know." Just the thought makes me want to cry. I'm empathetic that way. Sometimes I cry when I write emotional scenes, but I'm the only one who knows that. Well, Edith knows. But she's my editor. I square my shoulders. I can do this. For some reason, I need to do this for Marsh. And it isn't about getting in her pants, or her getting in mine.

"We'll take your car." Marsh makes it clear she's still calling the shots.

Chapter Eight

I bring my car to a gentle stop but leave the engine running. Afraid the absence of the motor's faint purr will wake Marsh, I want a moment or two to observe her.

She's propped against the passenger door, her face relaxed and long-fingered hands resting on her thighs. Her short hair is dark blond, naturally streaked an array of shades by her hours in the sun. At least, that's how I add up the clues. Amy's first riding lesson—the day I initially laid eyes on Marsh—was nearly three months ago. During that time, I've seen her stylishly messy hair cut long enough to hang over her sunglasses, short right after a trim, and longer again. But I've never seen any telltale dark roots of beauty-shopped color.

Her face is a geometric study in arcs and planes. Her darker eyebrows are elegant arcs ending near the curve of her perfect high cheekbones. Her jawline and chin are squarer than the feminine ideal but combine with that brow and those cheekbones for a striking visage. And those sky-blue eyes—currently hidden behind thick lashes—are breathtaking. At least they steal my breath. I have a sudden longing to see them.

"Marsh. We're here." I keep my voice soft so I don't startle her from the all-too-brief nap.

I expected it would take some convincing to get Marsh to rest, but she took the pillow I pushed into her hands without protest and tucked it between her head and the passenger door while I input the address of the animal surgery center into my GPS. She was out minutes after I pulled onto the highway. More than exhaustion, it's like she is so in command of everything that she simply told her body to sleep. And it did. Now she tells her body to wake, and I marvel as I watch her systems come back online.

I can discern the very moment my voice rouses her. She becomes absolutely motionless for a brief second while her brain goes from off to on. Her eyes don't open, her breathing doesn't change. Then her nostrils flare as she sucks in a deep breath. Her eyes spring open, clear and cognizant. No fluttering of the eyelashes. No yawn or stretch. No eye-rubbing. It's like a switch flipped. Asleep. Awake.

She clears her throat. "Are you sure you want to go inside?"

"Of course." I didn't drive ninety minutes to sit in the car. Okay. I drove ninety minutes to be here with Marsh. For Marsh. "I won't get in the way. I promise."

She opens her door. "Stick close, then."

The lobby feels like any other hospital lobby, except for the tile floor instead of sound-softening carpet. Several animal patients wait to be admitted while their human companions fill out the necessary paperwork. I follow Marsh to the reception desk, where four clerks are either registering someone, answering the phone, or digging through file folders. A young man finishes his phone conversation and looks our way.

"Can I help you?" he asks.

Marsh shakes her head and points to an older woman who is registering a middle-aged woman's cat. "I'll wait for Celia."

The woman, Celia, looks our way and gives a little wave. "I've got her paperwork right here. I'll just be a minute."

We step aside to let the young man help another client.

"If you'll wait right over there, someone will call you back in a few minutes. We're on schedule today, so it shouldn't be long," Celia dismisses the woman she just registered. She shakes her head as she waves us over. "Marsh. You look like hell." She holds up the folder that apparently is Butter's medical record.

Another woman appears, and Celia gives up her post. She apparently had been filling in during the other woman's break, because Celia's name tag identifies her as the operations manager. I note that it doesn't say chief of operations. A typical ploy to keep from paying what a man would earn in the same position. I mentally scoff. And a male COO wouldn't deign to work the front desk so the front-line employees could take a break.

"I'm pretty sure Dr. Michaels is still finishing up a surgery. I'll let his staff know you're here."

"I'd like to see Butter before I talk with him."

Celia purses her lips. "Okay. I've put the word out, but my contacts are already stretched thin. Nobody's in the position to take on a horse that's a medical liability. This latest recession has left too many healthy horses homeless because their owners can't afford to care for them any longer."

"Thank you," Marsh says. "I want to see where we stand before any decisions are made."

"Go on back. He's in C barn."

Celia swipes her security badge and lets us into a maze of hallways that Marsh navigates like she lives here.

I'm tempted to trail Marsh so I can stare at her butt, which looks great in those tight jeans. But many of the rooms we're passing have huge viewing windows so you can see into the operating rooms and laboratories. A dog is getting acupuncture in one room we pass. Another is laid out on an operating table while a surgeon works on his back leg. We take a left down another, wider hallway, and I nearly stumble when we pass a huge operating room where a horse is anesthetized and positioned on his back with his legs cuffed to chains that dangle from the ceiling, holding him in place. Sounds like BDSM but isn't.

"Do you have to come here often? They seem to know you." I've held back my questions as long as I can. "And you seem to know your way around."

"No." Her answer is terse, her lips drawn into a thin line.

Stupid, stupid, stupid. I'm thinking about her ass and making casual conversation while she's facing a decision that may break a fourteen-year-old's heart. I want to hang my head and slink back to the car. "I'm sorry." I keep my voice low, as if I might wake up an anesthetized patient if I speak too loudly. "I run off at the mouth in tense situations. I'll shut up."

Marsh doesn't answer but slides open a barn-type door at the end of the hallway and motions for me to go through first. A light touch to my back tells me I'm forgiven. I turn to catch her eye and acknowledge her unspoken message, but Marsh is already searching for Butter.

The stalls are concrete block on three sides and hard wire mesh on the side that fronts the barn's corridor. I think of those space movies where one side of a jail cell is just a force field so the jailer has a clear view of the captive. The empty stalls have concrete floors, with drains in the middle like a really big shower stall. Some have rubber mats covering the concrete. The occupied stalls have a thick layer of sawdust on top of the rubber mats.

Marsh lets out a short whistle, and an answering nicker farther down the corridor locates Butter for us.

A tall chestnut with a gorgeous head and ears that tip inward nickers again as Marsh approaches.

"Hey, old man. How's the gut feeling today?" She opens the door to the stall and steps in, holding it open for me to join them.

Butter searches her hands, then looks at me, as if evaluating whether I might be carrying one of those dreaded tubes they feed through a horse's nose to get to his stomach. I hold out mine, showing I have nothing in them, and he snuffles my fingers.

"So, you're feeling hungry?" Marsh coos to the horse in soothing tones. "That's a good sign. They told me you haven't been eating yet."

"He hasn't."

We both turn toward the voice behind us, where a man in rumpled scrubs stands. He reaches up to pull off a surgery cap that has *E. Michaels* embroidered across the front.

"Dr. Michaels." Marsh holds out her hand to him as he enters the stall. He shakes it and looks my way. "This is Lauren, one of my clients."

"Nice to meet you." I shake his offered hand and bite down on my tongue. A client? Is that what I am to her? Driving her here should at least rate a friend label. If the circumstances were different, I might have left her there to find her own way back to the stables. Butter seems to catch my change in mood and moves closer, snuffling my jeans, then lipping at my shirt. The big shit. It's hard to hang onto my dark cloud with his whiskers tickling my ear as he tries to nibble my hair. I scratch his withers to distract him.

"So, his prognosis?" Marsh isn't going to waste the doctor's time.

Doctor Michaels shakes his head. "He seems to be recovering fine, except that he isn't eating. We've given him electrolytes several times to make sure he doesn't dehydrate. But if he won't eat…" He smiles when he notices me fending off the inquisitive horse. "He does seem to be feeling better."

"He's a social eater," Marsh said. "He's used to being in a barn where he can see the horses in the stalls next to him. It might help if there was a horse across the aisle where he could see it."

"We can try that, but I think he's happy enough with the present company. Maybe we should keep her in the next stall."

I feel something scratching my arm and nearly fall when Butter, stalks of hay sticking out of his mouth as he munches, tries to rub his itchy head against my shoulder. Thank God. My brain had instantly screamed spider, and a scream would have come out of my mouth if it had been a leggy arachnid instead of hay stalks tickling my arm. It's not that I'm afraid of spiders, but the thought of one crawling on me makes me shiver.

"Hey, he's eating." I'm stupidly stating the obvious.

Marsh smiles, and I realize how much I want to see that expression on her face again and again. It's a rare occurrence, and I'd last seen it when I choked on the Jägermeister. No. That wasn't entirely correct. She smiles at the kids in her riding classes and at their parents when she talks with them. But this is a genuine one that lights her fantastic eyes. It's like the sun dawning. I'm so enthralled with it I almost miss what Dr. Michaels is saying.

"I wasn't sure surgery was a wise choice at his age, Marsh,"

Dr. Michaels said. "Especially given his history of colic. I guess he's proved me wrong."

"I'll talk to the owner about retiring him. I just haven't been able to get in touch with him yet."

"That would be best," Dr. Michaels says. "Give him another couple of days with us. If he continues to eat and produces manure, someone here will call you to come get him."

"Thanks, Doc." Marsh shakes his hand. "I appreciate everything."

❖

The silence stretches uncomfortably long as I drive us back to Langston Stables. Uncomfortable for me, at least. Marsh seems perfectly content with the silence. When I can't stand it any longer, I search for a conversation starter.

"So, if the owner retires Butter, will they take him from your stable?"

"Probably. Butter is no longer the eighty-thousand-dollar eventing horse he bought when his son was starting out in the sport. He has several months of healing, and then he could be a dressage horse for a beginner. But the guy who owns him is paying board and training fees on the horse his son is currently riding. I'm guessing he'll look for a buyer and sell Butter off cheap to someone who can wait months for him to heal and take the gamble that he won't colic again."

"It's a shame Grace can't get her dad to buy him for her. She really loves that horse, and I can see why. He's a sweetie."

Marsh stares out the window, her face mostly turned away from me. "Grace has the potential to ride at the top of the circuit. Her father showed on the amateur circuit until he went to law school and didn't have time for horses anymore. He knows that moving up in the sport means finding the next horse that can take you closer to the top tier. Butter is a second-tier horse that peaked at least six years ago. He was perfect for Grace to learn on and win some local ribbons with, but she'll need a better, younger horse to move up in the rankings. And I think, skills-wise, she's ready to do that in the junior competitions."

"What if she doesn't want to give Butter up?" I know it's silly to equate the two, but this sounds too much like dumping your girlfriend for the next hot woman who comes along. "What if keeping him is more important to her than winning trophies?"

"That's not her decision to make. She's a kid. Her father's the one footing the bill, and he knows what she needs to succeed. It's what I would recommend, too."

"That sucks." I knew I was scowling, but damn, it wasn't fair.

"That's how you make progress." Marsh's face was stone. "She'll get over him once she mounts a prime-eventer and feels what that kind of ride is like."

I grind my teeth to keep from screaming at her. How could she hold that crying child and comfort her, then conspire with the father to take her horse away. I was that kid, then that teen, and finally that young woman who was managed by the men in my life. I feel sick to my stomach. I want to save Grace from all the people who think they know what's best for her. But she isn't mine to save.

Stony silence prevails for the rest of our ride, and I don't turn the car off or get out when we arrive. Marsh doesn't move either.

"I'll see you Wednesday. You've learned all you can from Alex, so I'm taking over. Your morning lessons will switch to four in the afternoon from now on."

Just like that? She isn't asking. She's instructing without regard to the fact that equestrian lessons are not a priority in my life. I didn't like being told what to do. Too many people have done that most of my life.

"I'll check my calendar to see if I can come then." I stare straight ahead. I will not look at her. I will not look at her. But, damn, I can feel her studying me. Inexplicably, my eyes are drawn to hers by some magnetic force, some power she seems to have over me.

"I'd like you to come, Lauren. But the choice is yours." She gets out of the Volvo.

It's my choice, except that she seems to dictate what choices I have available. I don't care how sexy her ass looks as she walks into the barn without so much as a glance back or a "thanks for the ride." I feel like poor young Grace with other people making decisions for her. I have vowed that will never happen again.

Maybe I'll choose to not come back.

CHAPTER NINE

I don't need to look at the clock again because it will read 4:05, just like it showed four o'clock five minutes ago. Sleep is not going to happen. I'm wide awake after three hours of restless dozing. No matter. I don't have anything on my calendar for the day ahead, and since I live alone, I can prowl the house, work in my office, and nap the next day as I want. Nobody's here for me to disturb or to ask why I'm sleeping in the middle of the day.

Lying in bed and staring at the ceiling isn't productive, so I rise and throw on my worn, well-loved Pride T-shirt and baggy athletic shorts. Dressing shabby is another holdover from my rebellion against my father.

I flick on the coffee machine and roam through the house while it heats. The sprawling, two-story farmhouse situated on ten acres of expansive lawn and hardwood forest is my fortress against the world. I've spent a year personally supervising its renovation so it's exactly as I want. I contemplate taking a cup of coffee to my favorite rocking chair on the wide wraparound porch and watching the sun come up. But it might be a couple of hours before sunrise, and the dark outdoors doesn't call to me. My office door does. I need to work. Coffee first.

I nibble on buttery toast and sip my coffee while I scan the news headlines, then several "true" crime sites for ideas. My mind, however, keeps drifting back to Marsh. Damn her.

I change internet browsers to see if a search on her name will bring up anything my default browser doesn't. Bingo. Most results are the same, but the new search turns up an item in a gossip blog called *Paddock Talk*. I have to subscribe to get into their archives, but I'm finally having some success.

According to this blog entry, a gelding named Jakobi, owned and trained by Kate Parker and ridden by Marsh Langston, was favored to win an international competition at the Carolina Equestrian Park in North Carolina. Marsh and Jakobi had won the dressage and the cross-country phases, but on the morning of the final phase—show-jumping—Jakobi was found dead in his stall. The official necropsy deemed the cause of death was an overdose of selenium, the same thing that had killed twenty-one polo ponies in Wellington, Florida, several years before.

According to the blogger, Marsh normally rode for Margaret Talmadge, who also had a horse favored in the competition. Ms. Talmadge implicated Marsh in the crime, telling local law enforcement they had argued because Ms. Talmadge had ended a personal relationship with Marsh, who was desperate to get back in her favor—possibly desperate enough to poison Ms. Parker's horse to clear the way for Ms. Talmadge's horse to win. Marsh was arrested and jailed when a syringe and empty selenium vial were found in the pocket of her barn jacket.

Marsh was released after one night in jail when the district attorney announced he would not prosecute the charges, because no fingerprints—Marsh's or anyone else's—had been found on the vial. Several witnesses, the DA pointed out, testified that the jacket had been hanging in the tack room since the first day Marsh and Jakobi arrived, providing ample opportunity for anyone to slip the vial into the pocket and implicate Marsh. The rest was simply unproven accusations by Ms. Talmadge.

The blogger hints, however, something was kinky about the personal relationship between Marsh and Ms. Talmadge. Something more than the fact they are both women.

I shudder, but not in a bad way. More like intrigued and possibly turned on. *What are you really like in bed, Marsh Langston? And how deep into kink?* I'm not into pain, but the thought of a little role-play and light bondage wakes up my libido, which normally is averse to mornings. Stop. I do not need to go there. I still haven't decided if I want to go back for another lesson. I'm angry with her, my brain insists. My libido, however, isn't on board. What if sex with her is really hot? I don't know what appeals to me most—getting topped by her or maybe topping the top.

Stop. Right now. Work. I'm supposed to be working. Edith will be expecting some chapters to edit soon, but I don't even have an idea fleshed out. Or do I?

If I take a step back and ignore my personal interest—okay, infatuation—with Marsh, this cold case is the perfect grain of truth to turn into a pearl of best-selling fiction.

❖

Alex holds up a finger for me to wait, changes to another contact, and moves the phone to his ear. "Hey, where are you?" He listens, then curses under his breath. "I was hoping you were still at the house. Marsh has a migraine. It's bad. I know. I have no idea. Does she still have meds? Good. I'll just need to figure out how to get her to her house. A dozen kids are here waiting for their lesson." He listens for a bit. "No. I'll manage here at the barn." He looks at me, his ear still to the phone.

"Where's Marsh?" Contrary to my many, repetitively reviewed reasons of why I should stop my riding lessons and forget about Marsh, I have arrived for my four o'clock lesson on Wednesday as instructed...I mean, invited. But Alex is telling me that Marsh is sick. I flash back to how tired she looked the last time I saw her, how faded her eyes appeared.

Alex's frown softens, then relaxes into a smile. "Don't worry about it, babe. I have someone here I can enlist to help," he said into the phone. "Love you back, handsome." He ends the call and looks at me.

"What?" I don't mean to sound so demanding, but my impatience is getting the best of me. "Marsh is sick? Where is she?"

He puts his hands up, and I realize I've pretty much backed him up against his horse, who is patiently waiting to be unsaddled, hosed down, and turned out. "Down, Sherlock."

Did he just call me Sherlock?

He points to where a group of eight-to-twelve-year-olds are grooming and saddling horses. "Marsh needs me to handle her next class."

"Where is she? Is she all right?" I'm starting to sound like a continuous loop. Where is she? Where is she?

"She's in the barn office." He grabs my arm when I turn to go there. "Wait."

I want to stomp my foot like an impatient horse. I'm filled with an unreasonable sense of urgency to find her. Jesus, we haven't even had a real date, and I'm acting like...like...I don't know what. Like we are lovers. I force my emotions down and turn back to him. "What can I do to help?" I'm positive I was the one he mentioned on the phone as the intended help.

"Marsh occasionally suffers from debilitating migraines." He shakes his head, looking at his feet as he combs his fingers through his hair, his body language screaming frustration. "It's been a couple of years since she's had one. Not since..."

He clamps his mouth shut so abruptly the click of his teeth is audible. What did he almost say? He stares at his feet and shakes his head once, as if to reset.

"I have no idea what could have triggered this one, but it would have to happen when Harrison is tied up with a waiting room full of patients."

"Harrison?"

"Her brother, my husband. He's a doctor." He looks at me, clearly apologetic. "I'm sorry you drove all the way here, but do you mind if we put off your lesson for a couple of days? I'm going to have to teach her junior hunt group. You can't imagine the wailing if I tell them there's no class today...and that's just the mothers." He gestures to the group of women settling into lawn chairs under a nearby tree.

After six weeks of sitting on the edge of that group—close enough to be polite, but far away enough to avoid engaging much in their conversation—while my niece was in that class, I know too well how these women value their hour of idle gossip, adult conversation, or just sitting still to catch their breath from the rush of managing jobs, kids, husbands, and households. I can't much blame them.

"It's not a problem, Alex. We can reschedule. How can I help?" I ask the question again.

He looks toward the gaggle of noisy kids gradually migrating from the mounting area to the riding ring, then at the barn entrance. "I can teach this class and the one after it, but Marsh needs help getting up to her house." He wiggles his fingers as he waves his hand in front of his eyes. "She gets the blurry-vision thing, so she can't drive herself."

"I can do that." I know I sound overeager but don't care. I'm filled with an overwhelming need to protect and care for her. Weird. I'm a lousy nurse. The one time my niece Amy developed a fever while staying with me, I fed her ice cream. Something cold should help bring the fever down, right? Wrong. Milk and fever don't mix, and the kid promptly threw up in the middle of my living-room rug. I had to call my sister to come get her child. Katelynn also cleaned up the puke when I declared I was going to throw the expensive rug out and buy a new one because I was incapable of cleaning up the vomit without adding to it.

"Are you sure? She'll need help undressing and getting into bed." He scrunches up his nose and blushes. Alex is gay but not effeminate, and I almost laugh at his uncharacteristically cute expression. "Harrison always does that for his sister. Marsh isn't shy, but I am."

To my credit, I don't drool at the prospect of undressing Marsh. She's ill. This is serious. I offer Alex what I hope is a reassuring, not lecherous, smile. "Not to worry."

"Great." He glances at his watch. "Let me get the class started. That should clear the people and noise away from the barn. Harrison said he still keeps her meds up to date, even though she hasn't had one of these in a long time. She'll tell you what she needs, depending on how bad her head is."

I wave him off. "I've got this. I used to get migraines. I know what to do."

Once the students leave the barn, I park my car close to the entrance, get the super-dark wraparound sunglasses I saved from when I'd had Lasix surgery out of my glovebox, and go inside. I pull the huge barn doors closed on the back end, leave the entrance doors open just enough for a person to walk through, and make my way in the semidarkness to the door of the office. I tap very quietly on the door before opening it and sticking my head inside. "Marsh?"

A groan answers my quiet whisper.

My eyes are still adjusting to the dark room, but I don't see her anywhere. A gagging sound comes from the bathroom, where a tiny night light offers a bit of illumination. Another low groan. Missing-person mystery solved. I move quietly around the room, mostly from memory, collecting what I need—the small trash can next to the desk will make an excellent puke bucket for the back floorboard, her usual ball cap that hangs on a peg by the door, an ice pack from the refrigerator in the corner, and a bottle of water. Then I approach the small bathroom as quietly as possible.

"Marsh?"

"Go away." Her whisper is more of a plea than a demand, her breath coming in short pants.

I can see her outline slumped over the toilet and kneel next to her. "I told Alex I'd help you get to your house while he runs your class."

"Just leave me."

"Nope. Not going to. Give me your hand."

"I can't...I'm going to throw up." She groans but doesn't gag. "Please, go."

I ignore her, running my hand down her arm to grasp her hand. I pinch the pressure point between her thumb and index finger with one hand and gently place the cold pack on her nape. "I used to have killer migraines, so I can help."

We stay there for long minutes before her breathing slows and she sits back against the bathroom vanity. I release my acupressure pinch on her hand. Thank God. My legs are starting to cramp from squatting. I stand to get the blood circulating to my toes again.

"Thanks. That helped." I can barely hear her faint admission. "Do you think you can make it to my car? I parked right by the barn door. We should try to get you out of here before Alex finishes the class and the kids are swarming the barn again."

My eyes have adjusted to the dark enough to see her slow nod, so I offer my hand to help her. She ignores it and uses the vanity to lever herself up. I grab her hand and put the bottle of water in it, then flush the toilet for her. Another slight nod, and then she takes a minute to rinse out her mouth and drink some of the icy water. I hand over the dark glasses and ball cap. "I have some Vicodin in my pocket. But Alex said you have your own medicine at your house. Is there anything here you need to take with you?"

"Phone." She takes a few steps, then sways and grabs the bathroom door frame to steady herself. "On the desk."

I grab the phone, stuff it into my pocket, and return to pull her arm across my shoulders and wrap mine around her waist. Instead of the protest I expect, she leans heavily on me. "I've closed the barn doors, so it's pretty dark in the corridor, and I parked so you can get right into the back and lie down. The windows are tinted back there, but if the light is still too much, you can cover your eyes with my jacket that's on the seat."

I don't know if she's listening or how much she's absorbing through the pain. I do know I couldn't make decisions when I was in that kind of agony, so I grab the little trash can as a precaution and guide her out.

The slow trip up the rutted drive to her house is a series of groans, apologies for hitting potholes, and a gagging sound or two. I'm as relieved as she must be when I finally park at the back entrance to the house.

"The sun is bright today. Close your eyes and let me guide you inside." I speak as quietly as possible, and Marsh doesn't argue when I again slide under her arm to help her into the house.

"Bedroom," she mumbles.

Under any other circumstance, that instruction would have

thrilled me, but my libido for once is taking a back seat to an urgent need to relieve her suffering.

Inside the master suite, a queen-sized, four-poster bed covered with a luxurious Sherpa comforter sits to my right, and two doors are at the other end of the room. I figure one is the bathroom and the other a closet. I help her sit on the side of the bed where, judging from the book and water bottle on the bedside table, she normally sleeps, then kneel to tug her boots and socks off.

Marsh pulls the cap from her head, and her short-cropped hair sticks up in several directions. I want to reach up and smooth each roguish lock back into place. *Quit.* The woman is suffering. I can't see her eyes behind the dark glasses, but her face has gone from pale to chalk white. I grab a small trash bin that's nearby and push it into her lap just in time. Nothing's left in her stomach but bile. Strangely enough, I don't gag with her. I'm too consumed with concern.

"Where's your medicine?" God, I hope she can keep a pill down. She'll probably have to be unconscious before she'll let me administer a suppository. It's a little soon in our relationship for that sort of intimacy, no matter what the medical emergency.

Her head still bowed over the trash can, she pants out instructions. "Medicine cabinet. Syringe, top shelf. Already loaded."

I walk carefully on the balls of my feet to the indicated door so my riding boots don't clomp so loudly against the hardwood floor, then chide myself. The chance is slim she can hear me over her gagging into the trash can.

A bottle of pills and a pre-loaded syringe are, indeed, on the top shelf when I open the medicine cabinet. I search the drawers of the bathroom vanity and also find some alcohol wipes. It's been a while, but my college roommate during my sophomore year was diabetic and taught me how to give her insulin shots during my brief flirtation with pursuing a career in medicine. Turns out my flirtation had more to do with a girl in my chemistry class than an actual interest in medicine. More gagging and a groan come from the bedroom. *Focus, damn it.*

I soak a washcloth in cold water and hurry back to Marsh. Her gagging apparently is dry heaves—thank God—since the trash can is mostly empty. I gently take it from her and set it on the floor, then hand her the cold washcloth to mop her face. She shivers. This is as bad a migraine as I've ever witnessed. Her teeth begin to chatter with chills, which means she's beginning to run a fever.

Still wearing my dark glasses, Marsh turns her head toward me when I hold the syringe up and tap it to make sure there's no air bubble. She begins unbuckling her belt. "Hip," she says, her voice hoarse from throwing up. She hesitates. "Can you...do it?"

"Yes. I've given shots before." I catch myself before launching into an explanation. She isn't in any shape for conversation.

She puts a hand on my shoulder, and I steady her as she stands and pushes at her riding breeches. "Off," she says, her teeth clenched against the chills rolling through her body. She's still giving the orders even though she can hardly stand. I hold the shot at the ready while I use my free hand to peel the stretchy material down her long, leanly muscled legs. *Focus, Lauren. Stay focused.* Fuck. When I bend to free her feet from the breeches, I find myself eye level with the most perfect bare ass I've ever seen. She's wearing a thong. Just kill me now. At least that explains why her skin-hugging breeches never show panty lines.

Marsh turns and pulls the covers back on her bed, at the same time putting one glorious gluteus maximus perfectly in my strike zone.

"Brace yourself on the bed and hold still for two seconds," I say, tearing open the alcohol wipe with one hand and my teeth. I surprise myself at my lack of hesitation. It's been nearly twenty years since I've done this, but I administer the injection like a pro. Funny how a crisis helps you act without the usual burden of overthinking. Well, okay. Helps me act without my usual uncertain analyzing and projection of outcomes. I tear open another wipe with my teeth and swab the puncture mark again for good measure. "Done," I announce needlessly.

Marsh doesn't make a sound but turns slowly to sit and starts to lie down. I drop the spent syringe into the trash can and stop her.

"Let me take your shirt off so you'll be more comfortable."

She doesn't reply but lets me slip the cotton polo over her head, careful not to dislodge the dark glasses before I have a chance to close the blinds and darken the room. Shirt off, she eases down onto the bed. That answers my question about whether she wants her sports bra off, too.

I cover her quickly and hurry to darken the room, then gather a few things to make her more comfortable—an ice pack from the fridge in the therapy room, the Sherpa throw draped over the back of the sofa, and a thick hand towel from the bathroom. Marsh is lying on her back, still shivering. I add the Sherpa throw to the comforter covering her and gently trade the dark glasses for the towel to block out even the faint light seeping through the window blinds.

"I know you're cold, but this will help numb the pain," I whisper, tucking the ice pack under her head at the base of her skull. Then I stand by the bed, uncertain what to do. Marsh's bedroom decor is rather minimalist—a bed, bedside table, and chest of drawers. There's no chair for me to sit in and keep vigil, but I'm loath to leave.

Marsh's shivering has almost stopped, and her breathing slows and evens out. Whatever cocktail of medicine Harrison had loaded in that syringe is already working. I have no doubt it includes something for nausea, but I leave the small trash can next to the bed anyway.

I walk as softly as possible to the bedroom door. I could hang out in the living room in case she needs me. Maybe I'll find a book from her shelves to read. Damn. If I had my laptop, I could work on my book. That thought is barely finished when I find myself toeing off my boots and climbing onto the other side of the bed to gently lie down facing Marsh. She might need something. She is lying on her back. What if she starts throwing up again and is too drugged to turn to her side? I killed one of the characters in my first book by having them choke on their own vomit.

My writer's brain is mapping out possibilities when Marsh stirs. She draws her arm closest to me from under the covers, and I grasp her searching hand in case she doesn't know I'm still here. "What?" I whisper. What does she need? What does she want?

Her fingers curl around mine, squeeze, then relax without

releasing me. A soft sigh escapes from her lips, and after a few long moments, I hear a faint snore.

I draw the Sherpa throw over her exposed shoulder and arm, and then with fingers still entwined with hers, I close my eyes and relax, too.

❖

I wake, instantly alert, to the quiet murmur of voices and movement next to me. Marsh's hand is gone from mine, and a handsome man, his resemblance to Marsh unmistakable, is kneeling at her other side. This must be her brother, Harrison, the physician. He's inserting an IV into the bulging vein in her other arm.

I raise up on one elbow and mouth a "hello" to Harrison. He nods in return before speaking quietly to Marsh.

"I'm sure you're dehydrated from throwing up. These fluids will make you feel better. How's your nausea?" he asks as he draws up another syringe and lays it on the bedside table.

"Better." The strain in Marsh's faint, slurred response makes me wince.

He takes a penlight from the requisite black leather satchel at his feet. I didn't know doctors still carry those. "I need to check your pupils, but I'll be as quick as I can," he says, removing the hand towel covering her eyes.

Marsh squints and groans when he flicks the light over one, then the other, of her eyes. "Equal and responsive," he says, then reaches for the syringe on the bedside table.

"I gave her the injection that was in the medicine cabinet," I whisper to him.

He smiles. "Lauren, right?"

I nod.

"Thanks. I saw the empty in the bin." He gestures to the trash can. "That was mainly for her nausea and a little something to take the edge off the pain." He holds up the syringe in his hand and injects its contents into the port on the IV line. "This will put her out until the migraine subsides."

Marsh's hand that isn't hooked to the IV opens, palm up, and moves a few inches across the bed toward me. I immediately entwine my fingers with hers at the unspoken request and wonder what the gesture costs this proud and intensely independent woman. "Thanks." The whisper is so soft, it could have been a sigh. But I hear it. I feel it in the fingers that are squeezing mine. I open my mouth to assure her I've been in her place before and understand, but her hand relaxes, then goes limp as the medicine Harrison injected into the IV port takes hold. I don't care that he's watching. I give in to my impulse, swallow the assurances she won't hear, and instead stroke her now-slack face with the back of my fingers. I've never been so intrigued, so fascinated, so drawn to a woman before.

❖

"Surf and turf for Harrison, a ribeye for me, and for you..." Alex holds a Styrofoam meal container aloft. "Grilled salmon, sour-cream potatoes, and fresh broccoli."

I frown from my too-comfortable seat on Marsh's leather sofa. "I don't remember ordering dinner."

"Did I guess wrong?" he asks, puzzlement written all over his face.

"No. It sounds delicious." People ordering for me is a pet peeve, but I can see this is a sweet gesture from Alex, not a controlling one. Besides, I was with Marsh and not available to consult about menu items. "You didn't have to."

Harrison dismisses my protest with a wave of his hand. "Come on. I owe you for helping my sister." He sets out napkins and silverware for three at the L-shaped island that separates the kitchen from the living area.

"You don't owe me anything. Like I told Alex, I used to get migraines, so I know how painful they can be and what to do to cope with them."

Alex shoots Harrison an exasperated look. "Get some plates, Harrison. We are not going to eat out of the cartons like cavemen when we have company."

I chuckle. Alex's masculine demeanor around the barn becomes a little swishy in Harrison's presence. He smiles at me. "You saved my ass today."

"And I'm quite fond of that ass," Harrison says, giving Alex's butt a squeeze before obediently opening a cabinet and retrieving three plates. "Especially in those tight riding breeches."

Alex gives him a quick smooch for the compliment, then turns back to me. "I could have never concentrated on that kiddie class if I had to worry about Marsh blowing an aneurysm while puking her stomach up in the barn office."

"Thank you. I needed that picture in my head while I try to eat dinner." Harrison's chiding is warm with affection.

"Please, you see much worse than that every day, then wash your hands and eat a sandwich in your office."

I like Alex already, and it's hard not to like Harrison, since he looks almost like Marsh's twin. But I really like them now as a couple. I wonder how long they've been together because they're like a vaudeville act or an old married couple finishing each other's thoughts.

"Dinner is served," Harrison says, sweeping his arm in the air over the place settings.

The aroma of the food wafts my way, and I realize I'm really hungry. I rise and circle around a recliner but snag my toe on the edge of the area rug. I teeter for a long second, then grab the bookcase next to me to steady myself. I'm not normally clumsy, but I've felt off-balance since I first laid eyes on Marsh. The bookcase is tall and wobbles only a little as it bears my weight. Whew. I straighten, glad to avert a most embarrassing face-plant. My relief is short-lived. I watch in slow-motion horror as a silver tray—a trophy from one of Marsh's many wins—slides from its display on the middle shelf, bounces off the hardwood with a loud crack, and clangs against a metal floor lamp. My eyes instantly go to the closed bedroom door.

"She won't wake up until morning," Harrison said. "We could host a rave in here, and she wouldn't know it."

I watch the door anyway as I bend to retrieve the silver tray.

Alex beats me to it, snatching up the tray, turning it in his hands to inspect it.

"God, I hope I didn't hurt it. If it's scratched or dented, I'll pay to have it repaired."

Alex shakes his head. "I swear this thing could be used for armor. It can't possibly be even sterling silver. I personally think it's some kind of cast-iron alloy that just looks like silver."

"Does it matter?" Harrison pours iced tea into glasses. "Let's eat."

"It matters if it was passed off as valuable silver." Alex returns the tray to the shelf. "I can't tell you how many times it's slid off that shelf and still not a mark on it. I told Marsh to get a plate holder for it, but she still just props it up. I guess I'll have to get one for her. She's not very good with details unless it has something to do with horses."

I don't point out that the trophy is from a horse show.

"Don't bother her about it, Alex. She doesn't care about those trophies anymore." The sudden edge in Harrison's tone surprises me, and I log it in the mental notebook writers tend to keep in their heads.

Alex sighs loudly, making clear his exasperation with the unspoken of Marsh. "If she didn't care, her trophies wouldn't still be displayed all over her house and office."

I add a few exclamation points and a red underline to the mental note I've just made.

Harrison either doesn't hear Alex's mumbled response or chooses to ignore it. "Come on," he said. "The food's getting cold."

The salmon is delicious, and I hum my approval with the first bite, then dig into my meal while I listen to Alex and Harrison catch up on each other's day. I'm biding my time. The silver-tray trophy, ironically, is the door I've been looking to open and quiz the guys about Marsh's past.

I drain my glass of tea and get up to pour refills for all of us. "So, if Marsh won all these trophies riding, why doesn't she still compete?"

Alex and Harrison look up from their meals, then at each other. They need more prodding.

"I'm just a beginner, so it doesn't take much to impress me, but I've seen her ride. Why would she retire at what seems to be the peak of her career? She won a spot on the US Equestrian Team, for the second time, but she quit for no apparent reason less than a year before the Olympics."

Harrison stares at his plate while he chews his last bite of steak, but Alex puts his fork down and meets my eyes.

"Marsh likes you, Lauren. She's beautiful and confident and has never lacked for a bedmate when she wants it. But you're the first woman she's looked at twice." He shifts in his chair as if buying time to choose his words carefully. "You're the first she's looked at and *seen*. She seems strong, but she's so fragile."

"Alex."

He shrugs off Harrison's warning. "No, Harrison. I love your sister as much as you do, but sometimes she needs a little nudge. I know how private Marsh is. I'm not going to empty her panty drawer."

I almost laugh hysterically at his metaphor. Instead, I drop that one in my mental "save to use in a manuscript later" box and focus on what he's about to say next.

This time, Harrison is the one to heave an audible sigh. He stands and begins clearing our plates. "Coffee?" he asks.

"Please." I respond politely, glad he isn't going to shut Alex down. I refocus and return to our conversation before Harrison interrupted. "Then Marsh and I are on the same page." It was my turn to take care with what I said next. "Given my modest success as an author, I don't struggle for hookups either…when I want one. But Marsh isn't a one-night bedmate."

I look to Harrison, who makes quick work of the dishes and leans against the granite-topped counter, drying his hands. "At least I don't want her to be. Something about her makes me…" To my dismay, heat creeps up my neck and flushes my cheeks. "She makes me want…more." I stare down at my hands. How did my interrogation about Marsh become a confession from me? "But she won't let me in. Sometimes, I feel like I'm getting close, but then she backs away."

I raise my eyes to Alex-the-tell-all because Harrison is still silent and won't meet my gaze. "Has she always been this closed off? Or did some woman break her heart?"

Alex nearly growls. "Broke her heart? She goddamned betrayed her."

Harrison practically bounces up from his casual slouch and jumps back into the conversation. "That's Marsh's story to tell, not ours…if she ever wants to dig that up for you."

His tone and the loud silence that follows leave no doubt this conversation is over. Shame at prying into her life again scorches my cheeks. I feel like a scolded child. No. Harrison isn't my father, and I'm no longer that child. But I have willfully invaded her privacy for my gain—whether for a chance at something more with Marsh or for a pivotal chapter in my next book. My remorse comes from my own sense of guilt. I'm suddenly filled with the need to be near her.

"Maybe I should stay with her tonight to make sure she's okay."

Harrison shakes his head, but his expression and tone soften. "Thanks, but Alex and I have already planned to spend the night."

Alex stands and wraps one arm around my shoulders. "We spent a lot of nights here when her migraines used to be frequent. We still have pajamas in the chest of drawers in the guest room."

I eye him. "You guys wear pajamas?"

Alex throws his head back and laughs. "You are priceless. Isn't she, Harrison?"

Harrison chuckles. "A handful, I'll bet, for any woman who gets tangled up with her." He cocks his head as he meets my gaze. "Maybe just what my sister needs."

Drawing a modicum of confidence from his observation, I gesture toward Marsh's bedroom. "Okay if I just check on her before I leave?"

"Sure. Go ahead. I'm going to gather a few things from her therapy room to take that IV out with before we settle in for the night."

I leave the door ajar so the trickle of light lets me see my way to her bedside. I sit carefully on the bed next to her. She stirs at the movement, and I still until she settles again, then gently lay my hand on her forehead. It is damp with sweat but cool under my palm. I hope that means her temperature is back to normal. I give in to my need to kiss her lightly, a brush of my lips against her soft cheek, then her dry lips. The murmur of male voices tells me Harrison is ready to come remove her IV, so I stand. Unable to resist, I bend once more and touch my lips to her forehead. "Sweet, pain-free dreams, sweetheart. I'll see you soon." My next lesson is scheduled three days from now.

Her answer is a soft snore.

When I walk out of the bedroom, they're waiting, just as I expect. "The IV is almost empty," I say to Harrison. "Good timing."

Instead of replying, he nudges Alex. "Go ahead and tell her. I'm going to see to Marsh." He disappears into the bedroom, and Alex comes over to hook his arm in mine.

"I'll walk you to your car," he says, his tone light but serious.

When we reach my car, I turn to him. "What are you supposed to tell me?"

He clears his throat and looks everywhere around us, but not at me. I wait, unwilling to leave until he coughs up whatever is stuck in his throat. He finally meets my gaze.

"You shouldn't come around until your next lesson. Don't call, either. She'll be embarrassed that you saw her so vulnerable and probably withdraw a bit."

"She shouldn't—"

He puts up a hand to stop me. "I'm rooting for you to break through the walls she puts up, but you need to listen to me. Don't call or text over the next couple of days. And when you do see her at your next lesson, don't say anything about today unless she brings it up first."

"Alex, she'll think I don't care if I don't call tomorrow and check on her."

"I've known Marsh for a long time. Before I knew Harrison. She introduced us, but that's neither here nor there. What I mean to say is that I know her better than anyone except Harrison. She'll be embarrassed that you saw her so vulnerable and act like a grumpy old bear. If you call, she either won't answer or will say something to hurt your feelings so you'll back off. When you show up for your lesson, just act like nothing happened. Don't even open the door for her to push you away."

I mull this advice over. "Okay. I'll try."

"She's worth the trouble, Lauren. But you're going to need a lot of patience and a thick skin if you want to hang in long enough to get past her walls."

I nod, still processing his suggestion. "Okay." I narrow my eyes at him. "But you better be right."

"Trust me on this," he says, squeezing my shoulder.

I get in the Volvo but power the window down when he knocks on it. "Yes?"

He grins. "We wear pajamas only when we sleep over here."

TMI. I did not need that image in my head.

CHAPTER TEN

My heart leaps at the sight of Marsh looking strong and healthy as she encourages and instructs Grace in the dressage ring. It's been torture to not call or drop by to check on her—especially after I had to cancel my last lesson because of a last-minute change in the production schedule for my appearance on Oprah's book club. I've typed out *how are you* at least twenty times, then erased the text without sending. I sent texts to Alex a dozen times, to which he patiently answered *she's good as new* or *she's fine, don't contact her...I know you can do this* to each of my texts. But I need to see for myself.

In her compromised state, Marsh let me in a little. Marsh's offered hand, the small squeeze of my fingers, and the whispered *thanks* have played over and over in my daydreams...and night dreams. Those small gestures make my heart race and fuel a yearning that good sex never has. I can't even put a name to what I'm feeling, just that it's...more.

Marsh glances my way, and I wave, aware that a stupid smile is splitting my face and I'm helpless to tone it down.

She acknowledges me with an all-business nod. "Go ahead and saddle Fancy," she calls out. "We'll be done by the time you're ready."

Okay. Marsh is all business. She hasn't offered the smile I'd expected, hoped for. A smile that acknowledged something *more* had happened between us. But she's busy with a client. I can respect that. Business is business, after all.

Fancy whinnies when I near her stall, more for the apple I always bring than happiness that I'll spend the next hour bouncing around on her back, I'm sure.

Alex, his back to me, is prying a nameplate from the stall directly across from Fancy's.

"Alex?"

Spying the bud in his ear when he didn't respond, I arc a wave to get his attention.

He looks over his shoulder but keeps prying at the nameplate with a flathead screwdriver. "Hey." His smile is quick as he takes his phone from the back pocket of his jeans, pauses the app he's using, and removes his earbud. "I'm listening to the audio version of your latest book. I read last night until I couldn't hold my eyes open. This morning, Harrison announced that he'd downloaded the audio version onto my phone so I could finish it before he got home tonight." He rolls his eyes. "He apparently was offended last night when he wanted sex and I said only if he didn't mind me reading while he did what he needed."

I laugh, leading Fancy out of her stall and clipping her into the corridor's crossties. "Are you saying my book is better than sex?"

"Of course not, but I think he took it that way." He grins. "Anyway, I'm down to the last chapters—don't tell me how it ends. And I'll make it up to him tonight. Maybe I'll serve dinner wearing a French maid's apron and nothing else."

I cover my eyes as if he's wearing that now. "Yuck. I really didn't need that image in my head, Alex." Actually, it's tough to picture, given his current very masculine clothing. It's his day for teaching western-style riding classes, so he's decked out in his cowboy attire—jeans, Justin boots, a tight black T-shirt, and a well-worn Stetson hat. He's male-model handsome.

The nameplate pops free, and Alex checks the number of small nails in his hand to make sure he holds all that had attached the plate. Even the tiniest nail can puncture a foot and lame a horse. A weird sense of pride wells up that I know this from being around the barn over the past months. Thinking about this subject is also providing a good distraction. I'm uncharacteristically nervous about my lesson with Marsh. Crap. Now I'm thinking about her again.

Fancy shifts away because my brush along her sleek body has grown too vigorous as my nerves resurface.

"Sorry, girl." I drop the brushes in a bucket and turn my attention back to Alex, my distraction. He disappears into the tack room and returns with Fancy's saddle and bridle for me. "Thanks," I say.

Alex holds the saddle while I position the pad that will absorb her sweat.

"Whose nameplate were you taking down?" I don't really care. Horses come and go with their riders.

"Butter's," he says.

I whirl. "Oh, no. Did he…"

Alex hands me the saddle. "He's fine, but he was sold, and the new owner picked him up from the veterinary hospital."

"I thought he was coming back here. Does Marsh know who bought him?" I'd bonded with him during that short visit at the hospital and had talked myself into believing he'd started eating because he liked me. I'd even thought about trying to buy him once he returned to the barn.

Alex shrugs. "I don't know. She hasn't said much about it." He glances at his watch. "You better get out there. It's almost time for your lesson, and you know Marsh is a stickler for punctuality."

I wordlessly unclip Fancy from the crossties, and she obediently takes the bit in her mouth and lowers her head so I can slip the bridle over her ears. My heart is pounding again, and I pray that I don't swoon or faint or, more likely, say something stupid. The questions I want to ask are in my throat. How's she feeling? Did Butter go to a good home? But I swallow them and lead Fancy into the sunlight and toward the smaller of the oval rings, where my lessons are held.

Grace is mounted on an elegant, sixteen-hand-tall bay mare, and Marsh is walking next to them as they approach. Grace's smile is beaming, her eyes alight.

"She's a dream, Marsh. Her flying changes are so smooth."

Marsh smiles up at her. "I knew she'd be a good fit for you. But you still need to practice a lot to learn each other's signals. I'm seeing hesitation at some changes, and you need to work on your corners." She pats the horse on her shoulder. "If you work hard, I think you'll be ready for the next level by the spring tests."

"Awesome."

I can't help but smile at Grace's excitement, even though I'm put off by how easily she's left Butter behind for this new horse.

"Now, go give her a warm bath and a good rubdown," Marsh says, stopping near me and lightly slapping the mare on the rump to send them on their way.

I can't contain myself any longer. "Ready for me?"

Marsh keeps her eyes on Grace and her new horse a few seconds longer, I suspect to mentally adjust from teaching a promising young equestrian to spending the next hour with a middle-aged novice. But, with a nod and final look, she comes over.

"Has your post gotten any better?"

I put my left knee in her cupped hands, and she boosts me into the saddle. "Nope," I say happily. "I need lots more instruction."

She looks at the ground and shakes her head, but not before I see a small smile twitch the corners of her mouth. "Then we better get to work."

An hour later, I'm sweaty, Fancy is sweaty, and Marsh is still shaking her head.

"You post like a piston in an engine," she says. "Posting a trot is a dance that the horse leads." Marsh holds the gate open so I can exit the ring. "I thought all debutantes had to take ballroom-dancing classes, but you either skipped out or were a disaster."

"I was not a debutante." I put every ounce of indignation I can summon into my denial. "My mother said it amounted to parading girls around like the next cow to be bought, and my father was happy he didn't have to fork over a couple thousand dollars for a fancy dress I'd wear once." It was the only time I can remember that my mother stood up for me. Years later, I came to realize it wasn't much of a stand. My father wasn't that keen on the old society tradition to begin with. More to the truth, he was glad he didn't have to lean on a business acquaintance or golf buddy to make one of their sons escort me because I didn't date or have a boyfriend. "So that's why you lack rhythm. No dance lessons." She closes the gate and walks beside me as she'd done with Grace.

"I had ballroom-dance lessons."

"Ha. You must have crushed your poor partner's feet."

"No. In fact, I was much sought after as a partner," I say, my tone teasingly flippant. Alex was right. Marsh seems to have relaxed once it was clear I'm not going to mention the migraine incident, and we've easily returned to the teasing banter we had before my temper fit over Butter being set aside for a new, better model.

She looks up at me, one skeptical eyebrow raised. I stare back defiantly for a long second but can't keep up the façade. I laugh and confess.

"I went to an all-girls school, and the other girls were happy to always let me lead. I just never got the hang of following someone else's." I dismount but keep my hands on Fancy's flank to steady my wobbly legs.

"That's your problem, Lauren." Marsh's breath warms my ear. "You have to let go a little."

Holy mother. I freeze as my arms pebble with gooseflesh. God, I want her to press me against this horse, lick the sweat from my neck, and slip her long fingers into my breeches. I almost whimper at the loss of her heat when she steps back.

"Give her a good wash," Marsh says, her voice still low. "She's pretty sweaty, so be sure you scrub between her thighs or she'll chafe."

I nearly groan because the image her words conjure has nothing to do with a horse and everything to do with Marsh between my thighs. Maybe after Fancy's bath, I'll turn the water to cold and hose myself down.

❖

Fancy is silky clean and happily munching her dinner in her stall, but I'm a mess of dirt, hay, and dried sweat. Even that isn't enough to keep me from finding out if Marsh has dinner plans. She retreated to the barn office after our lesson but left the door partially open. I take it as an invitation, since she normally keeps it closed against the dust in the rest of the barn.

"Hey," I say, waiting in the doorway to be invited inside. She looks up from the laptop where she's entering information. Alex has warned that working on the business's quarterly taxes sometimes puts her in a bad mood, but she waves me in.

"What's up?"

God, what isn't up? My need to have her mouth on me, my neck, my breast, my... I mentally shake myself from those lascivious thoughts.

"Do you have plans for dinner?"

She points to the computer. "Paperwork. There's a local show Saturday, and I've got to finish registering the kids from our stable who want to compete. The event is a fund-raiser for a program that arranges pony camps for underprivileged kids, so we encourage as many as possible to sign up." She grimaces. "Their parents write the entry-fee checks, but I have to decide which classes they're qualified to enter and fill out all the registration forms. Then I have to get started on the quarterly taxes."

Wow. That does seem like a lot. I've never thought about all the work that goes along with running a show barn. But I'm selfishly not ready to end our time together today. I bend over and massage my right calf.

"Well, darn. I was hoping to buy you dinner in exchange for use of your therapy room and maybe get that massage you promised me before."

Marsh's nostrils flare, and her blue gaze practically scorches my backside. I feel no shame for taunting her like this.

She clears her throat. "Your offer is enticing, but I've already called Alex. He's bringing me a sandwich from the roast he and Harrison are having for dinner. And this paperwork has to be done tonight."

I straighten. The child in me pouts that I'm always at the back of the line. The grown-up in me, however, recognizes we are adults with adult responsibility. The shoe would be on my foot if she were inviting and I was up against a book deadline. "I understand."

Crap. With her at a show all day Saturday, I probably won't see her again until my lesson on Monday. I want to say more, but Marsh has returned her attention to the laptop. I turn to leave.

"I'm free for dinner tomorrow."

I pause mid-step, nearly stumbling, and my sulk vanishes like mist in the sun. "I'm also free tomorrow."

Chapter Eleven

I pull my Lexus next to Marsh's truck and put it into park. We had a wonderful dinner at one of the few five-star restaurants in town, talking easily about horses, books, movies—anything but our pasts or families—over an amazing five-course dinner. Now we sit in my car, outside Marsh's home, and I want more. More time with her. More of her rare touches like her hand on my back as we wove between tables to our intimate booth in the back of the restaurant. I want to warm myself against her leather blazer and sneak my hands under it to caress the cashmere V-neck that's the same blue as her eyes. Damn, she is so sexy, I can barely contain myself.

Normally, it would have been my hand on her back, guiding her to our table. I'd issued the invitation and picked her up for our date. But Marsh has a natural aura of command to which I instinctively, unconsciously, and willingly submit. That's why I'm hesitating now when all I want to do is draw her to me and kiss her senseless. She seems to sense my dilemma, her eyes darkening to a royal blue as they hold mine.

"Come inside for a nightcap." She's unbuckling her seat belt and putting her hand on the passenger-door release as she issues the invitation Marsh-style—not a question, but not a command.

Every fiber in me wants to scream yes, but I call on my last thread of control. "I will." Reassured by the calm I manage in my voice, I add, "As long as that nightcap isn't Jägermeister."

Marsh doesn't answer, but before I can unbuckle my seat belt and reach for my door handle, she's out, circles to my side, and opens my door for me. She holds out her hand, and although I don't need assistance, I give her mine. Her warm fingers loosely clasp mine, clearly not an assist but a gallant courtesy. I shiver when she drops my hand to unlock the door and wrap my arms around myself. Although the days are still pleasant, autumn has begun to chill the nights. Her warmth immediately returns, and the hand is back—on my elbow this time to guide me inside.

She flips a switch that bathes the living room in soft light, and then another that ignites the gas logs in the fireplace. "Have a seat." She indicates the living-room grouping that faces the fireplace. "I have a very good Napa brandy I purchased last time I visited the West Coast," she says, going over to a beautiful oak cabinet to extract the brandy and two medium-sized snifters. "Are you a brandy drinker?"

"Mostly wine," I say. "But brandy is a liqueur, isn't it? Sort of like a condensed wine, right?"

"It's not concentrated wine, but it is a liqueur," she says, sounding pleased that I know, well, guess that.

"I drink Fireball."

She laughs as she shakes her head. "You are such a contradiction—a rich debutante who drinks Fireball."

"I'm not a debutante." I poke my lips out in a mock pout.

"Forgive me. Socialite, never a debutante." She tilts her head and gives one nod, but her amused expression discredits her polite concession. "I can see where you could mistake it for a liqueur or a wine concentrate. Brandy is made from a blend of fruit and spices. Fireball is cinnamon-infused whiskey."

My cheeks heat, even though her correction is gentle, not ridiculing. "Am I about to get a lesson in brandy?"

She pours a generous serving in each glass and hands one to me as she joins me on the sofa. She crosses her long legs in an uncharacteristically feminine gesture and sits at an angle that allows her to observe me. I like being reminded that she's a woman, no matter how handsome she is or how much power she exudes.

"I spent more than a few summers when I was younger working

and learning from an equestrian master in Germany. Horses were her passion, but exporting and importing liqueurs was her family's business."

I was intrigued. "That's why you're fluent in German?"

"And French. I'm passable in Spanish and Italian. I also know enough Greek to order in a restaurant, ask for the ladies' room, or swear at a taxi driver."

"Wow. You didn't say anything before when I was bragging about speaking all the romance languages. And I've never studied Greek. You're making me feel like a rube."

Marsh cocks her head, her expression assessing. "I don't know a word of Russian, like you do, and I'm a horrible speller in any language. You certainly are not a rube, as you say. I'm completely in awe of your novel-writing talent, if that makes you feel any better."

"It does." Her compliment warms me more than the fireplace, and my heart goes from a walk to a trot when she puts down her glass and edges closer.

She takes my glass from me. Is she finally going to kiss me?

"This is the way you hold a brandy snifter," she says, placing the glass so I cup it in my hand rather than hold the stem with my fingers. "Your hand warms the glass, therefore the brandy, which enhances the taste."

She picks up her glass again, and her eyes hold mine as she lifts the snifter to her nose and inhales. I mimic her action, then hold mine out to swirl as I would to judge a wine. Her hand on my arm stops me.

"While there are two schools of thought on this, I was taught that swirling brandy breaks down the flavors to escape into the air. That explains why brandy is served in snifters. The larger bowl of the glass allows for cupping it in your hand to warm the brandy, but the mouth of a snifter narrows to keep in the flavors." She brings her glass to her nose again. "Unlike some wines, brandy doesn't need to breathe. You should drink it as soon as it's poured."

I'm mesmerized by her knowledge, by the flare of her nostrils when she inhales, and entranced by her mouth as she tilts the glass to take a sip. She closes her eyes for a long second before swallowing, and then her lips part, and her chest rises with a deep inhale. I lick my dry lips, and my own throat convulses with my urgent need to also taste that brandy, but on her lips and on her tongue. Hell, on her tonsils. I reach to cup her cheek like she cups the snifter, but she stops me.

Marsh folds her hand around mine to gently restrain it. Her eyes are bright. "Sip your brandy, Lauren. Hold it in your mouth to fully experience the flavors before you swallow. Then part your lips and inhale to let the air ignite the flavors across your tongue."

I do as she instructs, just as I've seen her do. I hold it, thick and smooth on my tongue, then swallow. The burn comes with my inhale and leaves the distinct flavor of... "Orange peel. And a hint of cinnamon. No, ginger."

She smiles and takes my snifter to place it on the coffee table next to hers. "Maybe I should taste for myself." I watch her lips form the words, barely comprehending before they brush against mine. Her tongue bathes mine when I open to her. The burning isn't on my tongue or even in my throat now. It's in my belly, lighting a fire in my sex. God, I want her. I reach for her, but she withdraws an inch, her breath still warming my face and filling my nose with the aroma of oranges, ginger, and Marsh's own earthy scents of leather and fresh-cut hay.

"I can see you're used to taking what you want, but that's not what you need, Lauren." She captures my hands in hers and holds them.

"What do I need?" I'm still breathless from the kiss and my desire to have her mouth again.

"You need to trust yourself."

What? Trust myself? I trust very few people, but I count myself at the top of the list.

She picks up a remote, and the room fills with a soothing piano waltz. She holds out her hand. Bedroom? Yes. To hell with sipping. I pick up my glass and throw back the rest of my brandy, then lay my hand in hers. She leads me around the sofa and out of the furniture grouping to the open floor between the fireplace seating and the kitchen. Then she pauses, turns, and draws me to her. I go willingly into her arms. I'll be happy if she just marches me into the bedroom and tears my clothes off. But this slow seduction has my heart tripping over itself.

Instead of her lips, I get her hips pressed against mine. She begins to sway, her hands on my hips keeping me tight against her while the pressure of her hips guides mine in a slow, sexy, swirling motion.

"See? You can let someone else lead."

God, her mouth is so close to my ear. If she will just bend her head a little and suck that sensitive spot on my neck. I close my eyes when she lays her cheek, soft and warm, against mine and sink into her long, lean body that fits so well against my curves. Our movements widen with the music washing over us, and then our feet are moving. My eyes pop open.

We are dancing and I panic. I try to concentrate, to anticipate her movements and pray I won't...damn. I step on her foot. I mean really step squarely on it. And stumble. Marsh, of course, catches me before I mutilate her other foot.

"God, I'm so sorry. Did I hurt you? I warned you I can't dance unless you...unless you let me lead." My words start out in a fast jumble, then trail off because she's staring at me with an expression I can only describe as hungry. She is a wolf about to swallow the canary who is singing nonsense.

"Wait here," she says, and disappears.

I stare after her. She finally goes into the bedroom but doesn't take me with her. My plan to get her naked body next to mine isn't going well. I've worn my sexy silk blouse and fine linen pants—not to mention my sexiest underwear—for nothing. God, she might as well turn that damned music off. My agitation swells, and I start to look around for my purse. Clearly, the spell is broken and the evening is over.

Then the music changes, and Norah Jones purrs for me to come away with her as Marsh emerges from her mission.

"Turn around," she says.

I protest. "Maybe I should go before I mutilate your other—"

"Lauren." Her fingers press against my lips to silence me. "I let you invite me to dinner, choose the restaurant, and drive us. You were in control. I am in control here. You can choose to leave if you really want, but my foot is not hurt, and I'd like you to stay." She caresses my cheek with the lightest of touches. "As always, it's your choice. If you stay, I'd like to teach you something about yourself."

I tremble at her touch. How can I refuse? I turn slowly to give Marsh my back as she asked. Hands gently arrange my long hair to drape behind my shoulders, and then moist lips trail along my neck. Swoon is no longer just a word I use in my novels, because I feel it to my very toes.

Then everything goes dark.

CHAPTER TWELVE

Complete darkness.

I suck in a surprised breath, and then her lips are on my neck again, her arms wrap around me from behind, and Norah is crooning for someone to take her home and turn her on.

"You're okay," Marsh whispers in my ear. "I've got you."

I am okay. I just wasn't expecting the blindfold Marsh slid over my eyes, leaving me totally in her control.

I clutch at her arms when they loosen, but she only lets go enough to slip around to face me and move down me. Holy Mother. I want to yank open my pants, just in case she's unsure she has my permission. I've been ready for her, hot and wet, since she kissed me on the sofa. I moan my disappointment when I realize my shoes—not my belt and zipper—are her intended target.

"So you won't be worried about stepping on my feet," she says as she removes my low-heel ankle boots. Shoes gone, she moves back up me, always keeping some point of contact so I don't feel adrift. I don't even try to hold back the impatient grunt when she bypasses my belt again. The deprivation of sight and anticipation of where I'll feel her next has me throbbing. I'm close to begging for an old-fashioned slam-bam, thank you, ma'am.

She soothes my frustration with a brush of her lips against mine as she places my right hand on her shoulder and takes my left in hers to tuck it against her chest. I can feel the swell of her breast against my forearm. Her free hand presses against my lower back to snug my hips against hers, and Marsh begins to sway with Norah's bluesy tune. Her cheek rests against mine as we move together. This is so nice.

Then her right hip presses so that I have to take a small step back to keep my balance. I stiffen. I can't do this. I can't do this. I'll trip and fall in an embarrassing tangle of legs, or I'll stomp her foot again. Thank God she removed my shoes.

"Don't think, Lauren. Just feel. Let me have you. I won't let you fall."

Oh, yeah. She can have me all right. On the sofa. On the floor. In her whirlpool. On the massage table. That thought opens the door to a whole new set of mental images that makes me press my breasts against hers and my nose to her throat, where I inhale her scent. The leather of her blazer mingles with the aroma of orange brandy and the smell of soap. I'm puzzling over which soap has that clean, fresh scent when I realize our sway has graduated to small steps, then slightly larger ones, from a small circle to cover a larger area. I start to stiffen, but her lips on my neck again distract me from my fear of tripping.

"You're a wonderful dancer." I'm almost startled by my own voice. I can talk and dance at the same time. I am so busy marveling over this discovery that she steps back, raises my hand over my head, twirls me away, and then pulls me back into her arms before I can freeze up. I'm smiling and a little breathless when she does it again.

"You are, too," she said. "When you stop thinking and give yourself permission to feel."

It's then that I realize that, without my sight, I'm responding only to the pressure of her hands and body against mine. I'm not giving a single thought to where my feet go. Until now. Because thinking about *not* thinking about my feet makes me stumble slightly.

Marsh hums her disapproval and tightens her arms. Her lips cover mine, not a gentle brush as before, but a kiss with purpose. I eagerly open to her questing tongue, cupping her nape to encourage her plunder. Then I'm spinning again, more forcefully than before, and find my back to her front when she guides my return. Nora is still asking for her lover to take her home and turn her on.

"You are a conundrum, Lauren Everhart. So beautiful and spirited, but so hobbled by your fear."

Her teeth nip at my earlobe. Her strong arms pen me against her so tight I can feel her nipples harden through the silk of my blouse. I press my butt into her crotch.

"Imagine how it would feel to surrender, to free yourself of those bonds."

I turn my head, but she silences my intended denial with a deep, forceful kiss that makes me whimper. She grinds her hips against my ass, and her hand is on my belt buckle.

"Lauren?"

Is there really any question about my permission? "Yes. God, yes." I guide her hand under the waistband while I release the belt, button, and zipper to give her fingers room to slide into my panties and between my legs where I need her.

"Tell me what you want, Lauren."

I moan because I can't form words. Arousal from her long seduction is drenching my panties, making my sex throb and my heart pound in my ears.

"Tell me."

I make a guttural sound of frustration when her fingers stop just short of their goal, and then, like a breached dam, words pour from my mouth. "I want your fingers on me, in me. I want you to stroke me, fill me. I want to come with you inside me."

"You're so sexy when you ask for what you want." She takes my mouth again, and I moan into hers as her fingers slide over my aching clit.

I'm so primed my legs begin to quiver on her third stroke, and I can't hold back when my belly tightens and the pressure builds. It's too soon, but it's too late. "Marsh. Oh, Marsh." Release bows my body, and my startled cry rings out. She plunges one, then two fingers inside and strokes through my orgasm until I'm limp and, I think, sated in her arms.

Before I can catch my breath, her arm is behind my knees, and she's lifting me. She's walking, and then I'm lowered onto something flat and soft. Her bed?

Wordlessly, she strips my linen trousers and panties down my legs, and then my silk shirt is opened, and my bra is gone. Her cashmere sweater is soft against my breasts, her nipples hard against mine.

"I'm going to put my mouth on you." Her words are low and smooth and certain. "And I'm going to fuck you."

"I might need a moment to recover." She isn't listening. She's moving down my body, tasting my nipples, dipping her tongue into my navel and pushing my thighs toward my chest, opening me to her. "Yes, please."

I reach to take the mask from my eyes because I want to see her between my legs. I want to find her eyes and hold on to her gaze. But she's atop me again in a flash, grabbing my hands and pinning them over my head.

"I didn't tell you to take that off." Still dressed, she grinds her pelvis against my sex, then plunges her tongue into my mouth, matching the rhythm of her hips humping against me.

We both suck in deep breaths when she withdraws. "Keep your hands off that mask." This is an order, not a request. I whimper because she is repeating her journey down my body. I have no time to protest or contemplate why my legs automatically open in a wanton display of where I want her most.

Then that tongue is doing delicious things to my clit and thrusting inside me. It isn't enough. I raise my hips. "More. I need more." I'm pleading.

"More of what, Lauren? I want you to say it."

"I want you to fuck me."

Her finger, then fingers enter me, and I gasp. So full, but her languid strokes are driving me mad. "I want you to fuck me hard." I moan out the words. "Hard and fast."

"Good girl." Her thrusting gains momentum. "See? You can ask. Now, give yourself to me." She adds a third finger and fucks me harder and faster. I'm so full, stretched so tight.

"Oh God, oh God. Marsh, I'm going to come."

"Not this time, but maybe next time I'm going to flip you over and fuck you from behind," she says. Her words ignite my orgasm, a flame burning sharp and hot through my belly when her mouth finds my clit and sucks hard.

It's probably seconds, but it feels like I'm hanging helpless in a hurricane of sensation for long minutes before it releases me, boneless and drained by spent pheromones.

"You are so spectacular when you let go, Lauren. Why do you keep such a tight rein on your need?"

"I...I don't." The murmured lie hangs between us.

Her sigh is a whisper across my lips before she gives me a taste of myself on her tongue. Then the bed jostles as she removes her boots and climbs up to spoon my naked body against her clothed one. She tugs a very soft blanket up from the foot of the bed and covers us.

"You do." Marsh's low burr holds no judgment. She nuzzles my neck and cups my breast in her hand—not in a way that excites, but in a move to possess. "I'd like to help you unbridle your passion."

Drugged by exhaustion, her words and my mumbled "yes" are the last thing I remember.

I stretch languidly in the sun that streams in through the window and warms the bed. I'm not surprised to wake alone. I know Marsh's days begin at sunrise with horses to feed, stalls to muck, and schedules to check. And I have a vague memory of murmured instructions that I should go back to sleep.

A chair has been pulled close to the bedside. Did she sit there to watch me sleep while she pulled on her boots? I've never slept so soundly, and no matter how badly I wish she were sitting there now so I could drag her into bed with me, the chair holds nothing but my clothes with a paper folded neatly on top. I reluctantly sit up, draw the blanket around me, and reach for the paper. My name is written in Marsh's perfect, bold cursive, so I unfold it and begin to read.

You are a temptress curled so innocently on my bed, in my blanket. But Langston Farms is one of the sponsors of Saturday's fund-raiser, so I'll be at the show grounds in Cherokee Falls much of the day to make sure everything is ready. I could use some help tomorrow if you're free and undaunted by chaos. I'll pick you up at seven in the morning if you're game. Also, there are bagels and cream cheese in the fridge. Keurig is on the counter. You're welcome to help yourself to breakfast and a shower before you leave.

Marsh

P.S. Your clothes are on the chair, except for the black lace panties. I'm keeping those.

My belly clenches, in a good way, and an involuntary shudder runs through me. I can't think about what she'll do with my underwear, or I'll throw myself at her the minute I see her. Images of her naked and hovering over me fill my languid mind. What had she said?

...next time I'm going to flip you over and fuck you from behind...

Last night had been perfect, except for one thing. I flush with shame. I fell asleep and left Marsh wanting. Damn. She must think I'm a pillow princess, which is far from the truth. I'm dying to get her naked and touch her everywhere. I want to cup that firm ass in my hands, wrap my legs around those slim hips, and dig my heels into her muscled thighs.

I shake those lascivious thoughts from my head and stand before I leave a wet spot on Marsh's sheets. Still wrapped in the blanket, I walk out to the kitchen and push the button for the Keurig to heat. While I wait for the coffee—a necessity for starting my day—I find a pen and add a reply to her note.

I'd love to spend Saturday helping you at the show. I'll be ready at seven.

Lauren

P.S. Since you've confiscated my black panties, I'll have to wear my red lace ones next time. Oh, and I'm going to steal a pair of your boy-short underwear to wear home.

Pleased with my note, I brew myself a cup of French roast, skip the bagels, and head for the shower.

CHAPTER THIRTEEN

M arsh wasn't kidding when she described shepherding a dozen youngsters, their horses, and a sidecar of parents among four simultaneously working show rings as chaotic. She appointed me as ringmaster since she, Alex, Harrison, and the parents with horse experience had their hands full keeping the beasts calm and safe among the chattering, giggling kids and nervous teens.

My job involves wielding a clipboard of schedules noting what classes are happening in which ring at what time and who from Langston Farms is entered in each. I make sure each participant is in the right ring at the correct time. I'm also guardian of the fix-it box, which holds hair ties, bobby pins, nail clippers, scissors, a sewing kit, a variety of safety pins, and first-aid supplies. I can repair a ponytail or nail-torn breeches and the scratch to the human skin underneath the damaged cloth. Also, I can safety-pin together what I don't have time to sew or tape.

I accepted the invitation to spend time with Marsh. But we've barely had time to speak since she handed me the clipboard, fix-it box, and brief instructions. She's around all the time, but we're both swamped answering questions, handling crises, and directing horses and riders from the massive Langston Farms seven-horse trailer where we've set up our base of operations.

The trailer is so large, Alex towed it with a semi-truck like a tractor-trailer rig. *Langston Farms* is painted on the cab's door and emblazoned in fancy script on both sides of the trailer. The front section holds a tack room, a small bathroom—reserved for Alex, Marsh, and myself—and built-in bunk beds. A couple of other smaller trailers belonging to some of the students and towed by pickups are parked to create a semicircle with the Langston Farms trailer. In that semicircle, two tent canopies are erected where people rest in lawn chairs among drink-filled ice chests when they aren't competing in a class.

Like a movie star, I sit in the center of it all in a tall director's chair. Alex has written "Lauren's Chair" in beautiful cursive with a thick black marker on the front and back. The scene would have seemed so elitist if we didn't all smell like horses and the manure shoveled out of the trailers. Everyone is wearing boots and pants spattered with mud from last night's rain.

Besides her students and their parents clamoring for her attention, a parade of attractive women—some younger and some older—keep showing up to flirt with Marsh. She's polite but never encourages them, no matter how much they bat their eyes, no matter how many times they grasp her arm, lean in to whisper in her ear, or kiss her cheek. One went for her lips, but Marsh neatly dodged. For God's sake, impressionable kids and watchful parents are milling around her. Do these women have no shame? They practically throw themselves at Marsh, but she is all business.

"Lauren." Grace tugs on my sleeve to get my attention. "I thought my hunt class was at two o'clock in ring three, but I just went down there, and the miniature horses are lining up to show there next."

I consult my clipboard, then my phone, where I pull up the show's website for last-minute updates. "Oh, your class was just moved because ring one is too soft for the wheels on the minis' carts. They're in three now, and your hunter class will be at the indoor ring."

"Sweet." Grace, who has stepped close to look over my shoulder while I consult the schedule, waves her arm over her head and yells loud enough to be heard in the next county. "Mom. We're changed to the arena. Over there to your right." Mom is diverted, and Grace leads her new horse to intercept her. She calls back over her shoulder. "Thanks, Lauren."

At least that's what I think she said. I'm not sure because my ear is still ringing from her screaming while standing next to me. Teens. Geez. I scan for Marsh again because I'm hungry. The delicious bacon-and-egg biscuit she got for us when we first arrived is a distant memory. Bingo. I spot her carrying two cardboard take-out trays and coming straight toward me.

"I guessed and got you a cheeseburger rather than a hot dog," she says, handing over one of the trays holding a large burger and piled high with French fries. She sets her own lunch on top of an ice chest and shows me how to flip up the small side shelf on the arm of the chair, then retrieves her own director's chair from the trailer to set up next to mine. She gets drinks for both of us from one of the chests, and we settle in to eat.

"You sure know how to treat a girl," I joke. The burger is one of those pre-molded, fifty to a box—tasteless if not for the cheese, tomato, onions, mayo, mustard, and ketchup piled on top. But the fries are still hot and incredibly good. Or maybe I'm incredibly hungry.

"Is that sarcasm? Is it the paper carton rather than china?" She waves a fly away from her food. "Or the pesky uninvited guests that want to share your meal?"

I laugh. "Well, I could do without the fresh, outdoor fragrance of manure, and the service is a little slow. I don't mind mid-afternoon lunches, except when breakfast is served at dawn. However, the sexy waitstaff pretty much makes up for my meal's late arrival."

"Your standards are very high," she says with an exaggerated frown. "I don't know if I can meet them." She wolfs down her last bite of burger and gives the rest of her fries to Alex's terrier tied to one of the larger coolers.

"I think further evaluation is needed," I say, struggling to look serious.

Marsh cocks her head, her smile amused. "I would agree." She steps close and bends to put her mouth next to my ear. "I think I'd like a chance to study this writer species further. Perhaps in her own habitat."

Her words send a chill down my arms and flames to my crotch. "I think that can be arranged." I am so easy. I wipe nonexistent food from my lips, just in case I'm actually drooling at the suggestion.

Marsh straightens. "Alas, I have to spend the next hour judging two beginner equestrian classes, so I must leave you to your own devices. I think everybody is already lined up for their last class or two, so you're done with your duties. If you're tired, you can nap in the trailer."

"I think I'll wander around a bit. I haven't had a chance to check out the vendor booths, and I might watch a bit of the minis' class. They are just too cute pulling those carts. I can't believe two of them can haul an adult person around."

"They may be small, but they're horses and very strong. I can promise that you wouldn't want one of them to kick you." Marsh peers across the grounds toward the indoor arena, where more experienced riders are competing in show-jumping and dressage. "Jules is here, by the way."

I stand and stare in the same direction. "Is she? Where? I might want to make a massage appointment with her."

Marsh's frown is genuine this time. "I have it on good authority she's booked solid for the next year." She turns to me and raises an eyebrow. "Perhaps you'll have to make do with her massage instructor."

It's my turn to lift an eyebrow at her. "You?" Holy mother. Is there anything this woman doesn't do exceptionally well?

"Unless you inherit wealth, which I didn't, most equestrians have to work some job to support themselves. Massage is one of those professions where you can make your own schedule and work as much or as little as you need."

"Then I, of course, would rather go to the source, rather than the student." I revel in her unexpected display of possessiveness.

Marsh tips her head toward me in acknowledgment. Is that a flicker of relief before her expression turns smug?

"But since you brought her up, where has Jules been lately?" I've gotten used to seeing her around the stables. Marsh has been contracted to train a couple of the horses at her barn and Jules assists by exercising them, sometimes riding them in their training sessions while Marsh watches to correct movements.

"She's been traveling on the show circuit, campaigning a stallion for Skyler Reese. Sky and her wife, Jessica Parker, own and manage Cherokee Falls Equestrian Center," she says, sweeping her arm around to indicate the huge facility where the show is being held.

"Campaigning?"

"People are going to pay top dollar only for the little swimmers of a proven champion, so you have to show a stallion to gain attention and ratings that improve his worth as a stud. Selling sperm is the big moneymaker in the equestrian world."

Marsh glances at her watch. "I'd better head over there." She picks up our trash to toss in a nearby receptacle, then turns back to me. "Jules is show-jumping in the class that's about to start in the indoor ring. You should watch her. She has excellent form."

I slide out of my chair. "I think I will. I've only watched that on television. I'd love to see what it's like up close."

She smiles again, but this smile holds a bit of secrecy. What is she plotting? I like this new Marsh, relaxed and flirty. I love intense Marsh in the bedroom, too, but this version of her is more open. The intense Marsh always feels like a dam holding back...I don't know...her true self, her passion, her heart?

"Keep your seat after Jules's class, and you'll see some real jumping," she says. She moves quickly to plant a light kiss on my lips, and then, with a wave, she's gone.

Stunned, I glance nervously around. Oddly, we're the only two people in this area. The day's crowd has thinned considerably since the classes that hold mostly kids concluded around lunchtime. I touch my freshly kissed lips and feel them stretch in a what I'm sure must be a silly grin. I'm glad nobody else is nearby to see it—the stupid grin, not the kiss. Damn. I'm not falling for her. I'm not falling for her. I. Am. Not. Falling. For. Her.

❖

The indoor ring has actual bleachers that are nearly full of people eager to watch the jumping event. I spot a few open seats on the sixth row and climb toward them, but when I get there, I spot a riding helmet and jacket reserving the places for someone else.

"There's room here." A woman on the third row a few seats to my left scoots over a bit and indicates the empty space next to her.

"Thank you." I smile at her and murmur a litany of "excuse me" and "sorry" for the toes I crush and knees that have to move as I make my way to her. Finally, I plop down on the metal bench. "I guess, judging from the crowd, this is the place to be?"

"A couple of Olympic hopefuls are in the class. I imagine that's what everybody's here to see." She hands me a program and points to the section that lists the upcoming class. Then she holds out her hand. "I'm Tallie." She has a faint European accent I can't place. Definitely not British, but too fleeting to pinpoint. French, maybe?

"Lauren." I'm relieved she only wants to swap first names, cursing for the millionth time my lack of foresight in not using a pen name on the books I write. Sometimes I love being recognized, but mostly I just want to be me, not Lauren Everhart the author. "Thanks for the seat."

"Not a problem. I'm pleased to meet you, Lauren. Do you know somebody showing in the next class?"

"Yes. Jules—" I don't know Jules's last name. "Sorry. Friend of a friend. I don't know her last name."

"Ah. Jules Ransom. She's a rising star on the circuit. I understand she's Marsh Langston's protégé."

"You know Marsh?" I hadn't realized I have a jealous streak, but this woman is an attractive brunette with hazel eyes. Older than I'd picture Marsh with, but judging by the women who've been popping up all day to purr in her ear, Marsh doesn't discriminate on the basis of age. And Tallie has the commanding aura of a woman who knows what she wants and goes after it—just the thing I imagine would attract Marsh.

Tallie shrugs. "The equestrian world is rather small. At the upper level, you keep competing against the same people at different shows, so it's hard not to at least be acquainted with almost everyone." She makes a show of looking me over with an appreciative gaze. Oddly, it reminds me of Marsh's. "But I don't believe I've seen you around. I would have remembered."

I wave a dismissive hand in front of me. "I'm just a spectator. My niece stayed with me this past summer while her parents were out of the country, and I enrolled her in one of Langston Farms' pony camps. She loved it so much, I decided to take a few lessons myself."

She nods knowingly. "It sort of sucks you in, doesn't it? I think females are most attracted to it for a lot of reasons. There's nothing like a thousand pounds of beautiful horse under your control to make you feel powerful."

"Yes." My answer is an afterthought because the first rider is being announced. Like a professional golf tournament, etiquette requires that all conversations pause so neither horse nor rider is distracted. Several of the jumps seem dangerously high, and I hold my breath as a young man navigates the course astride a dappled gray mare. He takes down two of the rails on the higher jumps, and the audience seems to let out a collective breath when he exits the ring.

"Still rushing the jumps," Tallie observes. "He's never going to be a top-tier rider. He tries to muscle his horse over the course." She scoffed. "Men are so heavy-handed. They like to be in control but have no idea how to do it correctly."

I don't respond to her gross generalization of male equestrians. "You're a rider, too?"

She shakes her head, her eyes still on the horse as the rider exits the rear of the arena. "Not for many years. I teach some but mostly breed, buy, and sell top-tier eventing horses." Her eyes and jaw harden in a way that scares me a little. "The gray that just knocked down two poles is mine. Looks like I need to hire a different rider if I want to show her real potential and make a profit when I sell her."

"Why don't you still ride?" I catch myself. It's so hard not to slip into interview mode to mine information for future novels. "You don't have to answer that if it's too personal. Occupational hazard. I ask too many questions." Damn. I didn't mean to bring up occupations.

She looks at me and, with a smile and tilt of her head, answers. "I was never a top rider. Too big to be a jockey and too short to really get a good leg on the larger breeds preferred for eventing. So, rather than be one of the chess pieces, I decided to be a chess master—someone who moves the pieces around the board."

I open my mouth to respond, but another rider is announced, and we turn our attention to the ring where a young, slender blonde is mounted on a dark-gray roan with a black mane and tail. They are a gorgeous pair.

Even three rows back, I feel like we're ringside. The smell of dust and hay fills my nose as the horse and rider circle so close to the rail near our seats, I have to resist the urge to lean back away from them.

The pair completes the course flawlessly, and we join the rest of the audience in politely clapping our approval when their time and score flash on an electronic board hung on the wall near where the riders enter and leave.

The rider pauses the dancing stallion at the arena's entrance to speak to a tall woman carrying a child, probably about three years old, on her shoulders. The kid holds her fist out, and the rider leans down to bump it with hers. It's cute.

"I thought so." Tallie's checking the program. "That's Skyler Reese's protégé, Jaime Maddox." Tallie nods her approval. "I don't know why I didn't recognize it before. She definitely rides like Skyler."

That's the second time the name has come up, so I google her on my phone. "Skyler Parker-Reese?"

"Yes. I believe she married the Parker heiress, Jessica Black. That's a sad story."

Wikipedia has a long entry on Skyler. Gold-medal Olympian,

rider turned trainer, and now co-owner of Cherokee Falls Equestrian Center with her wife, Jessica Black Parker-Reese.

"Sad? Them getting married?"

"No. Jessica was a brilliant rider and had the horse who would easily get her to the Olympics, but a bad knee injury ended her professional riding career."

There's got to be a good story in all that. I tuck the information away for further exploration, because the announcer is introducing Jules as the next contestant.

"Ah, Marsh's girl," Tallie says.

We quiet as the timer buzzes when Jules enters the ring. She's riding a bay stallion with a black mane, tail, and leggings. He sports a thin white blaze from forehead to nose. Very flashy. They navigate the course of jumps with such casual ease they could have been on a Sunday joy ride. The stallion jumps big, clearing even the tallest obstacle by several inches. Their relaxed demeanor, however, is deceptive. They exit the ring almost two full seconds quicker than Jamie and her mount. While Jamie's and Jules's scores are identical, the faster time puts Jules in first place.

"A brilliant ride. She's almost as good as Marsh."

We chat and watch the rest of the field, only three more riders, before Tallie abruptly stands. "I need to go speak to someone before they leave about a new rider for my mare." She holds out her hand again, but this time it contains a card. "Tallie Bouling" is printed on one side and a cell-phone number and email on the other. "Please don't share this because it's my personal information, not my business card. I've very much enjoyed our conversation. I'm also a fan of your books."

My face heats, but I take the card and tuck it in my pocket. "Sorry. I always feel like a snob if I announce that before the other person brings it up. I don't normally get recognized, a lot of time, even after I tell someone my name."

"Totally understandable." She glances at something behind me, then picks up her shoulder bag. "Call me and we'll do lunch. I think we could become friends."

I smile up at her. "I'll do that." And I mean it. Since I'm afraid to let Marsh know the subject of the manuscript I'm currently working, Tallie could be a great source. She might even have some inside information on what happened to Marsh.

"What did she want?"

I swing around from watching Tallie depart and face a scowling Jules. "Who?"

"That bitch who was sitting next to you. Was she asking questions about Marsh?"

I scrunch up my brow, quickly reviewing our conversation. "If you mean Tallie, she did mention that she knows you're training with Marsh, but that's all." I hold up my hand. "No, wait. She also said your ride was brilliant and that you're almost as good as Marsh." I expect that to reset Jules's attitude toward my new friend, but she's still frowning as she plops down in the seat Tallie vacated.

"Just be careful if you run into her again. She's not a nice person and likes to use people."

"She was perfectly nice to me, but I'm always careful. I'm not going to give away any of your or Marsh's secrets." I feign surprise, my finger on my lips. "Wait. I don't know any secrets." I grin cheekily at her. "So, no worries."

Jules looks down and shakes her head, but I still see her smile. "Marsh said you're a handful. I can see she isn't exaggerating."

I narrow my eyes at her. "Now who's talking about people?"

Jules chuckles and grabs my arm to pull me back down when I try to stand and leave. "Wait. Sit. You don't want to miss this."

I check my program. The show-jumping we just watched is the last class listed. I'm about to ask what she's referring to when the arena announcer erases the questions in my head.

"Ladies and gents, don't leave yet. We have an unscheduled treat for you to wrap up a very successful event today. I'd like to remind you that all proceeds from today will be used to provide equestrian opportunities for financially underprivileged children and underserved minorities. The Parker Foundation, one of our most respected nonprofits in the equestrian community, has offered to oversee the distribution of the money. I have Jessica Parker-Reese's personal guarantee there will be no administrative charges. Every penny will go to the intended purpose. I'm reminding you of this because we'll have two tables set up outside the arena where we encourage you to make an extra donation by emptying your wallet of any cash into their bucket, swipe your charge card, or write a check for a little something extra in exchange for this big something extra you're about to see."

While he talks, a handful of people run into the ring and begin raising the jumps to what I think are impossible heights. Rumors have been circulating all day that something was going to happen, but nobody seems to know what. This has to be it.

"Jules?"

"Just wait."

We both whisper but still get shut-up looks from the people around us.

"Drumroll, please." The lights dim with the announcer's deep rumble, and then a video is projected from some place I can't discern onto a white wall at one end of the arena. We see and hear a closeup of gloved hands rolling out an intro on a snare drum, and then the voice-over begins.

"Cherokee Falls Equestrian Center presents the duel of Olympians. Two former Olympians competing against each other in a best two-out-of-three contest on a five-star course. Introducing gold medalist Skyler Parker-Reese…"

Images flash of Skyler on the Olympic podium, jumping a tall, black horse in the Olympics and other prestigious five-star events, then Skyler as a trainer coaching rider Jessica Black, who is riding a big stallion named Rampage, and finally, a segment on Skyler's work with the Young Equestrian Program targeting troubled children or ones living in troubled homes like she and her twin brother had. Wow. What an accomplished woman.

The drumroll shows again.

"And challenging Ms. Parker-Reese is former US Equestrian team member Marsh Langston, owner of Langston Farms, one of the sponsors of today's show. Despite injury and personal circumstances twice preventing her from actually competing at the

Olympics, Ms. Langston was a familiar face on the winner's podium while competing with the team at many international five-star shows leading to the Olympics. Today she…"

I'm mesmerized by the scenes edited into the video of Marsh clearing impossibly high jumps, riding a cross-country course that looks very dangerous, and winning accolades in the dressage arena.

The lights come back up when the video concludes to reveal both riders mounted at one end of the arena.

The arena announcer takes over where the video stops. "Ms. Parker-Reese will be riding Rampage, owned by Kate Parker and Jessica Parker-Reese."

The tall woman who'd been carrying the child around on her shoulders earlier is mounted on a huge bay that prances restlessly. They step forward as the announcer introduces them.

"This horse scored triple individual gold medals for the United States team in the last Olympics, his high scores enabling the US to take home a silver medal in team competition," the announcer says.

Skyler gives the stallion rein, and they circle the ring in a ground-eating canter, drawing applause from the audience that now is standing room only.

The applause cuts off as Marsh guides her mount, a fiery chestnut stallion that seems to glimmer under the arena lights, into the spotlight.

"Our challenger is Marsh Langston of Langston Farms, riding Crescendo. Imported from Germany, this is his debut in the United States."

Murmurs of exclamation accompany the applause as Marsh and Crescendo wheel in a showy circle, then take their turn around the arena. When they return to stand next to Skyler and Rampage, the older stallion pins his ears back and tries to take a nip out of the chestnut. Skyler tightens the reins to restrain him as the announcer injects a little fun into the show.

"Ho, ho. Looks like Rampage doesn't like sharing the spotlight. How about his rider? Ms. Parker-Reese, anything to say before we start?"

A helper hands up a wireless microphone to Skyler.

"First, I want to thank everybody for coming out today and contributing to a very worthy program. Kate Parker and her horses saved me when I was a troubled teen, and my life's mission is to pay that forward."

A small voice rings out when Skyler pauses. "Hey, Mom!" Skyler waves at the kid, and the audience titters with amusement before Skyler continues.

"Anyway, my friend Marsh shows up today bragging about this new stallion she's imported. She says he's the best she's ever jumped. Well, I couldn't let that go unanswered. Rampage is still the top horse on this farm, even though he's only lounging around the barn and servicing mares these days. So, I figured Rampage and I could knock the dust off and show these two youngsters a thing or two."

"Ms. Langston, do you want to answer that? Is Skyler Reese talking trash?"

The audience hoots and cheers, then quickly quiets to hear Marsh's reply.

"I bow to Ms. Parker-Reese's long list of admirable accomplishments and undisputed skills. But maybe it's time she should put the old man out to pasture and relax in her front-porch rocking chair while we youngsters break their records."

The crowd, buying into the hype, hoot and cheer again, calling out the name of the horse they favor. Shouts of "Rampage" are met by shouts of "Shen-doe," an apparent shortening of Crescendo.

I turn to Jules. "I think I like that. Shendoe."

"It is kind of cool." Her eyes are bright, never leaving the flame-colored stallion.

I find it amusing that this polite equestrian crowd has turned into a raucous mob. I could close my eyes and visualize a rock concert or two I attended in my younger years. Not that I'm old now, but old enough I don't enjoy freezing my ass off in an outdoor amphitheater or stadium to hear someone sing.

The crowd quiets when Marsh exits the arena to give Skyler and Rampage room to settle before crossing the beam to trigger the timer. Only an occasional cough breaks the silence as Skyler turns her mount in a few small circles until he settles facing the gate to the ring. They hold stock-still for a long second, and then Rampage leaps forward.

It takes a few strides, but Skyler settles him into a rhythmic canter as they approach the first jump. Up and over. Up and over. It looks like he's going to turn in a clean run, but his hind hoof grazes a pole on the highest jump. It wobbles and falls. The crowd groans as they break the timer beam and exit out to the connected warm-up ring.

Only a second passes before Marsh and Crescendo enter and head straight for the jumps. Marsh sends him around the course with an unfaltering confidence her mount seems to feel. Her form and his jumps are nearly perfect. His foreleg brushes the top rail of the highest jump, but the rail vibrates, then holds in place.

Their score and time beat Skyler and Rampage's first round.

They've barely exited when Rampage lopes into the arena for his second attempt. He appears more settled and gets down to business. Skyler guides him over the course with the precision of an exceptional equestrian.

"See her hands and legs talking to him?" Jules's whispered question is more of an awe-filled observation. "She's an amazing rider."

This time, Rampage clears the highest jump by several inches. The audience's polite applause is punctuated by restrained whispers of "he's still got it" and "that's what I'm talking about."

I want to stand and clap and cheer. I have no idea how these people can hold it in. But they're horse people and well-schooled about making sudden loud noises while the horses are performing. I wonder why the earlier cheering didn't spook the stallions, but I stay quiet, too, because I've watched too many videos in the past weeks of mishaps that broke bones, necks, and even killed horses and riders. I shudder and push that thought out of my head.

Skyler's second round is clean and her time better than either of theirs in the first round.

Marsh is back, gliding her shimmering mount fast and clean

over the course and matching Skyler's second-round score. That leaves Marsh with a small lead.

Rampage charges into the arena for his third try, sweaty and snorting. Skyler fights to rein him in, but the big stallion shakes his head and takes the first two jumps at a fast pace. He shakes his head again, and Skyler lets him have it. His bay hide is dark and gleaming as he practically gallops the rest of the course, clearing the jumps like they're anthills and he has wings.

I grab my phone and type out my question to Google. "Jesus. Her time is only a second off that horse's Olympic time."

My stage whisper prompts several people sitting around us to also check their phones to see if I'm right.

Jules shakes her head, her expression disbelieving. "She just gave him his head and let him go. I swear, that horse might have run the course clean with no rider at all. Just for the joy of it."

Someone sitting nearby shushes us because Marsh and Crescendo are starting their third round. Marsh is obviously pushing him to match Rampage's speed, and they nearly do. But the young stallion rushes the last jump, and two poles fall.

The crowd waits as his time and score flash on the light board, then the final scores.

Skyler and Rampage have edged them out by a few points.

"Let's give them both a round of applause, folks."

Skyler reappears, and both riders take a turn around the arena to accept the applause before they stop and dismount.

The young blonde who'd ridden against Jules earlier comes into the ring and gives Skyler a fist-bump, then leads Rampage away. Alex comes in behind the blonde, and Marsh hands Crescendo over to him.

Marsh walks over to Skyler and holds out her hand. Instead of a handshake, Skyler yanks her close to fling her arm over Marsh's shoulders. Someone puts the wireless mic in her hand, and Skyler addresses the crowd.

"I guess the old man still has it in him," she says. With the horses gone, the crowd is more raucous than ever, cheering and stomping their feet on the metal bleachers. After a minute, Skyler waves for quiet. "I want to thank Marsh for participating in our little contest. Folks, that stallion just came out of quarantine this week and arrived at Langston Farms yesterday. Marsh literally rode him once in Germany and a second time yesterday at her farm."

The crowd rumbles with surprised and appreciative remarks.

"After seeing him perform today, I'm looking forward to sitting in my rocking chair and watching Marsh collect the blue ribbons and maybe a few gold medals over the next couple of seasons."

The crowd applauds with a few whistles thrown in as Skyler hands the mic to Marsh, who shakes her head as she accepts it.

"Thanks, Sky," Marsh says. "And thanks to all of you. I hope you enjoyed the show, and please be generous on your way past the tables mentioned earlier. It's for a very good cause."

CHAPTER FOURTEEN

Marsh puts her truck in park but leaves it running as she twists toward me. "Thanks for helping today." Her face is unreadable in the dim light.

"Come inside. I have chicken Alfredo we can heat for dinner. I might even have a German wine you'll like." Actually, I found a highly rated wine from a German winery located in the area where Marsh said she'd spent summers training and riding, and I paid a small fortune for a case of it. I already tried a bottle, and it's very good.

Marsh doesn't move or answer. She studies me. "Tell me what you want, Lauren. What do you need?"

I want her to stay. I hesitate to admit what I need because need gives away power. My brain insists I don't need anybody or anything. My body is screaming a completely different story. I've been thinking all day about this chance to be alone with Marsh, and I'm not going to mess up this opportunity, even if it requires a little role-playing. I lower my eyes to my hands. "I want you to stay. To share dinner and conversation with me." I raise my eyes to hers. "I need you to fuck me senseless afterward."

I swear that her blue eyes grow bright with that last admission, burning with a hunger that makes me catch and hold my breath.

She lifts her hand and caresses my cheek. "Thank you. I will stay for dinner…and after."

Saints above, I am so instantly wet I practically slide off the seat and out of the truck when she comes around to open my door. Dinner is a simple salad and two plates of chicken Alfredo. I'm a pretty decent cook, but I'm lazy and haven't been home since Marsh picked me up at seven this morning. So, the housekeeping and chef service I use came while we were at the horse show, cleaned the house, and left the dinner I requested in the refrigerator. Mr. Microwave is my friend.

We make small talk while I set the table and heat our dinner. The main part of my house, like Marsh's, is an open concept, which lets Marsh peruse the artwork on my walls and the bookcases that flank my fireplace. I watch her circle the room, peering out the large windows even though it's too dark to see anything, examining the book titles—all classics—on my bookshelves, and picking up the framed photo of my nine-year-old self hugging my grandmother while we smiled for the camera.

Her house decor is sort of a modern-cabin, L.L.Bean style. My home is more Martha Stewart–Southern casual with color-coordinated throw pillows placed strategically around the room and on the window seat, a Sherpa throw tossed casually over the back of the sofa, and my reading glasses perched atop a book on an end table. I become uncomfortably aware it all seems too perfect, like the house has been staged for some tour-of-homes fund-raiser.

"Don't be deceived by how neat everything is," I say. "My housekeeping service came today and cleaned up my usual sloppy chaos." Truth is, I'm fairly neat when I have time to be, which is any time I'm not up against a book deadline.

"It's a beautiful home," Marsh says. "How much acreage do you have?"

"Just ten. I didn't want to be too isolated, but I wanted to sit on my porch and see nothing but woods and meadows, not another house a hundred yards from mine."

Marsh nods. She understands. We're both fairly private people.

"Can you open the wine?" I ask, plating our salads and placing the warmed mini-loaf of sourdough bread on a small cutting board with a crystal dish of Irish butter. Martha Stewart would be so proud.

She picks up the bottle of wine and smiles. "A very good vintage. I'm truly impressed." She uncorks it and pours a bit into one of the glasses I've set on the table. She swirls it, takes in the aroma, then tastes. She takes time to roll it on her tongue, then gives an approving nod and fills her glass and mine.

When I bring the warmed plates to the table, she holds my chair for me to sit. Although it's my house, she makes it clear who's in control here. The warm, relaxed Marsh who kissed me briefly at the horse show is transforming before my eyes into the intense, enigmatic, and commanding Marsh.

We talk about her new stallion, the equestrian center where the show was held, and the story behind the Parker-Reeses. We're both hungry, so our plates and wine bottle are empty too quickly.

"Would you like coffee? Or some dessert?" I'm about to die for sex, but not sure how to transition from dinner to naked. "I have several flavors of ice cream."

Marsh stands. "I'd like to see the rest of your house."

Her request surprises me. Maybe it's a polite way of asking to go to the bedroom, and I'm on board with that.

My bedroom is a lot of white—white sheets, white duvet, white sheer curtains, and a white faux-fur rug next to the side of the bed where I sleep. All the white is accented by blues—a country-blue dresser, a royal-blue wing-back chair, and, of course, a variety of strategically placed pillows in various shades of blue.

To my disappointment, Marsh gives my bedroom only a cursory look. She seems fascinated, however, by my office.

"This is where you really live." It isn't a question.

"Well, yes. This is where I usually work. If the weather's nice and I'm writing rather than researching, I sometimes take my laptop out to the patio. I like the fresh air and watching the birds and squirrels that come to the feeders."

She nods, trailing her fingers along the rows and rows of books I have on the shelves that line two entire walls. She gives a quick look at my collection of mysteries. "You like British mysteries. Good choice." She slows at my library of fantasy. I'm not much for science fiction. "Impressive," she says. "And surprising. I wouldn't have pegged you as a fantasy reader."

"I like the fantasy genre. It's freeing and often an insightful vehicle for social commentary."

"I agree. Don't ever bring the subject up around Harrison unless you have a couple of days to discuss it. Fantasy is his genre of choice."

I'm pleased that she takes my reading choices seriously but wait impatiently for her to reach the second wall of books, which consists of almost exclusively lesbian titles.

She moves to the other wall, where she scans the titles more carefully. She glances my way once, and I don't try to hide that I'm watching her. She takes a book from the shelf, reads the summary on the back, then thumbs through to read a few passages. She raises her eyes from the book, and her gaze is so piercing that, after a long second, I lower mine. Heat crawls up my neck, but I watch again—more discreetly this time—when she returns to the shelf to select another for examination. She repeats the process of reading the back of a book, then thumbing through it several times before she suddenly wheels and exits my office. What the hell?

Startled, it takes me a few seconds to react and follow. I burst into the hall just in time to see her disappear into my bedroom. Weird, but I'm going to go with this because I'm absolutely dying to see her naked, and watching her read my erotica collection has turned me on like I'd never imagined.

I find her standing at my two-drawer bedside table. She holds my gaze for a moment, and I know what she's going to do. Probably the most private thing in the home of any single woman—gay, straight, or bisexual—is the contents of their nightstand. I meet her gaze, then submissively lower my eyes. My heart pounds with this game we're playing. Although I rage at the thought of anyone trying to control my life, I can't deny that my deepest desire is to give over that control in the bedroom. Marsh somehow sees this need in me, and I realize at this very moment that I trust Marsh's discretion enough to give it to her.

She opens the top drawer and extracts my bedtime reading material for the past month, *Riding Passion*. She raises an eyebrow and hums her approval of the horse on the cover. Then she digs around among the sex toys, uh, stimulation aids. I'm not ashamed of what she finds. I'm an adult, and women have a right to pleasure themselves. I'm sure she does it. Still, my face heats when she holds up the cylindrical vibrator. I keep my eyes averted, but not so much that I can't watch her in my peripheral vision. She watches me as she smells, then licks the length of the vibrator.

I can't hide the shudder that runs through me, but I bow my head to stare hard at the floor and resist the impulse to widen my stance because of the throbbing between my legs. I'm concentrating hard on this and miss her crossing over to me until the vibrator appears under my nose.

"Is this you I smell and taste on this? Or some other lover?" Her tone is curious rather than accusing.

Still, I stiffen with indignation. "I don't bring women to my home." As soon as the words are out of my mouth, I realize what I've revealed.

Marsh says nothing, but grasps my chin and tilts my face up. She looks briefly into my eyes, hers so fierce and hungry I don't know whether to back away or fall at her feet. But I don't have time to do either because her mouth is on mine, devouring and claiming. Her hands are on my hips, pressing me against hers. Her hands move to my ass and lift me off my feet. I instinctively wrap my arms and legs around her as she steps over to the bed.

She lays me on the bed and leaves my mouth to kiss and suck at my neck—Goddess, I love that—while she unbuttons my shirt and opens the front clasp on my bra to bare my chest to her. She pays only small attention to my breasts before kissing down my belly, dipping her tongue into my navel while she makes quick work of my belt and the zipper on my pants.

Marsh yanks off my boots while still leaning over my half-naked body, then slides my pants and panties down my legs to toss them behind her. Her mouth is on me again, but she does not linger or tease. My clit, turgid with arousal, is between her lips. She alternates between sucking and licking, sometimes scraping her teeth against my singing bundle of nerves as she sucks and licks, sucks and licks. I don't last more than sixty seconds before I'm bucking and screaming at the ceiling in the clutches of a blinding orgasm.

Her mouth, her tongue is glorious. If she were mine, all mine, I might be inclined to have it insured. I'm still riding the aftershocks when she claims my mouth again. Her cheeks are slick with my cum.

"Don't move," she commands.

As if I could.

"I'll be back."

She strides out of the bedroom, leaving me in my post-orgasmic stupor. My shirt and bra are still on my shoulders, but laid open, and I'm naked from the waist down. I'm too boneless to even cover up, although Marsh remains fully clothed.

Languorous, I relax into my plush bedding with my legs still half hanging off the bed. I wonder briefly where she put the vibrator. I'm still singing with arousal. But then the vibrator would be a disappointment after Marsh's cunnilingus skills. Did I mention that her mouth is spectacular? I drift through that savory memory, then jerk back to the present when Marsh is again hovering over me.

She tugs me up to a sitting position and fully divests me of my shirt and bra, then cups my ass to lift me. I demur even as I'm again wrapping my arms and legs around her, but she ignores me and carries me back to the dining-room table. She has cleared our dishes and prepared a bowl of pistachio ice cream. I'm intrigued.

She rests my butt on the table and lays a long finger against my lips when I start to protest for sanitary reasons. "No talking." Her stern words rather than her finger stop my protest. "You're sitting on a place mat because I'm still hungry, and you, Lauren, are going to be my dessert."

"Yes." Only a whisper, but I know she wants to hear my

consent. Marsh has always emphasized choice in every step in our relationship.

She holds up a spoonful of ice cream for me. It's smooth and cold in my mouth, and before I can swallow the melting treat, Marsh's lips are on mine, her tongue mining mine for all the sweet goodness.

"Marsh, please." I tug at her polo shirt to pull it from her pants, but her hands stop me. She steps back, her eyes smoldering. "Please," I repeat. "I want to feel your skin."

She doesn't allow me to undress her, but she pulls her shirt over her head and tosses it to the floor. Hot damn. Not the ripped six-pack of a starved body builder, but the faint outline of abdominal muscles under her smooth belly. She pauses, and I hold my breath. I'm not sure if she's deciding or simply torturing me, but she finally peels her sports bra up and over her head. It joins her shirt on the floor.

Her breasts are high and small, her nipples rose-colored to my paler-pink ones. And her shoulders are wide but not bulky. Her shoulder muscles are pronounced and her arms sinewy. My mouth waters. I see a woman warrior before me. She stays just beyond my grasp to retrieve the bowl of ice cream, then uses her fingers to paint her nipples with icy pistachio. "Come here," she says.

I hop off the table, still a little self-conscious but sure she's going to join my nakedness in the next moments. My eyes are drawn to her belt buckle in anticipation of its unfastening. It glistens with my juices from her carrying me from the bedroom.

Marsh, though, has a different plan, catching and holding my hands when I reach for her. "Taste my breasts," she says. Again, her tone is commanding, not requesting. My traitorous libido loves it when she wraps her hand around my nape and guides me to her left nipple.

The pistachio is melted and warm from her heated skin. I lap every bit of the stickiness off, then suck her into my mouth. She doesn't make a sound, but I feel her breath hitch when I flick my tongue over the hardened nub as I suck. Then I give the same treatment to her right breast.

Having one hand freed when she released it to grasp my neck, I rake my nails across her abs and bend to lick the pistachio that has dripped down her ribs. She allows this until I touch her belt buckle. She grabs my wandering hand, spins me around, and pins both of my hands behind my back. The quick move forces me to stay in my bent position, and she uses her hips to push me a step forward. My belly tightens in a small orgasmic spasm when I realize I'm bent over the dining-room table.

...next time I'm going to flip you over and fuck you from behind...

I squirm when her fingers stroke my clit once, twice, and then I'm filled with one long finger. I'm ready, slick and open, and she's in up to her knuckle in one firm stroke. I gasp when she rakes her finger over my g-spot, which is so much more sensitive in this position, and reenters me with two, then three fingers.

I moan as the pressure in my belly begins to build. She's pounding her hips against the back of her hand to thrust into me harder and faster. "Marsh, I'm…"

"Don't you come. Not yet. I'll stop if you do." Her words come in short pants. She's getting off on fucking me, and that realization edges me even closer to orgasm. She's bent over me, her hard nipples raking across my shoulders with every thrust. She's slamming her hips into my ass, her fingers into my sex so hard, her thrusts so erratic the table slides forward a tiny bit. It feels so good. So good. I lift my head, and movement in my peripherical vision draws my attention to the floor-length windows along the front wall. It's dark outside now, so windows mirror back our image—me bent over the table and her bent over me, fucking me with her hand and hips. Stars above, I'm going to die if she doesn't let me come. I hear her breath catch and feel her body begin to stiffen against mine.

"Come for me, Lauren. Come for me now." She groans her words out through clenched teeth, and I am helpless to refuse her.

"Marsh. God. Oh, Marsh." I'm coming so hard and long the room fades from me. Then I realize my eyes are closed because my body is on sensory overload after spying us in the windows. I'm not a religious person, but sex with Marsh makes me want to scream "Praise Jesus!" Not that he has anything to do with it, but those words are entrenched in the DNA of all Southerners and seem to surface during moments of extreme gratitude.

I open my eyes to our reflected image. We lie half on the table, her bare flesh hot against mine, our sweat mingling. I jerk when her fingers, still inside me, twitch with the aftershocks of her orgasm. I feel smug that I made her come, too, even though I regret not being able to watch her face when she climaxed.

I moan when she withdraws her fingers and wipes them on the cloth napkin I used at dinner.

"You are so goddamned beautiful," Marsh says, leaning over me again to kiss my shoulders. My back goes cold when she straightens and steps away. Before I can protest, she's back with a soft throw from the sofa. She gathers me in her arms, wrapping the throw around my naked body. I lay my head on her shoulder, and we stand there, her holding me for several long moments.

Finally, she speaks. "I need to go check on things at the barn."

Actually, I was surprised when she accepted my invitation to dinner. I know she trusts Alex to handle the stables in her absence, but I've observed that her need to be in control isn't limited to her sex life.

"It must be killing you not to be there when the kids and horses return from the show." Neither of us have moved, despite her announcement of her imminent departure.

"You're a powerful incentive," she says.

I'm pleased enough to release Marsh to her duty, so I raise my head and kiss her. I mean it to be a light, brief kiss, but she deepens it until my head is swimming again. When she gives up my mouth, I step back and out of her arms. "Now go. It's getting late. I have a book signing tomorrow, but I'll see you Monday for my lesson."

Marsh nods. "You still need to work on posting a trot." She narrows her eyes at me. "I'm starting to wonder if you're purposely bad at it." She picks up her sports bra from the floor and tucks it into the back pocket of her jeans. When she turns to retrieve her shirt,

I see a flash of red lace peeking out of her other pocket. I smile to myself. It's an unspoken gesture of ownership. Who owns whom is the unanswered question.

"I'm not above that sort of thing if the incentive is spending time with you. But in this case, I really just can't find the rhythm."

"You will," she says with her usual complete certainty.

If only I were that certain about her, about this—whatever it is we're doing.

CHAPTER FIFTEEN

I loved this book so much, I downloaded the audio version and listened to it after I finished reading the ebook version." The woman gushes while I sign my latest book for her. Some of the top best-selling authors roll their eyes at this type of fan. She's overweight, has a bad haircut, and is dressed in a style not outdated enough to be retro chic.

"Thank you, Emily. I'm so glad you enjoyed it." I give her a genuine smile, because I love this type of fan. I wouldn't care if she were wearing a clown suit. She bought my book three times—first in ebook, then audio, and now the hardback version I'm signing for her. "I'm thinking I might revisit that same detective character in another book."

Her eyes go round. "That would be so terrific," she says, breathlessly. She leans over the table where I'm seated and stage-whispers, "But she needs a boyfriend. A big, hunky one."

I've been thinking the detective needed a hot girlfriend, but I nod earnestly at Emily. "I'll have to consider that suggestion. Thanks for the idea."

The bookstore manager steps up next to me and addresses the line of people waiting to get signed copies of my book. "The store is closing in fifteen minutes, folks. We need to move this along so everybody can get their books signed."

This is one of the big chain stores accustomed to author signings and equipped with stanchion posts and black ropes to keep those waiting in an orderly line. While the manager is making the announcement, a store employee is pulling one of those ropes across the entry point and posting a sign telling people they can buy a pre-signed copy at the register.

I give Emily a little wave as she's ushered away.

The store manager reminds me of my eighth-grade French teacher, who used to sit on a tall stool in the corner of the room with her dark sunglasses on during tests to catch anyone who cheated. No dark sunglasses, but he stands a few feet away to discourage any fan like Emily who wants to chat with me. Yet he's gracious, thanking me after the last person walks away with their signed copy. He waves an employee over to collect the few unsigned books left, so I begin to gather my messenger bag and prepare to leave.

"Could I talk you into signing one more?"

The store manager has gone to manage someone or something else, but the clerk who is collecting the books protests. "I'm sorry, but Ms. Everhart is leaving, and the store is closing. You can—"

"Tallie, it's so nice to see you." I grab a book from his arms and dig my favorite signing pen and my credit card out of my bag. "Of course I'll sign one for you."

I haven't worked up the courage to tell Marsh about the book I'm working on, so I've decided that Tallie will be a fantastic source for the details on how the eventing circuit works. I'll crosscheck what she tells me, but googling things is just not the same as knowing someone who has actually been involved. I have so many questions for her. I hand the clerk my credit card and begin writing an inscription in the book for Tallie. "Will you ring up this book for me, please?"

The clerk looks uncertain, then takes the card. "Sure, Ms. Everhart. I'll be right back."

"You didn't have to do that," Tallie says when I hand her the signed book. "I can well afford the price of a book."

I smile at her. "Consider it advance payment. I need a consultant on the book I'm currently writing."

"A consultant?"

"Do you have time for me to buy you dinner and explain?"

Tallie smiles back. "Why, yes. I do. In fact, I was going to invite you."

"Excellent." I shoulder my messenger bag. "There's a Thai restaurant a few doors down."

"Perfect," she says. "Lead the way."

❖

"The manuscript I'm working on now is set in the eventing world, so I could use someone involved to check my details, answer my late-night questions, give me the inside on how things work... that sort of thing. You can only piece together so much from YouTube videos, and it's hard to find current information. My questions might be as simple as 'do you have to wear a certain color blazer when you show dressage' to 'what kind of security would they have in a show barn.' You can waste a lot of time trying to search for details on the internet, and the information you get isn't always reliable. It's quicker and easier if you have an expert to consult."

Tallie cocks her head, chewing her curried chicken before answering. "I was under the impression you were friends with Marsh Langston and Jules Ransom. They won't answer your questions?"

"I am." I shift uncomfortably. How much should I reveal? "I take lessons from Marsh and met Jules just from her being around the barn." I didn't want to reveal that Jules had given me a massage once, because that might generate more questions I didn't want to answer. "But I asked Marsh once why she doesn't ride in competition anymore, and she won't talk about it. She got rather touchy, so I'm thinking it's better if I find someone else for a consultant."

Tallie sips her tea, looking thoughtful. "I'm not surprised she's closed-mouth about that. It was a nasty mess all around—that horse being found dead in its stall."

"I read something about that, but there's not much information about what actually happened."

"Marsh threw away a very successful career in one misguided moment. She's lucky she's not in prison. She probably would be if Kate Parker hadn't stepped in to get her off the hook."

I can't believe it. I'm staring across the table at a gold mine of information. Hot damn. "Kate Parker?" I scoop some jasmine rice into my mouth, trying to appear only casually interested.

"Living this close to Cherokee Falls, I'm surprised you haven't heard of Saint Kate," Tallie says. She looks like she'd just eaten something bad in her curry.

"Saint Kate?" I'm starting to sound like a parrot. "I bought my property less than two years ago and am afraid that—even though Cherokee Falls is only forty-five minutes from here—I've only been there once to speak to a class at the college, and then on Saturday for the horse show. So, no, I don't know Kate Parker."

"Kate, and I guess her wife Laura Black Parker, owned the equestrian training center, where the show was held yesterday, until they signed it over to Kate's heir, Jessica. Anyway, Kate is a hurricane—always stirring things up, butting in where she shouldn't, and throwing her influence and money around. The Parkers are old money, and Kate gives to so many charities that people around here think she's a lesbian Mother Teresa. She can afford the best attorneys in the state and golfs with every important judge in three districts."

"You have a problem with lesbians?"

"Not at all. It's well known that you prefer ladies, and I asked you to dinner, didn't I?"

I laugh, but being a stickler for details and accuracy, I correct her for no real reason. "I asked you, although you did mention that you intended to ask me before I beat you to it."

Tallie's smile is warm. "I enjoy your books and our new friendship. We're becoming friends, aren't we?"

"Yes. I think we are." I'm pleased that she understands I'm only interested in friendship. Tallie is maybe twenty years older than I am, but very attractive. If I weren't so enamored with Marsh, I'd definitely consider her for some recreational sex. Then again, maybe not. Tallie has an edge that surfaces briefly when she talks about Kate Parker, and I wonder who else might put that hard glint in her eyes. "I have to ask you, though, never to repeat anything we discuss. You'd be surprised at how cutthroat the publishing business and the media who follow publishing can be."

"I understand completely." She holds up one hand, her fingers arranged in what I surmise is a "Girl Scouts' honor" pledge of silence.

She doesn't explicitly say she won't repeat our conversations, but I brush that detail aside because I don't want to be a diva about the issue. "Back to Kate Parker and Marsh. What's their connection, other than their interest in horses?"

"It's all very incestuous, if you ask me. Kate mentored Skyler Reese, who married Kate's and Laura's daughter, Jessica, who manages the equestrian center. Skyler runs the Youth Equestrian Program for troubled and disadvantaged kids that Kate and her mother started. Skyler and Marsh are friends, so I'm sure that's how Kate got to know Marsh."

"Was Marsh part of that program? Is that how she knows Skyler?" I frown. Marsh has never mentioned her family, except for Harrison. Had she been a troubled kid, or disadvantaged?

"No. Skyler and Marsh were always competing against each other on the eventing circuit and somehow became friends. I think Skyler was Marsh's connection to Kate, because not long after Skyler and Marsh became friends, Marsh started campaigning a horse or two for the Parkers. I still can't figure out why Kate came to Marsh's rescue. It was one of Kate's horses that was killed."

"Oh." She'd captured my full attention when she'd labeled the situation incestuous, and I'm disappointed I can't whip out pen and paper to take notes. "You said Kate's lawyer swooped in and got Marsh off the hook. That sounds like you think Marsh was guilty."

"Nobody will ever know. Sheriff Kate rode into town, and everything was okay at the corral again." That hard glint flashes in her eyes again, then disappears.

"Except one of the circuits' top equestrians isn't riding anymore. I have a really hard time believing Marsh would ever harm a horse. What was the evidence pointing to her?"

Tallie shrugs again. "I don't want to gossip. A lot of theories were flying around, and it became hard to separate the truth from rumors." Her tone is dismissive, but I'm not ready for a change of subject, so I make a show of nodding thoughtfully.

"But in your estimation, what rumor sounded most plausible?"

Tallie chews for several long minutes—on the food she's just put in her mouth and, if I'm reading her stare correctly, on how to answer my question. Then comprehension dawns in her eyes, and her expression changes like someone flipped a switch.

"You're basing your next book on this crime, aren't you? That's why you're so curious. It's not because you have the hots for Marsh."

I nod, then shake my head. I still have reservations about admitting the subject of my next book, but it might be more dangerous if I don't qualify my questions. "I think all books, especially mysteries, start with a grain of truth. Truth rarely makes a great story, so the facts are embellished and sometimes discarded or distorted to make a boring true story into fantastic fiction." It's a dodge, for sure. I try again. "Yes, I'm hoping to construct an interesting mystery from the bones of what happened that day. But you're wrong about the other. I *am* curious because Marsh and I are involved—sort of."

The confession comes with a flitter of nerves and a sense of foreboding. I brush it away as me being paranoid. What possible motive could Tallie have for violating my confidence?

A frown instantly replaces Tallie's smile, and her eyes harden. "How involved? You know she has a stable of women, right?"

I force out a laugh and lie like I'm CIA. "Of course I do. I'm just having a little fun. Well, a lot of fun because that woman has skills. And I have my own stable, thank you. A willing woman at every book signing." Okay. I'm stretching the truth a little too much, but she has no way of verifying what I say.

Tallie turns her head to look at me sideways, amusement playing over her features. "So, you're using Marsh, then?"

I sputter. "Nuh-n-no. I wouldn't call it that. Not at all." I start shoveling a load of shit to get out of the corner my lie has backed me into. "I should have said that we're mutually enjoying each other. Nothing more."

She turns back to me. "Good. I wouldn't want my new friend to fall victim to the circuit's biggest Lothario. Where were we?"

"Rumors." This is the information I'm waiting for, but all I can think about is what Marsh might be doing right now and who she might be doing whatever with. I must be covering my turmoil well because Tallie seems oblivious to it.

"So, as I said, Marsh was contracted to ride Kate's horse at the show but flirting her ass off with me."

"You dated Marsh?"

"Marsh doesn't date, and I wasn't interested in a hookup. So, no. I think she was infatuated with me because she's always been able to seduce whoever she wants." The hard glint returns to her eyes. "In fact, Marsh came to me the day before the horse was found dead in his stall and offered to ride my horse. That was no surprise because I had a better one than the Parkers, and Marsh hates to lose. But I already had a rider familiar with mine, and she didn't take being turned down by me again very well."

"That could be a motive for an unstable person, but I've never thought of Marsh as unstable."

"I'm not saying she did it, but I had to tell the police when they asked. I didn't really think it would matter because I also told them I didn't think Marsh had it in her to kill a horse."

"Okay. What else?"

"The horse was being fed a selenium supplement, which is pretty common for show jumpers. It helps their leg joints and is safe in small doses taken orally. However, the vet who did the necropsy on the deceased horse said lab specimens showed levels of selenium in the horse's blood stream so high, it had to have been injected. According to the security guard assigned to that stable, Marsh was the only visitor to the barn that night."

"What about security cameras?"

"Each of the two premium barns where they house top tier competitors is equipped with one surveillance camera that shows if anyone comes in the barn and walks down the center corridor."

"Did the stalls have exterior-access doors?"

"Not in those two barns. You'd have to walk in front of that camera to get to a stall, but the camera in the barn where the horse died was out of order. So, while the guard was assigned to watch over two barns, he stayed in that one all night and watched the other one on a security monitor."

"Why was the security camera not working?"

"They said a rat or something had chewed through the wiring that ran along the rafters to the barn's office. It went out that evening, and a repairman was scheduled to fix it the next day."

"This all seems very circumstantial. Even a mediocre lawyer could have had the charges against Marsh dropped."

"They also found a box of latex gloves and syringes in her trunk."

I'm puzzled. Marsh drives a truck. Did she drive a car back then? "Trunk?"

Tallie leans forward over the table, her eyes glittering. I think she's enjoying this retelling. "Every horse travels with a trunk that holds their tack, blankets, leg wraps, and basic first-aid stuff, along with any special medicines, vitamins, and supplements the horse might be taking. The gloves and syringes are unusual. A veterinarian, not the trainer or rider, would treat any injury requiring injectable drugs or gloves."

"And Marsh's fingerprints were found on these items?"

"Other than leaving them in plain sight, Marsh isn't stupid. There were no fingerprints, but the box of gloves was open, and several were missing."

"Still circumstantial."

Tallie shrugs and sits back. "I'm sure there must have been other incriminating evidence the rumor mill didn't circulate. Why else would the police arrest her?"

That's the big question. Only I can answer the bigger one. Do I convict or acquit the Marsh character in my manuscript?

CHAPTER SIXTEEN

W e're going to take you back to basics," Marsh says. She gives me a leg up to mount Fancy. "This mare has a very smooth, floating trot. If you can't eventually get how to post on her, then you're a lost cause."

"No pressure there." I'm whining, but I really, really don't want to disappoint Marsh. Will she still want me if I turn out to be hopeless as an equestrian? Will she see me as her one failure? Maybe she's had other failures, so it won't be a big deal if I can't get the hang of this. Yeah, right. The softer Marsh, the one who hugs the kids she teaches and talks to horses and plays with Alex and Harrison's little terrier mix, has transformed into the other Marsh. The other Marsh is a general in the training ring, a stickler about a clean and orderly stable, and a dominating sex partner. I shiver at the last thought and shift in my seat to relieve the instant throb in my crotch.

"Are you listening to me?" Marsh's stern tone brings me back to the present. "Because if you're not focused on this lesson, then I've got a lot of paperwork I could be clearing from my desk."

I suck in a deep breath, clear my mind, and then visualize correctly posting Fancy's trot. "Sorry. I'm totally focused now."

"Good. We've talked about leads, which leg strikes forward first."

I nod. "And changing leads." Maybe I can impress her with how much I have learned as opposed to how much I can't do.

"Right. So, when you post a trot, you want to rise and sit in sync with the outside foreleg of your horse. Keep your hands steady and your legs from the calf down stationary."

I'm trying to cram the instructions in my head into muscle memory. Damn. It's a lot to remember. It's like that swimming lesson when you first learn to freestyle and have to remember to stroke with your arms, kick, and turn your head to breathe.

Marsh puts her hand on my thigh. "Relax, Lauren. You're already tensing up. Maybe I should feed you a couple of my favorite shots beforehand, so you'll be relaxed."

I don't think she's aware her fingers are tapping out some tune on my thigh as she seems to mull something over. Is that the *Jeopardy* tune? I want to laugh.

"Before I forget to ask, we have another big show in three weeks. You were a great help at the last one. You game to do it again? It's out of town, though, so you'll have to spend a couple of nights in a hotel."

My brain cuts right to the good part—several nights in a hotel with Marsh. Surely she wouldn't want separate rooms. "Yes. Definitely, yes. I enjoyed helping out. I'd be glad to do it again."

"Great. Now close your eyes," she says. "Think about how you rise from a chair. You bend forward just enough to put your center of gravity over your heels, and then you straighten to a standing position. Try that now in the saddle."

I open my eyes.

"No. Keep your eyes closed, and imagine you're getting up from a chair."

I close my eyes again and visualize sitting in a straight-backed chair. Then I rise.

"Now sit. Don't flop into the chair. Sit softly."

That's easy. One of the things my mother drummed into my head is that ladies do not flop into a chair.

"Very good. See? You can do this."

I open my eyes and beam a smile at Marsh. "I can do this."

She lets General Marsh retreat long enough to return my smile.

Then the general is back. "I don't know why Alex thinks you're hopeless."

"Maybe I don't take direction well from men...a subconscious thing."

Marsh ignores this comment. "I want you to start off walking clockwise. When you're ready, ask Fancy for a trot. When she puts her front leg on the rail side forward, you rise out of the chair. When her back leg comes forward, you sit...not completely, but with about a third of your weight on the saddle."

I take a deep breath. I'm swimming again. Stroke, kick, breathe sounds simple in contrast to rise with leg, sit with leg, don't sit all the way, hands steady, shins stationary. I'll never remember it all. Timidly, I direct Fancy into a clockwise walk. Marsh moves to the center of the training ring and waits. I'm two-thirds around the ring when Marsh barks the order.

"Trot, Lauren."

I'm not sure I would have ever asked Fancy for a trot if Marsh hadn't ordered it. The past five years have been a rebellion against taking orders from anyone, but I find that I want Marsh to tell me what to do. I know I don't need someone to do that, but it's different with her. It's like she's taking the heavy load of decision off my shoulders. I feel like she's my protector, my shield from the world. I want to relax and put myself in her hands. Oh, yeah, her hands. Warm and sure. Her long fingers. Shit. I'm supposed to be posting. I rise when I see Fancy's left front leg go forward, then sit, then rise, then sit.

"Don't force it. You look like a jack-in-the-box. Let your horse's motion carry you forward until your legs are straight, then sit...softly. That's better. Keep your hands steady and don't swing your legs back when you sit. Your lower legs should stay stationary, shins perpendicular to the ground."

I lose my rhythm when I try to concentrate on my hands and legs. Fancy shakes her head at my awkward efforts.

"Stop, stop." Marsh walks over to me and takes my hand.

I'm sweating more from nerves than effort, but she doesn't

seem to mind sweaty hands. Or maybe she does because she's frowning.

"You need to be wearing gloves." She pulls her riding gloves and the bandanna I gave her from her back pocket. "Give me your hands." When I obey, she dries my sweaty hands with the bandanna, then hands me the gloves. "Put these on, and then bend down here."

Yes! She's going to kiss me to get me to relax. I'm totally into that, so I hurriedly pull on the butter-soft, thin leather gloves and lean down while offering her my most sultry smile. She reaches up for me and everything goes dark. She's tying the bandanna over my eyes.

"I can't see, Marsh." Being blindfolded indoors, in Marsh's arms, is one thing, but I'm outdoors and sitting on the back of a horse. I don't feel secure on horseback yet even when I can see. I grab her forearms to steady myself, but she peels my fingers from her arms, puts the reins back in my hands, then guides the heels of my hands to rest on the pommel.

"After you pick up your hands to ask for a trot, then barely rest your pinkie fingers on the pommel and let the contact keep your hands still when you post."

Okay. That grounds me a little. Park my pinkies on the pommel. I wonder how many times I can say that really fast without tying my tongue up, but I voice it only once. "Park my pinkies on the pommel."

"That's right."

"How will I know when to rise if I can't see her step forward?"

"Feel her, Lauren. Let her lead the dance. When we danced, you stopped trying to anticipate my moves after I blindfolded you. You concentrated on the motion of my body to let me move you. Fancy has been schooling riders for more than seven years. You can trust her to stick to the rail of the ring and to keep her pace. Relax, and you'll feel the shift of her shoulder and the forward flow of her motion. You can do this."

"Let her lead. I can do this." I vocalize these instructions to reassure myself as much as Marsh.

I feel a tug on the reins as Marsh turns Fancy in the correct direction, then hear her click her tongue to set the horse in a calm walk. After a moment, I began to relax. I can't see, but Fancy can. She won't let me fall. I screw up my courage and ask for a trot. Fancy responds immediately. Pinkies on the pommel. I feel her shoulder shift, but is that forward or back? Hell, I don't know. I quiet my mind and concentrate on her motion. I can feel as she propels forward, so I rise, then sit. I'm doing it!

"That's it. You've got it."

Then I lose her rhythm. Marsh sounds far away, so I figure I've reached the other end of the ring.

"You had it. Sit for two beats, then rise. You'll find her rhythm again. That's right. Remember how to do that because that's how you'll follow her when she switches leads."

Her instructions make me think too far ahead, and I lose the rhythm again. I sit two beats and manage to pick it up again, only to lose it after three or four steps. My legs are already aching. Then Fancy suddenly gives a little buck and dances sideways. I rip off my blindfold. Yellow-jacket wasps are swarming around us.

"Wasps! Run for shelter." Marsh is already opening the gate when I turn Fancy toward it. The wasps aren't that easy to shake. They're back again, and Fancy takes off, bucking every second step. Before I realize it, I'm flying through the air. Damn English saddles. Nothing to hold on to. And damn, that ground is hard. I land on my back, and all the wind is knocked out of my lungs. Marsh is at my side when I open my eyes.

"Are you okay?" For the first time, I see a flash of panic in her eyes, so I nod. She presses on my diaphragm, and I suck in air on my third attempt because five or six wasps are swarming around us, and one stings me on the neck. Marsh slaps one that latches onto her cheek, and it buzzes away, only to come back and sting her forehead. She slaps harder this time, and when it falls to the ground, she squashes it with her boot.

"Fancy." I gasp out her name. Are they still chasing and stinging her?

"Can you make it into the barn by yourself? I need to get her."
I struggle to my feet. "Go. Hurry." Then I stagger away,
slapping at the wasps dive-bombing me.

When I reach the barn, Marsh is already running my way with
Fancy in tow and a huge swarm of wasps following. I know they'll
follow us into the barn, and while Marsh and I can hide in the office,
we can't seal a stall to protect Fancy. I run into the barn office. My
breath is still shallow, but urgency is pumping adrenaline in my
muscles, and I shove against Marsh's desk.

"U-u-u-uh." I don't know why, but yelling seems to help. I
don't have incredible upper-body strength, but my legs are pure
muscle, and I use them now to push the heavy desk against the wall.
Thank the stars for my running addiction. I've gone from panting to
gasping as my diaphragm loosens.

Marsh and Fancy are just reaching the barn door, and I wave
them into the office. Marsh looks confused but doesn't stop her
forward momentum. The wasps are still following, so I grab the
hose coiled in the wash stall.

"I cleared enough room for Fancy in the office," I yell at Marsh
as they pass me. I turn the water wide open and adjust the nozzle.
They aren't quite past me when I start knocking down wasps with
my water cannon.

"We're in. Come on," Marsh yells from the door.

I feel like I'm in a sci-fi novel, shooting down aliens as I back
away to the wash stall, shut off the water, then run into the office.
Marsh slams the door behind me.

"Are you okay?" Marsh is checking my arms, face, and neck.
"You've got a few stings."

My adrenaline is waning, and I'm starting to feel them. "I'm
all right. What about you?" Marsh has several red welts on her neck,
forehead, and cheek. "And Fancy?"

She's running her hands over Fancy. I see four or five swelling
bumps on her rump. "There's a set of clean sheets in the trunk over
there. Get the flat sheet out, and then look in the bathroom closet for
a sleeve of two-by-two gauze, tweezers, and the steel bowl. They
should be on the middle shelf."

I'd always thought the office was roomy, but it got small really quick with a thousand-pound horse taking up space. I edge around Marsh and Fancy to get the sheet. The closet mostly holds meds and other first-aid items for horses and people. Something tells me to grab the scissors, too, because three of us have stings, and I'm pretty certain Marsh intends to divide the sheet. I take the items to her.

"Thanks. It looks like they got Fancy in five places on her rump, once on the inside of her leg, and once about midway up on her face. You've been stung twice on your neck, once under your jaw, and once on your arm. You're not allergic, are you? Any shortness of breath? Can you swallow fine?"

I catch her hands in mine to stop them from continuing to check my scalp and under the collar of my polo shirt. "I'm not allergic, and the only places stinging are the ones you mentioned." I start my own exploration of her body. "Stand still. You've got four stings on your neck, one on your cheek, and one on your forehead that I can see."

She grimaces. "One got in my shirt and stung me a couple of times. The one in my armpit really hurts. But let's help Fancy first."

Marsh pulls away from my examination and rummages in the bottom drawer of her desk before holding up the object she's been looking for.

"Meat tenderizer and a magnifying glass?" I'm stumped.

"A few hours from now, you won't even know you were stung," she says, taking the steel bowl from me and going into the bathroom. She fills the bowl with water and dumps a handful of the gauze pads in the bowl to soak. "The best thing to draw their poison from the flesh is to wet the spot, make sure no stinger is left in there, sprinkle a lot of meat tenderizer on the sting, then cover it with a damp cloth for a few hours."

We go to work. I hold the bowl and tenderizer while she searches for stingers with the lighted magnifying glass and tweezes them out. Then she takes a square of gauze and wets the swollen tissue, sprinkles on the tenderizer, and lays another wet square of gauze on top to let it cook. We find a rhythm to our work—check, wet, sprinkle, cover. We joke about Fancy looking like an appaloosa before we lay a huge piece of wet sheet over her rump to hold the individual squares in place. We tie strips of the sheet around her leg and jaw to secure those squares.

I doctor Marsh first because she has more stings than I do and is feeling a bit nauseous. She slips her shirt over her head without hesitation. Much to my disappointment, she doesn't have any stings under her black sports bra, so she keeps that on. I don't find any stingers still in her flesh except for one of the two stings in her armpit, which she said hurt way more than the others. I tie a strip of sheet around her head to hold the gauze against her forehead sting and tape the square to her cheek sting because we can't figure any other way to secure it.

Then she doctors me, her hands gentle and sure. Our necks are easy to wrap in sheet strips, but the sting under my jaw is a conundrum. We don't have any paper tape, and I'm very allergic to the adhesive in other kinds. So Marsh wraps a sheet strip under my jaw by tying it in a bow on top of my head. She smiles as she leans back to observe her handiwork. "Very cute."

I slap her shoulder playfully, then snatch her phone away when she picks it up. "You are not taking a photo of me like this."

She chuckles. "I was going to call Alex and have him send out messages that the stables are closed tomorrow for extermination."

"Oh." I hand her phone back to her.

"But since you mentioned it…"

I whip around to stand at her side and wrap my arm around her waist to hold her there. "Only if you shoot a selfie with me and send it only to Alex. And both of you have to promise this photo will never show up on any social media or real media without my explicit consent."

Marsh holds up her phone for a selfie. "Done." She snaps the photo.

We are a sight to behold—like walking wounded in a World War II movie.

She texts the photo to Alex with an explanation and instructions, specifying that the photo cannot be shared because of my celebrity status. Harrison is an exception.

"The wasps should be gone back to their nest now," Marsh

says. "Will you put Fancy in her stall and give her a scoop of feed and fresh water?"

"What are you going to do?" I don't want Marsh to put herself in danger again. Even if she isn't allergic, I've read that too many stings can make you very sick.

"These wasps that make their nest in the ground are particularly mean. Alex and I have a system for getting rid of them."

"Just be careful."

"It's nearly dusk, a time of day when they're sluggish. They'll have retreated to their nest." She stares at me for a moment, something between hunger and...and...something else I've never observed in her eyes. "You be careful, too."

After I take care of Fancy, scoop up the manure gift she left in the office, then mop the area, I search for Marsh. She's just returning to the stable. What the hell? "Is that the shop vac sitting in the ring?"

She's plugging a long orange cord into an outdoor electrical outlet, and I can hear the vacuum come on. "It's pretty simple and very effective. You lay the nozzle of the vacuum right next to the hole leading to the underground nest and leave it running for twenty-four hours. As the wasps fly out of the nest to feed, they're sucked into the vacuum. If any are still outside the nest, they get sucked in when they try to fly back into it. You cap the hose so they can't come out through it after you shut the vacuum off and set the vacuum in the sun for a few days. Kills all of them without using insecticides or anything else that might poison the ground or harm people, pets, or wildlife."

"My dad used to pour gasoline down the hole and toss in a match."

"First of all, that's dangerous. Gasoline can explode on you. Second, that doesn't take care of any flying outside the nest, and they'll just dig in somewhere else. Third, gasoline pollutes the ground for a long time."

Marsh looks in on Fancy, who's already cleaned up her grain and is taking a standing nap.

"I didn't know you were such an environmentalist." I toss the tease over my shoulder as I go into the office but stop when I realize

Marsh isn't behind me. I poke my head back into the barn's corridor and find her staring at the entrance leading to the wasp ring. It's never going to be the training ring in my head anymore. It's the wasp ring. "Marsh?"

She continues to stare out into the dusk. "I don't know how you managed to get down here so fast when you couldn't even draw a complete breath. You even had the presence of mind to grab the hose and keep them back so we could get in the office." She turns that look on me...the one I couldn't decipher before. It's respect, no, admiration.

I take a step back into the office. Marsh follows like a big cat stalking prey, smooth and measured. She comes closer, eyes glinting, and closes the door quietly behind her. Then she pounces.

Her arms are around me, and she's kissing me. Her tongue pushes into my mouth, and her hips are grinding against mine. I'm instantly wet and my belly tightens. "Yes," I breathe when she takes her mouth, that wonderful mouth, from mine.

"You were fearless today. A warrior. A wasp warrior. I never realized that was inside you. Knowing you're the same woman who submits to me, gives me her trust, makes me crazy hot." She whirls us around so my back is against the door. "I'm going to fuck you, Lauren the Brave."

"Yes, please." I'm helpless against her frenzied onslaught and so turned on I'm afraid I'll come the minute she touches me.

She claims my mouth again while she unbuckles, unzips, and pushes down my pants. Her gloriously long fingers are between my legs, cupping my sex, then plunging inside me. She doesn't tease. Her thrusts are forceful and fast, her fingers filling me, her palm massaging my clit.

Too soon, way too soon, my orgasm is upon me. The spasm holds me in an iron grip while Marsh plunges into me. Then everything bursts free, and pure tingling pleasure flows through me like a drug spreading through my veins. One orgasm leads to a second. I may have briefly blacked out, because the next thing I feel is Marsh holding me up and my head resting on her shoulder. Consecutive orgasms don't happen to me. Sure, like most women,

I can have more than one orgasm in a single night, even a second shortly after the first with the right stimulation. But I've never had one orgasm flow into the next. Wow. My strength is returning, and I lift my head from her shoulder to kiss her. She accepts my kiss and deepens it until we break apart, needing air.

I slip off the stupid sheet strip that's tied in a bow on top of my head. I can't believe I could turn anyone on while wearing that. "Marsh, please let me touch you."

She narrows her eyes, studying me for a long moment. Then she rotates us so her back is against the door and begins to unbuckle her belt. "On your knees."

I snatch a saddle blanket from the top of the trunk and throw it on the concrete floor, where I sink to my knees. I'm nearly blind with arousal, but not stupid. Marsh and I both need her to dominate, but neither of us is into pain. I wait on my knees for her permission, her order while she pushes down her jeans, then her black boy-short underwear.

"Just your mouth," she says.

I tickle my nose against her dark-blond curls and inhale like testing a glass of fine wine. Her scent is intoxicating. The insides of her thighs shimmer with arousal, and I lick them clean before moving upward. I lick all of her and she moans, then grabs the back of my hair.

"Suck me." Her voice is hoarse and tight. Her grip on my hair guides me to her clit and holds me there. So, I do her bidding.

I suck her turgid flesh into my mouth, scraping my teeth lightly over the top of her clit as I suck and release, suck and release. Her hand in my hair begins to tremble, and her thighs go rock hard. I look up without taking my mouth from its task, but her head is thrown back, her face to the ceiling, so I'm cheated of seeing her eyes as she comes. Instead, I draw my satisfaction from her loud, growled declaration that comes next. "Mo-ther fuck-er."

I continue to suck until her thighs soften. Then I begin to lick away the spoils of my success. Her hand on my cheek stops me, and I put my hand in the one she offers to help me stand. She wraps her arms around me and holds me tight against her. I curse that I didn't have the presence of mind earlier to pull my shirt off, because she's still in her sports bra, and I can feel the warmth of her skin through my shirt. And I can feel her curls against my belly because she's a few inches taller than me. I'm wet again, but too exhausted to do anything about it. I sense she is, too.

"I'd ask you to stay, but I'm not going to the house. I'll sleep here so I can keep an eye on Fancy." She squeezes me in a rare show of affection. "You're welcome to use the bathroom. I've got to feed the rest of the horses. But if you wait, I'll help you wash off that tenderizer before you go."

"I'll wait."

She nods and pulls up her pants, then disappears into the barn.

I know she won't be long because I'm familiar with the routine. Morning and evening feed rations are prepared in the morning. She just has to dump each one in the correct bucket. Hay bags are refilled as soon as all the horses are turned out or saddled for lessons by the boy who helps around the stable. Marsh has to bring the horses in, but it's later than their usual feeding time, so they'll be standing at the gate. All she has to do is open it and get out of the way. They all know which stall is theirs and that dinner is waiting. She follows and closes the doors on the stalls to keep them tucked in for the night.

So, I don't have much time. Bathroom first. I need to pee and clean up. Damn. I find it impossible to keep a dry crotch around her. I smell like sex, and my underwear and riding breeches are soaked through. Then I remember the stack of clothes in her trunk. Yep, two sets of clothes. Which for me? Another pair of boy-short underwear and a thong. I take the thong, the sweatpants, and the long-sleeved T-shirt, leaving her the boy-shorts, soft flannel pajamas, and a short-sleeved T-shirt.

I rinse out my underwear and the crotch of my breeches and hang them over the shower rod. I toss my polo into the laundry bag hanging on the back of the door. I hadn't realized how dirty it was from my fall off Fancy until I took it off to remove my bra. I feel that I'm running out of time, so I rush to open the sofa bed, put the fitted sheet on the thin mattress, and get the soft blanket from the trunk. I've barely sat down on the bed when the door opens. I wish for a moment that I had my toothbrush, then decide I don't want to wash the taste of Marsh from my mouth just yet.

Marsh enters with a canvas carrier filled with wood and sets it next to the stove in the corner. She looks me over. "You're staying?" I'm suddenly uncertain. Did I assume too much? "If that's okay with you. I'm concerned about Fancy. I guess I've gotten attached." She turns back to the stove and begins building a fire. The longer the silence stretches between us, the more my uncertainty grows. The fire blazes to life, and Marsh closes the door to the stove. I feel like she's closing the door on us, like she's regretting that she let me touch her. If only I could turn back the clock and never ask.

Marsh rises from her task and comes to the bed where I'm still sitting. Is the night getting colder, or is it just me? I can't look at her, so I stare at my boots and contemplate pulling them on and going home. A finger lifts my chin, and I stare into the blue depths of her eyes.

"Thank you." She bends down and places a light kiss on my lips. "I'd like for you to stay."

My anxiety deflates like a hot-air balloon with no flame. "Are you sure? Really, I can go home. I know you'll take good care of Fancy." Damn that tremble in my voice.

"Very sure." She touches her lips to mine again, then points to the stack of clothes I've assembled for her. "Are those for me?"

I grab the clothes and thrust them at her. "Yes. I hope it's okay. I wasn't snooping. I just noticed them when you asked me to get the sheet, and I thought…" My words come in a rush until I realize she might think I'm being presumptuous and sputter to a stop mid-sentence.

Marsh gives me a crooked smile. "Yeah, the wet crotch is a bit uncomfortable. I'll be right back." She disappears into the bathroom, and I scramble to get under the covers. Only a few minutes later, I realize the sweatpants are going to be too warm under the thick, soft blanket, so I scramble out again and take them off. Although the thong covers none of my butt, the T-shirt is plenty long since Marsh is taller than me, and I slide under the covers again.

The minute I settle in the bed, I realize the adrenaline rush of fighting the wasps off, the poison from the stings, and the post-battle sex have drained me. I must have drifted off and only partly rouse when Marsh slides under the blanket next to me. Her hand finds my bare butt and strokes me from hip to knee. I'm so glad I shaved and lotioned up that morning, but I'm too tired to even open my eyes.

"If I weren't so tired…" Marsh lets the sentence hang in the silence for me to finish in my head, and I think I smile. "Roll over to your other side," she says, guiding me so she can spoon me from behind. The flannel of her pajama pants is soft when our legs entwine, and her hand sneaks under my T-shirt to hold my breast. She yawns, her breath warm. "Attachment to Fancy is fine. Just remember that I don't do relationships." Her lips touch my cheek. "If I did, you'd be at the top of the list."

CHAPTER SEVENTEEN

The sun coming in through the single window is so bright in my eyes.

I wake with Marsh's words on a continuous loop in my head. My uncertainty has returned. Even after the intimacies we shared, Marsh still maintains that she doesn't do relationships. What does that mean? She wants an open relationship? Or maybe she's making it clear that she might walk away at any convenient point? I try to dismiss those insecurities and concentrate on her last words.

If I did, you'd be at the top of the list.

That's enough incentive to continue my pursuit of her, right?

I roll over to find her side of the bed empty and mentally scold myself for sleeping so late. I'm sure Marsh got up several times to check on Fancy, but I was dead to the world.

I rise and stretch lazily. I've got writing I need to do, and a business trip later in the week that I have to plan, so I pull on the sweatpants I'd shed last night, fold the bedding and put it in the trunk, then fold the bed up into a sofa again. I try to move the desk back in place, but it's too heavy now that I don't have wasp-induced adrenaline.

When I go into the bathroom to retrieve my clothes, I smile. My panties I left drying on the shower rod are missing. I go to the laundry bag hanging on the back of the door and dig out the boy-shorts Marsh had worn the night before. No. I'm not going to sit around sniffing her underwear or anything like that. It's a symbol of ownership. I chuckle at the thought of us in a wedding chapel, exchanging underwear instead of rings. My writer's brain sometimes conjures the most ridiculous images. I gather the rest of my clothing and decide I'm going to have to suck it up and wear my boots home. Sweatpants and boots. How nerdy is that? I shrug at my internal conversation.

I stick my head out into the corridor first to make sure a bunch of people aren't there to witness my walk of shame. No. No. This is a walk of triumph. Not everybody can say they're at the top of Marsh Langston's list. Whatever. It doesn't matter because the barn appears to be empty. I peek into Fancy's stall. It's empty, too. Hopefully, that means she's fine and was turned out with the other horses for some pasture time.

When I emerge from the barn, I shade my eyes from the bright morning sun. I'm startled at first that the area is empty of the usual groups who come for lessons. Then I remember Marsh told Alex to cancel today's classes. I'm about to head for my SUV when I spy Marsh and Jules over by Marsh's truck. Are they arguing?

Marsh is pacing, and Jules is talking fast, gesticulating with her hands as if trying to convince Marsh of something. Marsh slaps the truck's fender, and Jules barely hops out of the way when Marsh gets in the truck, slings gravel as she turns it around and speeds down the driveway. Jules is shaking her head, her face red. I don't have to go to her because she's heading my way.

"Go home, Lauren," Jules barks as she passes me.

I break free of my shock and chase her. "Wait. What's going on? Marsh looked upset."

Jules turns on me. "Haven't you pried enough into her life? Leave her alone. Forget you ever found this stable. If you want riding lessons, at least five other facilities would probably be glad to accommodate you."

"I'm not leaving until you tell me what's going on."

Jules slams the side of her fist against the wall. "It's none of your business. Marsh never was your business, so go. Forget you met her. She doesn't need another Maggie in her life. The last one almost broke her." She wheels and heads for the office door.

I'm sputtering at this sudden exile. "Tell me what happened." Jules ignores my demand, so I run to catch up with her, but she reaches the office door three steps ahead of me. When she slams the door behind her, I'm so close I have to put my hands out to stop myself from colliding with the door and maybe breaking my nose. The lock audibly clicks into place. I slap my hands against the door in frustration. "Jules. Calm down and tell me what's wrong."

Silence.

After ten minutes of pacing outside the office door, I sit down, pull off my boots, and take off Marsh's clothes, except for her underwear. I'm going to keep those, damn it. I leave her T-shirt and sweats and pull on my dirty clothes from the day before.

I pause at the door of the Volvo, then get in because my eyes are filling with tears. I'm not giving up. I'm going to talk to Marsh after she has time to cool down.

❖

I manage to drive home with tears running down my cheeks, reviewing over and over what Jules said to me. How can my life go to shit during the few hours I slept?

By the time I pull into my garage, I'm no longer crying. Instead, I'm sinking into a depression. Obviously, Marsh must have found out about the manuscript I'm working on. I open my liquor cabinet and bypass the flavorful Apple Crown Royal in favor of a full highball glass of Crown Reserve. I head for my luxurious master bathroom, begin filling the claw-foot tub, and toss in one of my favorite bath bombs.

I could have gone straight to the hot tub on my patio, but with my dark mood I don't want to be out in the cheery sunshine. And I don't want to bother with a bathing suit because the cleaning service is scheduled to show up in a few hours. I strip and climb into my tub, the water so hot it's almost scalding my skin. "Alexa, low lights, master bath." I have a smart home but rarely remember to use it.

As the lights dim, I take a big swallow of my drink, then cough at the burn in my throat. I begin a review of my situation.

Haven't you pried enough into her life?

Jules had undoubtedly been referring to the story I'm writing based on what happened to Marsh. Sure, I can switch to a different story—maybe something based on the electrocutioner who was paid by owners to kill high-priced horses for insurance money. Or the polo ponies that were overdosed when a compounding pharmacy made an error while mixing their feed supplements. But those cases were solved, and Marsh's incident isn't. That's what makes her story interesting to readers.

Maybe I'm wrong to be poking into Marsh's life, especially without talking to her first, but who could have told her? The only people I've discussed this with are my agent, my editor, and Tallie, who swore an oath of secrecy. Sort of. But what motive could she possibly have? There has to be some other person. Maybe Marsh or Jules has a contact in the police department who alerted Marsh that I'd requested copies of the police file on the investigation. Or maybe it was the local reporter I'd questioned. Geez. How could I have been so stupid to think Marsh wouldn't find out?

I send a quick text to Marsh's number.

I can explain.

Four hours later, I still haven't received an answer, so I text again.

Please let me explain.

I try to work, but writing isn't happening today. I'm too distracted. Instead, I call LaSalle and tell her I'll drive to Raleigh tomorrow for the book signing and stay with her rather than a hotel. She's my sister confidante, and Dorine's the mother I wish I had. I need my chosen family with me right now. The thought of never seeing, never kissing Marsh again causes an awful, hollow pain in my chest, like nothing I've ever experienced. Could it be? Have I finally, truly fallen in love? Or is this the way you feel when you betray someone you care about?

❖

"I can't finish this book." I'm driving to North Carolina and on a call with Edith after six of my eight pleading texts bounce back. Marsh has blocked my number.

"Calm down. You always panic halfway through a book, and they always end up being spectacular." I can hear Edith rustling papers while she talks.

"This isn't about my usual mid-book insecurities."

"Then what is it?" I can picture Edith putting down her papers and taking off her reading glasses to give me her full attention.

"It's about prying into something, into someone I never should have. It's about betraying someone I really care about."

"This story is good, Lauren. Really good. I feel confident in saying this book will slap down the critics who think you're only good for one best seller."

I'm surprised. "Who says I'm only good for one?"

"That doesn't matter. What matters is that you prove them wrong. This book can do that. I love the romance you're weaving into the mystery. That's going to greatly broaden your audience. You should do that in every book."

"Duh. How many times do you want my detective to fall in love?"

"Once. You can write a romance for her sidekick."

"She doesn't have a sidekick."

Edith lets out a sigh. "Write one. You're the author. You can create as many characters as you need to make this story and the next marketable."

We're getting off track. "Regardless, it won't be in this story because I'm going to shelve it."

Edith ignores my declaration.

"I'm about ready to send you some edits on the last few chapters. I normally wouldn't need them back for a month or so, but I think you should take a look. Reading what you've already written always seems to inspire you to finish more quickly."

"Edith." My tone is the one my mother would use when forbidding me to do something my father would hate, but I don't care at this point. "Listen to what I'm saying. I. Am. Not. Going. To.

Finish. This. Book." I emphasize each word like a separate sentence to get my point across.

"I want you to listen to what *I'm* saying. You signed a contract. You have a legal imperative to finish it. I'm sorry if you've hurt someone's feelings over this, but it's too late in the game to switch horses. The cover has been approved. We've already signed contracts for ebook formatting and an audio version. Marketing materials have been posted online, and thousands of bookstores have already put deposits on big pre-orders."

"What if I die or become incapacitated? There has to be a clause for that."

"There is, but you are not dead or incapacitated. And if you try to fake either, I'm obligated to report our conversation today."

Her stern lecture takes me aback. Edith has never been this hard-nosed with me. I feel like a child scolded for trying to get out of schoolwork. Silence hangs in the air.

"Look," Edith says, using her coaxing voice that I normally hear when she's trying to boost my confidence because I don't think I can write a sex scene or one that includes violence. "You can do this, Lauren. Finish the book, then go to your friend with your finished draft and let her see that it has only a grain of her experience. Then tell her about our conversation today. She'll realize you had no choice."

"Okay." My voice is small because I know my chance to explain has passed. I'm so stupid. Stupid, stupid, stupid. I intentionally dug up an unpleasant time in her life and will be exposing her again to gossip and rumor.

CHAPTER EIGHTEEN

LaSalle stares silently at me after I finished recounting the whole mess with Marsh, and then she rises and goes to the bar, where she pours us two shots of whiskey from a distillery in the North Carolina mountains. She brings both shots and the bottle labeled Defiant and sets them on the small table between our Adirondack chairs.

"So you're in love with this woman? Because if you aren't, she isn't worth risking your career over, no matter how guilty you feel." She lifts her shot and waits for me to do the same. We clink our glasses together, our eyes connecting in mutual understanding that dates back to our college days. Then we down our whiskeys.

"Wow. That's smooth. I'm going to have to buy a case of that and take it home with me." The slow burn warms my throat, but it has no bite like many whiskeys or tequila. I'm feeling more relaxed already. LaSalle refills our glasses.

"You didn't answer my question," she says.

I pick up my glass and don't wait for LaSalle this time. I down a second shot. "I'm afraid I am." I can't look at her. What's more pathetic than unrequited love?

LaSalle downs her second shot, then refills our glasses again. "Then fight for her. You solve mysteries. Find out who killed that horse and clear her name."

"I make up mysteries for books. When I write, I already know who did it and lay down clues to finally point to them. It's an entirely different thing."

"Go to the place where it all happened. You'll get some idea or find someone who knows something. Isn't that what cops do when they're investigating?"

I smile at her, my first glimpse of hope in days. "How would you know what cops do?"

She shrugs. "I might have dated a detective once."

I'm feeling a little giddy after only two shots, so I laugh. Not a polite laugh, but a full-out belly laugh that's part hysteria because her remark really isn't that funny. I waggle my finger at her. "You've been holding back. This is a girlfriend I haven't heard about."

LaSalle's eyes go wide, but she's looking at something over my shoulder rather than at me. "Shit. Here comes Dorine. Quick, down your last shot, because she's going to take our bottle from us."

I don't stop to think and do as LaSalle suggests.

"Uh-huh. I see what's going on." Dorine scoops up our bottle and shot glasses. "You bonehead. You know our Lauren is a lightweight when it comes to alcohol, and I didn't slave over her favorite meal just to have you two sit out here until you pass out."

"Fried chicken, mashed potatoes, and those little lady peas?" Nobody fries chicken like Dorine.

"Just for you, baby doll." Dorine pinches my cheek affectionately.

"Hey, when I ask you to fry chicken, you always say it's too much trouble to clean up later." LaSalle pokes her lips out in a pout.

Dorine scowls at her. "You are so spoiled already, I wouldn't be able to live with you if I catered to your every whim." She puts the whiskey bottle back in the cabinet and washes out the shot glasses in the small sink of the poolside bar. "Now drag your lazy butts inside. Dinner is ready."

The dining room is almost part of the kitchen in the open layout of the remodeled mansion. When LaSalle hired Dorine away from her parents, she made it clear that Dorine is family, along with me. So Dorine sits and eats with us, ignoring social protocol against dining with the hired help. While we eat, LaSalle gives Dorine a condensed version of my predicament.

Dorine looks across the table at me. "You know you should have asked before you started prying into her past."

I nod, my mouth full of food. I swallow and answer. "I had to do some investigating first to know if it was worth a book."

Dorine gives me a don't-lie-to-me look. I feel ten years old again, trying to make up a good story for something LaSalle and I had done.

I stare down at my plate. "Okay. Yeah. I should have talked to her first." I raise my eyes to hers and square my shoulders. "If I'd told her, she would have stopped me before I got started."

"And what does that tell you?"

I lower my head again, shame heating my cheeks. "That I shouldn't have stirred up things that aren't my business when I know she wouldn't want me to."

Dorine reaches across the table and pats my hand. "At least you understand and own up to your mistakes, not like the moose that lives here."

"Hey, I pay your salary. Don't be maligning me to my friends."

"Pooh. You know I don't need your money. I'm perfectly comfortable financially, but when your mother, my best friend, moved back to New Orleans, I promised her I'd look after you."

LaSalle blushes pink. "I know, Dori. And, honestly, I'd be lost and lonely without you." The two stare at each other with affection.

Dorine grabs LaSalle's hand and smiles at the use of LaSalle's childhood name for her.

"I know, baby. As much as I threaten it, I'm never going to leave you if I can help it."

"Stop it, you guys. I'm PMSing, and you're going to make me cry." The tears gathering in my eyes aren't because of their conversation. Their affection for each other, though maternal rather than sexual, makes me jealous. For the first time in my life, I feel destined to grow old all alone.

❖

"I thought you were going down to Southern Pines to investigate your mystery."

I'd intended to stay longer with her and Dorine, but after Dorine dragged that confession out of me, I felt a strong imperative to go home and apologize to Marsh. She can block my calls, but she can't stop me from showing up unannounced. I'll make her listen. So as soon as my book signing is over, I hit the road.

"I might be back. It depends on how my apology to Marsh goes. Edith says it's too late to back out of this contract, but by God, I can make the rest up if she insists and forget about using the details of Marsh's incident."

"Okay, pal. I'm here if you need me. Hell, if you need to get away, just come hang out for a month or however long you want. Dorine would love another person to boss around."

"Thanks, Sal. If I do need to run and hide, it's nice to know your luxurious cave is always open to me. You're better than a sister, you know? Not that anything's wrong with mine, but she's not really someone I can talk to about this sort of thing."

I hear what sounds like a little sniff from LaSalle. "Yeah, well. You're the sister I never had, Laurie. Dorine and I'll always be in your corner."

"That's good to know, pal." I need to get off this call before I start sniffling, too. "I'll give you a buzz and let you know how it goes after I see Marsh. And I'll be back in a couple of days, anyway, for the signings at your other two stores."

"I'm going to hold you to it, so don't let me down and cancel on me."

"I'll never let you down if I can help it." It's the truth because I don't have very many people in my life who I've let get close.

❖

When I reach Langston Farms, it's already dark and past feeding time, so I figure Marsh will be at her house, rather than the barn. I'm surprised to see a light on in the barn office. Can it be Marsh? It has to be, because I see Alex getting into his truck to head up to his and Harrison's house. I whip into the space next to him and hop out of my car. I stretch. My muscles are still stiff after the nonstop, five-hour drive. I wave at Alex to at least acknowledge him as I round his truck to go into the barn. He trots after me.

"Lauren, wait." He catches up and grabs my arm. "Wait, damn it."

"I know she's blocked my phone number, but I have to talk to her, Alex. That's her in the office, isn't it?"

"Don't go in there, Lauren. She's been really upset. You need to give her more time before you talk to her."

"I think I know what she's upset about. I have to explain and apologize." I brush past him and take two steps before he catches my arm again. "Let me go, Alex. I love Marsh, and I'm not leaving until I talk to her." I jerk my arm from his grasp.

"Oh, Jesus, Mary, and Joseph. Just listen to me, okay?"

I stop. "You've got one minute."

Alex wrings his hands in a very unmasculine way. "Marsh has been different since you came along. Different in a good way. She hasn't let anyone close to her—well, except for me, Harrison, and Jules—since, um, since the problem in North Carolina. Harrison and I've been scared to even say we like you, or acknowledge that anything's going on between you two, for fear she'll back off and close up again. Then you go and betray her. She's hurting, and Marsh strikes out when she's hurt. You do not want to go into that office."

"I don't care what cruel things she says to me. I deserve them, and I'll handle it." I stride purposefully to the door and begin to open it when Alex yells after me.

"She's not alone, Lauren."

I rap quickly on the door and open it as Alex's warning settles in my brain. Then I stand frozen in the doorway.

Marsh's jeans are sagged around her knees, her bare butt is framed in the black straps of a dildo harness, and she's pumping into a woman whose face is turned away from me. Even so, I'd recognize that voice and that hair anywhere. It sure isn't her clothes that tips me off to her identity because she isn't wearing any. Tallie?

"Oh, God, Marsh. I'm going to come." Tallie moans out her next words. "Harder, baby. You know what I like."

Marsh looks over her shoulder at me, her eyes hard and distant, but she never breaks rhythm as she thrusts harder and delivers several loud smacks to Tallie's bottom while she stares at me. Tallie howls and turns her head toward me, capturing my gaze.

"Yes, I'm coming. So good. It feels so good. Don't stop. Don't stop." Tallie's voice goes from a deep moan to a shrill scream. "Oh, God. Yes, yes, yes!"

I step back and slam the door closed. My guilt morphs into anger. Fool. What a fool I've been. I'm too tired to drive back to Raleigh, so I check in to a hotel on the off chance Marsh comes looking for me later. No way. She's already moved on. But I'm not taking the risk.

I'll swing by my house tomorrow to get some fresh clothes and go right back to North Carolina. I don't deserve this. I haven't accessed anything that isn't public record so far—things any member of the public could request to see.

I grab the bottle of Defiant I picked up on my way out of North Carolina, plus a glass, and sit on the small balcony of my hotel suite. I swig a mouthful straight from the bottle before pouring a glassful over ice.

God damn Marsh Langston. I was stupid to trust her. A plan begins to form in my head. I'm going to get to the bottom of this and clear Marsh if she's innocent. If she's not, well, then I've brought a horse killer to justice.

Chapter Nineteen

My first stop is the Cherokee Falls Equestrian Center after I've gone by my house to refresh my suitcase and eat lunch. Actually, I made a huge sandwich because I haven't eaten since an early lunch yesterday. But I still can't stomach food, so after a few bites, I wrap it up to take with me. Cherokee Falls is forty-five minutes northwest in Virginia's Blue Ridge foothills, and my ultimate destination—Raleigh—is five hours southeast of my home. But I'm hoping to interview Kate Parker. She has to know things that aren't in public records.

I'm awestruck again at the expanse of this place—five barns with paddocks extending from each, two outdoor rings, and the arena's indoor ring. Marsh told me on the day of the show that a sixth building houses an indoor pool and gymnasium. At the center of all that is a two-story, sprawling farmhouse with a wide porch that wraps around three sides of the bottom story.

The center is teeming with people and horses. When I knock on the door, the woman who answers seems familiar. Her dark hair is pulled back in a French braid, and her blue eyes are at least two shades lighter than Marsh's. Gah. Stop thinking about Marsh's blue eyes.

"Yes?" the woman asks when I don't say anything.

It dawns on me. "You're Jessica Black." I'd seen photos of her with the articles I read about the accident that ended her riding career.

She chuckles. "It's Jessica Parker-Reese, but you can call me Jess. Please come inside."

I hesitate, my writer brain flashing to all those scenes where the victim stupidly lets the killer in her house because he says his car broke down and needs to use her phone. "Do you always let strangers in your house without knowing who they are?"

Jessica smiles over her shoulder. "Oh, I know who you are. Skyler's read every book you've written, and your picture is on all the back covers. And Jules has gone on and on about the famous author taking lessons at Langston Farms. Skyler and I both wanted to meet you last weekend at the show, but everything was just too hectic."

"Is Skyler here?" I shake my head to reset my thoughts. "Actually, I was hoping to talk to Kate." I came here for a reason, and I don't need to drag this out. "I've been looking into the incident that happened in Southern Pines, the one that made Marsh quit riding professionally. I was hoping she might be able to answer some of my questions."

Jessica leads me into a home office and sits behind the desk. "Kate and my mom are in Greece, where they have a villa. We expect them back in about three weeks because they're planning to build another house on the back part of this property."

"It was Kate's horse that was killed, right?"

"Yes. Jakobi was Kate's horse, but nobody here thought for a minute that Marsh was to blame. I was too pregnant at the time to go to that show, so you really should talk to Sky. I'm sure she can fill in a few blanks for you." She stands again and gestures for me to follow. "She's at the gym, overseeing homework time for the kids in her program. I can't leave the house because our little one is napping, but I'll point out the building."

I find Skyler sitting at an old-fashioned, oak teacher's desk, tapping away on a laptop with a dozen kids sitting in student desks, their heads bent to their schoolwork.

Skyler looks up when I hesitate in the doorway and smiles. I speak quietly so I won't disturb the kids. "I'm sorry to interrupt, but Jessica said I'd find you here."

Skyler stands, and I realize how very tall she really is—at least six feet or more. She holds out her hand. "Ms. Everhart. It's so great to finally meet you. I looked for you after our little show Saturday, but Marsh whisked you away so fast, all I saw were the taillights of her truck." She cocks her head, her eyes filled with amusement.

"Yes, well." I debate how much to say. Skyler's students appear to be hard at work, but I feel like a dozen pairs of ears are also listening. "Do you have somewhere we can talk?"

Skyler looks over her group, then at her Apple watch. "We're almost done here. One minute and I'm all yours." She gestures to one of the students. "Jamie, bring your stuff up here, please."

The young blonde who I'd seen riding for the center at Saturday's show gathers her books and backpack and comes to the teacher's desk. She's clearly a teen but almost as tall as Skyler.

"Can you check everybody's homework and text their trainers that they're clear?" She hands Jamie her phone.

"Sure, Sky."

Skyler slides her laptop into a messenger bag and joins me at the door. "Let's go to the office."

❖

"So, does Marsh know you're poking around in this?" Skyler asks after I explain the information I'm trying to track down.

I stare out the picture window that looks into the pool area, then make a quick decision. Deceit has wrecked my budding relationship with Marsh. It's not that I outright lied to her, but I did through omission. I look up, directly into her eyes, and tell the truth.

"I didn't tell her at first because, if I'm honest with myself, I knew she wouldn't like it. Later, I was afraid letting her know would mess up the relationship developing between us. But Tallie Bouling told her. Now, Marsh has blocked my number so I can't explain...I mean apologize. I was wrong to not tell her."

"Why don't you just go to her barn and make her talk to you?" My cheeks heat with embarrassment and anger. "I did. But, only two days after we'd been together, I found her in the office fucking that woman, Tallie, who I'd confided in."

Skyler sits back and steeples her fingers. Will she help me? I've put my cards on the table, but I have the distinct impression she's going to refuse to talk to me until she consults with Marsh. Celebrity apparently does not trump friendship. Her loyalty to Marsh guts me. I've been such a selfish prick. My throat tightens and eyes well with tears. I busy myself with getting a notepad and pen from my shoulder bag as I brush away the few that trickle down my cheeks. When I look up, Skyler's expression is questioning but not judgmental. She silently hands me the box of tissues on the office desk.

"I'm sorry. I love her. I didn't even get the chance to tell her before I messed things up. It's probably for the best. She obviously doesn't feel the same about me, or she wouldn't have been with another woman just two days after..." I can't finish and wipe angrily at my tears. I don't deserve respite, but I feel a little lighter after confessing to this woman who's practically a stranger. "I'm sure that's more than you want to know."

"That's exactly what I wanted to know," Skyler says. "Things were not easy for Jess and me when we first got together. I didn't like her, and she didn't like me until we got to know each other. Then Kate didn't want me dating her daughter because, even though she was my mentor, she knew of my love-'em-and-leave-'em reputation. But in the end, we rode out the rough spots because we were destined to be together. Marsh and I are pretty good friends, but she's not really talkative. She doesn't need to be. Working with the troubled kids that I do, I've taken courses on psychology and how to read people. Marsh was different Saturday. She was more open and talkative. I haven't seen her that relaxed in years. Well, since Southern Pines. And she kept scanning the crowd. I'm guessing she was looking for you because she made one excuse after another to keep popping back over to her trailers. I'm guessing that's where you were most of the day."

"Yes." Just thinking about what I'd thrown away almost makes me burst into tears again.

"So, tell me what you want to do about it."

I take a deep breath and blow it out to collect myself. I look up and hold Skyler's gaze, hoping she can see the honesty behind my words. "I want to clear Marsh's name. I know Kate got her out of jail because they had no damning evidence, but without finding the real culprit, she'll always have a shadow over her and gossip around her. I want to find who killed that horse, because I can tell you with certainty that Marsh didn't do it."

"How can you be certain?"

"The same way you and Kate knew and fought for her even though it was Kate's horse that was poisoned."

That seems to be the right answer. We talk for another thirty minutes before Skyler stands. She has riding students waiting for her.

"Well, that's all I can tell you, but I'll pass along your phone number and email to Kate. They'll be in Greece for another couple of weeks, maybe a month. She'll get in touch if she knows anything more."

"Thanks, Skyler. Sorry for blubbering and laying this at your doorstep. If it goes even more sour than it already has, I'll never tell Marsh that you tried to help."

Skyler shakes her head. "Kate and I should have done this for Marsh back then. We were wrong not to. We got her out of the physical jail, but she's been in a jail of rumors and innuendo ever since."

CHAPTER TWENTY

"Y ou caught her fucking another woman less than two days after she's been doing the dirty with you, and you're still going to keep trying to prove her innocence? Seems like to me you should forget her and write the rest of the book off the top of your head."

I eye the nearly empty Defiant bottle between LaSalle and me, then drain the rest of it into my glass of diet soda. "I'm in love with her, Sal. I'm furious and hurt, but I've never felt this for another woman. I'm not ready to walk away."

"Lauren."

"No. Even if she doesn't feel the same—except I know she does deep down because I've seen it in her eyes, felt it in her touch—I'm going to do everything I can to clear her. I want to give this to her. This situation is crippling her emotionally and professionally. I want to free her of that."

"I still think you're crazy."

Dorine pokes her head into the great room. "Don't talk to her like that. A woman knows her heart, LaSalle. Now go get that extra bottle of whiskey you think I don't know about in your room and mix my bedtime toddy. I'm ready for sleep, and you should be, too. You both have to be at the Chapel Hill bookstore by eleven in the morning."

"Yes, ma'am." LaSalle slowly rises from her recliner and leaves to retrieve the requested, or rather demanded, bottle of whiskey. "I would've bought a whole case if I'd known everybody else was going to drink it up." Her mumbling fades as she climbs the stairs. Dorine looks at me with sympathetic eyes and pats my hand. "If it's meant to be, sugar, it'll all work out. You do what you have to, and don't worry about what other people think. The Lord will watch over you."

I'm feeling very tired and a little drunk. "He doesn't watch over lesbians and gays, Dorine. We're an abomination."

"That's just mean, insecure people talking. Jesus loves and watches over everybody. Didn't he stand up for the prostitute against people who were about to stone her? You who have committed no sins, cast the first stone, he told them. Of course, none of them could. And it wasn't Jesus who said all that stuff about gay people being abominations. It was those self-appointed men, especially that idiot Saul turned Paul."

Dorine always insisted that LaSalle and I go to church every Sunday morning until we were adults. Then it was our choice. I never felt comfortable, and once I started taking history classes and learned the truth about the Christian Crusades and the slaughter the crusaders committed in Jerusalem, I began to see Christianity in a different light. I'm no longer religious—not that I ever really was—but I am spiritual, and Dorine knows that.

"You just throw out every other part of that Bible and concentrate on what Jesus said. That's the important stuff," she says.

"Okay." My answer holds little conviction.

Dorine pats my leg this time and accepts the nightcap LaSalle brings her. "I know you don't believe me, but Jesus will watch over you whether you believe or not. I'll say a special prayer for you tonight to make sure he's paying attention."

LaSalle doesn't roll her eyes as I expect but helps Dorine to her feet with a murmured "Good night."

Dorine stops when she reaches the door. "Belgian waffles at nine thirty. You need to be headed to Chapel Hill by ten."

"Yes, ma'am," LaSalle and I chorus. Even hell freezing over can't keep me from Dorine's Belgian waffles.

❖

"Thank you for reading." My hand is cramping, and my smile is forced. I normally like book signings, even when my hand is sore for days afterward. Today, I'm having trouble focusing because I'm anxious for the day to be over so I can drive to Southern Pines tomorrow morning. I take another book from the stack next to me, open it to the title page, and look up with pen poised. "Hi. Who should I sign this...Anna, hey. It's great to see you."

My one-night stand—okay, a couple of nights since we met—book-club friend stands before me, clutching the hand of a beautiful African American woman. "Hi, Lauren." She seems a little nervous but gestures to the book I've opened. "You know I already have a signed copy. This one's for my mother, Ellen. Just write something about what an awesome daughter she has."

"That won't be hard to do."

We laugh as I begin to scribble. When I finish and hand the book to her, we both speak at once.

"I want to introduce..."

"I'd like to pick your brain..."

We laugh again.

"You first," I said.

"I want to introduce my girlfriend, Alisha. We met a few months ago when she joined our mystery book club, and it was, I dunno..."

"Love at first sight," Alisha fills in for her. "After my first book-club meeting, we literally talked all night." Alisha's voice is as rich and smooth as her complexion. I like her immediately. She hands me a dog-eared copy. "I've read it at least three times. It amazes me how when I reach the end, I can look back and see the small clues you left throughout the book."

"That's because she already knows how it's going to end." LaSalle's big voice comes from just behind me.

She holds her hand out to Alisha. "I'm LaSalle de Blanc, owner of this fine store."

Alisha returns the handshake. "Alisha Turner."

"My chef has informed me that she's prepared a dinner large enough for a mob, and since Lauren is staying with me, why don't you two join us for dinner? Lauren can tell you about the woman she's gone gaga over recently."

Maybe I could use a pair of objective eyes on the problem. Anna may be a physical therapist, but she has a keen mind for solving mysteries. "Please, do join us. Both of you, of course."

Anna visibly relaxes, her eyes finding mine. "Really? That would be great, if we're not taking up too much of your time."

LaSalle has conspired for them to be the last in line, so as I begin to clean up, she gives them the address and arrival time. I pause and try to rub out a sudden cramp in my hand, but Anna brushes away my good hand and begins her expert massage on the cramped tendon.

"Your tendons are as tight as my granny's garters."

The cramp releases my tendon under her ministrations, and I sigh with relief. "Thanks. But I worry about why you know how tight your granny's garters are."

Alisha laughs, and I smile at my tease because I'm feeling better. I'm surrounded by friends who will understand my dilemma. Friends who may be able to help my pursuit of justice.

With guests to entertain, Dorine is in her element. I'm not a guest, of course. I'm family, which she's made clear on many occasions. When Alisha stiffens at LaSalle having an African American working as a domestic, LaSalle and Dorine share a glance, and both go out of their way to make clear that Dorine is no maid.

"Anna, Alisha, this is Dorine. She's our chef and my personal assistant. Hell, she's more like my boss, and I just live here for her to have something to do."

For the first time, I see Dorine and LaSalle like others might. They're a comical match—Dorine diminutive and LaSalle tall and large-framed. Dorine is obviously in charge, and neither makes any attempt to hide that fact.

We all go straight to the informal dining area—a rarely used formal dining room is attached to the other end of the kitchen—because the aroma of Dorine's enchiladas has everyone's stomach growling.

"I'll set the table," LaSalle says, picking up the stack of plates, napkins, and silverware Dorine has placed on the kitchen island.

"No, you won't," Dorine says. "You never do it right. Lauren, honey, please set the table for us?"

I grin and accept the dinnerware from LaSalle. Anna and Alisha help, taking the place setting I hand them and arranging it exactly as I do because I'm the one Dorine has deemed worthy. I kinda feel like a kid doing what Mom wants. I grin at Alisha, and she gives me a toothy grin back. She's finally relaxing into the informal atmosphere and jumping into the teasing. I see the looks of affection passing between her and Anna, which makes me miss Marsh all the more.

We're lingering over scrumptious passion-fruit flan and coffee when Anna draws the conversation to my writing.

"So, *The Book Club Murder* is selling well? I saw it hit the top of the mystery best-sellers list."

I swallow the flan melting in my mouth. Damn. I'm going to have to get Dorine's recipe and give it to my chef. "Unbelievably well. It's broken into the top ten on the main *USA Today* and the *Readers Digest* lists. As we discussed, ten percent of the proceeds are going to literacy programs. I do that with all my books. And another ten percent is going to your book club to distribute how they see fit. Right now, that money is funneling into a bank account here, with only LaSalle or me able to make withdrawals, but we need to give your club access to the account. The withdrawals will require two authorized signatures." I gesture to LaSalle. "And Sal has another surprise for you."

Everybody looks to LaSalle as she explains. "The small store next to my Chapel Hill bookstore is going to be vacant by the end of next month because the current retailer is moving, and I've bought the space. I want to put a façade resembling a cottage in the woods on the front and call it A Murder of Mysteries. You know, like a murder of crows? It will have its own street entrance but be connected inside by an archway to my big bookstore, with all the mystery books shelved in that smaller space."

LaSalle is almost bouncing in her chair with the next bit of news, which is saying a lot for an NFL-linebacker-sized woman.

"Get to the point, child," Dorine orders her. "I swear, I'll be picking out my casket before she ever tells it."

I expect a comeback from LaSalle, but she's obviously too excited.

"The smaller store will have a room at the back just for your book club. It will have double doors that stay open unless you guys are meeting. You can have lecturers come, you know, like a detective who's solved a big murder. You, of course, can loan the room to anybody else you want, but that's totally up to you. Your club's name will be over the door, and you can use some of the money from the account Lauren set up to furnish it."

Anna's eyes are wide as she takes it all in. Alisha's expression is calculating.

"Would that account have enough money to donate to the local library system, so they can buy more mystery books?" Alisha asks.

Anna jumps in to clarify. "Alisha is a librarian. Besides working at the Chapel Hill Library, she's on the regional board that decides what books they buy each year."

I'm caught up in LaSalle's excitement, so my laugh is giddy. "That account already has several hundred thousand in it. As long as the club approves it, y'all can give as much to the libraries as you want. It doesn't have to be just for mystery books either."

Alisha puts her fingers to her mouth. "Oh my God. There's so much that could be done. More bookmobiles so we can get books out to remote areas. I don't know how to thank you...if the club is on board with making a sizable donation to the libraries." She looks to Anna.

Anna's mind, however, is clearly running on a different track. "We need to come up with a better name for our club. I love the store name, A Murder of Mysteries. We need something cool like that. I'll send out a group email and get everybody to bring suggestions to next week's meeting."

"The money's not likely to dry up either," I tell them. "I'm thinking that I'll want to do another book or two based on the club. It would be a series of lighter, fun mysteries—Miss Marple kind of stuff—between my more serious, gritty mysteries."

Anna actually claps in excitement. "I'm sorry. I'm just so overwhelmed. It's all so amazing."

Alisha is still wearing a huge smile but gracefully controls her enthusiasm. "Can we ask what you're currently working on?"

Here's the big moment. I'm perfectly comfortable dissecting and talking about other people's lives, but when it comes to sharing mine, I'm extremely private. I'm desperate, though, and feel like this Marsh situation isn't at a dead end, just a tree I can't see around because of the forest crowding in. I need a fresh pair of eyes.

My cheeks heat a little, and I use my fork to toy with the tiny bite of flan still on my plate. "As Sal mentioned, I've met someone, too."

Anna reaches across the table and squeezes my hand. "Oh, Lauren. That's so wonderful. What's her name, and why isn't she here?"

"It's a really long story, but the short version is that I met Marsh when she was running a pony camp I signed my niece up for last summer. I'm so shamelessly hot for her that, when the camp was over, I asked for private riding lessons for myself."

Anna smiles. "I'd love to meet the woman who's caught your eye."

"She's not speaking to me right now. Maybe never again."

"Oh, no." Anna's tone is so sympathetic, I would have curled up in her arms if her girlfriend wasn't sitting in the chair next to her. "What could you have possibly done to deserve that?"

"She's a professional equestrian, and something bad happened to her about four years ago. A horse was killed. I'm talking a very high-dollar horse. I started looking into it because I was curious. Then I realized the mystery of who killed the horse had never been solved. I'd been struggling with what to write next and realized this would be perfect to base my next fiction novel on. I almost always build my fictional books from the facts of a true story."

Alisha frowns. "There's nothing wrong with that."

"Marsh is very private, and I knew she wouldn't like me poking around something awful that happened to her. So, I didn't tell her. She still found out and is so furious, she's blocked my number on her phone."

Anna sits back. "Wow. You've got quite a mess, don't you?"

I hang my head. "I tried to quit the book, but my editor already has about twelve chapters of it and says I have to fulfill my contract."

Dorine takes my hand and squeezes it for support. I swallow my rising emotions.

"I intended all along to find the real killer to stop the rumors that Marsh did it and managed to wiggle out of any criminal charges. It's almost wrecked her career—and her personal life, I think." I straighten my shoulders and lift my chin. "I still intend to clear her, even if she never takes me back."

Alisha lifts an eyebrow and points out the elephant in the room. "You love her."

"I do." I meet her eyes so she can see the truth in mine. "I'm sort of stuck right now. I know I'm close, but I'm still looking for the key that will unlock this whodunit. I'm afraid I'm too involved to see it clearly, especially if the unthinkable happens and I find evidence that Marsh is guilty. I need a fresh pair of eyes looking over my shoulder." I shift my gaze to Anna. "I was hoping to persuade Anna to go with me to Southern Pines tomorrow to see the location where it happened and talk to people who might have been around then. I know it's really short notice, but you were incredibly helpful on the book-club-murder story."

"I can." Anna answers so quickly, she actually talks over my last few words, then catches herself and looks uncertainly at Alisha. "If it's okay with you, honey."

"Alisha, you're welcome to come, too. I mean, I'll pay for two rooms anyway."

Alisha is shaking her head. "I had one coworker fly out West to meet her first grandbaby. Before her plane's wheels touched down in Denver, another coworker was taken to the hospital and ended up getting an emergency appendectomy. There's no way I can leave work this week." She turns to Anna. "But you go, baby. Lauren's right. You're good at this sort of stuff."

Anna gives Alisha a quick kiss before looking at me again. "What time do we leave in the morning?"

CHAPTER TWENTY-ONE

We're hardly on the highway before I confess the rest of my story, that I caught Marsh with another woman. Anna's response isn't what I expect.

Instead of consoling me, she blurts out her own confession. "I told Alisha that I've...that we've slept together."

I stare at her for a few seconds before returning my eyes to the road. "And she still let you come with me?"

"She knows how head over heels I am for her. So, no. She's not afraid we'll sleep together again." She hesitates before continuing. "She also said she could see how in love you are with Marsh."

My cheeks heat a bit. "You have a very perceptive lady."

Anna looks shyly down at her hands folded in her lap. "She's really special."

"If you don't mind, I'm still going to get separate rooms for us. We can get connecting ones if the hotel has two available so we can brainstorm, but I haven't been sleeping well lately and often get up in the middle of the night to answer email or write, then go back to sleep for a few hours. I'd just keep you up, too."

Anna's voice is soft. "Whatever is most comfortable for you is fine." She flashes a smile that brightens our somber discussion. "Now tell me more about the fictional account of all this that you're writing."

❖

The Carolina Horse Park is actually about twenty miles from the better hotels of the Southern Pines-Pinehurst area, so we check into one of those "by Marriott" places in a small town closer to the park.

The horse park is an amazing two hundred and fifty acres, with three show-jumping rings, a show-jumping-slash-dressage arena, barns totaling nearly three hundred horse stalls, and at least six steeplechase courses, plus a driving course for horse carts, not golfers.

I had called ahead to explain that I wanted to use the park as one of the settings in the new mystery I was writing and asked if anyone would be around to give us a tour and answer questions. The guy who answered the phone wasn't very enthusiastic but said he'd pass the request along. The woman who called back was on their board of directors and thrilled to personally accommodate us. I have no delusions that there's a mystery reader behind every bush, but she must have at least googled me. True to her word, a petite, silver-haired woman was waiting for us at the announcers' building.

"Ms. Everhart, it's so nice to meet you." She reminds me of Barbara Stanwyck, the tough matriarch in the old television western *The Big Valley*. "I'm Victoria Banks. We spoke on the phone earlier."

I shake the hand she offers me. "Thank you so much for letting us take up your time." I gesture to Anna. "This is Anna, a friend who is helping me with research for my current project."

The two women shake hands and exchange pleasantries, and then Victoria pretty much recites the info we've already viewed on the park's website, with a little history thrown in.

"Now, what can I show you first?"

I scan the area, and Anna takes a yellow legal pad from her shoulder bag, both of us acting out the agreed pretense of simply casing the site. Anna, bless her, begins to draw a rough map of the park. "We'll want to estimate some distances between things, so I can get the timing right in my story, but we can add them later."

"I have just what you need." Victoria strides over to her Mercedes G-Class SUV, opens the back, and retrieves a range finder from her golf bag. She holds it out to Anna, but I take it instead.

"Of course. I don't know why I haven't thought to use one of these before." I hold the device that looks like a small, sleek pair of binoculars up to my eyes. "These are perfect." I give Victoria a beaming smile as I hand them over to Anna. "I'll have to get a pair of these for myself."

"Oh, keep those," Victoria says. "I've got a dozen of them. They're like reading glasses. You can never find a pair when you need it, so you buy enough to keep one in every room of your house and another for the car."

I laugh. "That's very generous. Thank you so much."

Actually, I learned from a psychiatrist friend that people will be more open with you when they believe you're indebted to them. Someone who owes you would never betray you, right? It's an old scammer's trick, my friend told me.

"We should look at the stables first," Anna says.

"Yes." I agree.

"This way," Victoria says.

The stables are long, shed-row-style facilities lined up parallel to each other and perpendicular to a large, grassy quad. Half are on one side of the quad and half on the other side, with about thirty feet between each stable. Rather than an interior corridor like Marsh's stable, the stalls of rough-cut oak open from the outside, with a six-foot roof overhang that shelters them from direct sun or rain. Thick boards go all the way to the roof on the back side to separate the stalls from the ones on the other side.

"I'm sorry. This isn't how the stables were described to me. I was told the barns had a center aisle, and the stalls opened only to the inside."

"Oh, you want to see the new stables with premium stalls. Well, they're not really new. I guess those barns are four or five years old. They're the last ones." She gestures for us to follow her, and we walk past three other barns to reach one of the two fancy ones. "They were built about five years ago with donations from the people who own the top-tier horses and come for the international and national shows. They wanted barns with security. Some of those horses are worth more than a million dollars, you know."

"Really?" Anna distracts Victoria as we had planned so I can poke around. "I know racehorses can cost a lot, but I had no idea." Victoria scoffs. "I personally think horse racing is disgraceful. They run those poor animals at top speeds before they finish growing. That's why so many break down on the track. A top-tier dressage horse is usually at least eight years old."

"Eight years?"

"That's because we don't ride them before they're at least three, and it takes that long to train them. As you can imagine, dressage takes a lot more training than just letting horses run fast around a track."

Anna apparently has hit a nerve with Victoria, and she's on a rampage about an equestrian sport she considers gauche. It's perfect cover to free me to explore. I walk down the corridor, looking into the stalls. No rough-cut boards in these. The inside is lined with finished oak, and the top half features vertical bars of black metal. These are nice, like the stalls in Marsh's barn. The barn smells of the wood chips, sweet feed, and leather.

I spy a security camera at one end of the long corridor. Midway down the corridor are a tack room and a walk-in, closet-size security office with a half-bath. The office consists of only a small desk, a trash can, and a computer wired to the security network for the two premium barns. The tack room is large and designed sort of like a pro-sport locker room, with each open locker wide enough for a standard tack trunk and two wall-mounted saddle brackets aligned vertically on one side. The other half above the trunk has a short shelf with space below to hang clothing. Each locker is numbered to correspond to a specific stall in the barn. I'm surprised I can see no security camera in this room, considering how much the saddles and bridles cost. There's a large window on the outside wall and several ventilation fans to keep mold from forming on the oiled saddle leather.

I'm by the window when I hear Anna's and Victoria's voices grow closer. I turn around, intending to rejoin them, when I realize I can stand by the window in the tack room and see right into the horse stall across the aisle—all the way into it if the stall door is open. Curious. My writer brain files this fact away as a possible plot point.

"What do you think?" Anna looks at me expectantly when I step out of the tack room.

I stand in the stall across from the tack room and point. "When you slide this stall's door back, you can see all the way through the tack room and out the window." The tack-room door is as wide as an exterior door, I assume to allow for large trunks.

Anna raises an eyebrow. "I can see several possibilities for that fact in your story."

I grin because I can tell our minds are running along the same track. I'm honestly looking for ideas for the book's plot as well as searching for clues to who killed the horse Marsh is blamed for.

Victoria looks from the window to where I am in the stall. "Too bad nobody was outside that window that awful night the Parker horse was killed."

Anna and I exchange surprised looks.

"You were on the park's board then?"

"Oh, yes. It was terrible. These premium barns were finished just in time for the international show. Actually, the stables were finished, but we were still deciding what horses should get priority in booking these stalls. I mean, you don't want a junior equestrian's twelve-hundred-dollar pony stabled here while a later booking comes in from someone with a million-dollar Olympic prospect, and all you have left are the basic stalls in the other barns."

"What about security?" I asked. "Do you have guards patrolling the grounds at night? And who hires them—the board or the event organizers?"

"Oh, no. Just like the sound system at the judges' building, we have a minimal security system the event organizers can make use of, but we decided from the outset that the legal pitfalls of the park providing security guards were too great. If the event organizers want security guards and to use our simple system of two cameras in each barn, they have to hire their own guards and sign an agreement that we're not responsible for anything that results from unreported problems with the security hardware, or within a reasonable twenty-four-hour repair period should the system become inoperable. We're a nonprofit, not a wealthy corporation, but we do have several attorneys on the board who ensure we're protected should something catastrophic happen."

"So the event sponsors hired the guards the night the Parker horse was killed?"

"Yes. We all felt terrible, of course, about what happened." She shakes her head. "I think everyone would have been less devasted if a person had been killed, rather than such a highly trained, beautiful horse."

My gut tells me she's hit on a truth at the heart of the dark deed. "We've run across several different rumors about who might be responsible. There may be more rumors we don't know about. Can you tell me what you've heard?"

Victoria studies me, suspicion creeping into her expression for the first time. "I'm not going to end up quoted on some true-crime television show, am I?"

"Absolutely not by talking to us." For once, I'm truly glad for the celebrity my success has brought. "You know who I am. I write fiction. I don't rehash unsolved murders on B-level television. In fact, I hate those shows. They're filled with sensationalist innuendo."

Victoria nods but still hesitates before she spills what she's heard. "I guess the main rumor is that Marsh Langston killed the horse to please Maggie Talmadge, who owned the next-best horse in the field. Maggie had pretty much groomed Marsh as a rider, and God knows what else, since Marsh was a young teen."

Whoa. What? "What did you mean by 'God knows what else'?"

"I have always heard whispers that Maggie has a kinky sexual appetite and always has a young woman or young man under her wing. She's a spider who uses her horses and money to lure them into her web."

I don't like thinking of a young Marsh under the spell of some rich sexual predator. "What other rumors?"

"Oh, things people wrote off pretty quickly as hogwash. Kate

Parker had her own horse killed for the insurance money. Nobody believed that, of course. Kate, like her mother was, is a horsewoman through and through. She loves her horses like they're her children."

"I haven't met her but have heard her referred to as Saint Kate." Victoria chuckles. "No doubt. She's given money to just about every horse-rescue group and charity on the East Coast. I heard they asked her to run for governor once, but she turned them down."

Anna is writing furiously while Victoria is talking, but I'm thinking we haven't turned up anything that really helps us clear Marsh. I glance at my watch. Time to begin disengaging from our chatty hostess.

"I want to thank you so much. Actually seeing a place like this helps me be authentic in my fictional setting. And those are some interesting rumors, uh, theories."

"Oh, two more ideas stuck around for a while. Some said the security guard was one of the young men Maggie supposedly mentored and was angry because she up and married some rich guy. They theorized that he meant to kill Maggie's horse in the next stall but mixed up the stall numbers."

Something niggles at my brain, a thought not yet fully formed. "And the last theory?"

"Some said Maggie killed the horse because she wanted Marsh to ride her horse, not Kate's, in the competition. Kate's horse had already won the first two legs of the competition—dressage, and cross-country. He was a shoo-in to win the show-jumping and the entire event the next day."

Anna is scribbling this information down, and I'm thinking it over when a vibration at my hip makes me jump. Then my phone begins to ring in my back pocket. I smile my embarrassment but frown when I look at the screen. Few people have my personal cell number, and Caller ID identifies the caller as an international number. I answer anyway.

"Hello?"

The voice is female but deep, with that warm quality that makes you want to trust it—like James Earl Jones or Cate Blanchett sound.

"Kate Parker. I'm calling for Lauren Everhart. Do I have the right number?"

My heart leaps. "Yes! Ms. Parker, thanks so much for calling." Anna and Victoria both pause their quiet conversation when I identify who's calling.

"It's Kate, please. And I couldn't avoid it. My wife's a bigger fan of yours than Skyler is, and that's saying a lot. Besides, Skyler told me what you're up to, and she's right. We should have kept at it until we found who did kill Jakobi. That was my horse. We've let Marsh down by not following through."

I turn my back to them and lower my voice. "I'm actually here at the horse park, and Victoria Banks is giving my assistant and me a tour. Do you mind if I put you on speaker?" Her answer will tell me how much she trusts Victoria. And how much I can trust any information Victoria gives me.

"Vic is there? Go right ahead."

I turn back to my companions and change the setting on my phone. "Okay. You're on speaker."

"Vickie, you old trickster. Are you still charming boys, or have you found a silver-haired fox like yourself to den up with?" Kate's previously smooth voice booms over the phone.

Victoria grins, her blue eyes glinting. "I see Laura's still sanding away at your rough edges, you old dog."

"She says I'm a lost cause. We'll call you when we're back and set up a time to come down and play golf."

"That would be wonderful. I'll look forward to it."

"But that's not why I called, Ms. Everhart."

"Please. It's Lauren. I'm guessing Skyler told you why I wanted to talk to you?"

"Can you tell me what you've found out so far?"

"It's easier to tell you where we're stuck. I need to find two people I think are key to this case, if not suspects. I'm trying to track down Maggie Talmadge and the security guard assigned to the barn that night. I got his name from the police report, but it's a dead end. He's disappeared."

"Yeah. That's pretty much why I stopped looking into it. I was about to hire a private detective to find him, but Marsh was so hurt, she just wanted it to go away."

"It hasn't gone away, Kate. It's a weight that's still crushing her."

"Again, I feel really bad that I haven't done something before."

We all go silent for a few seconds.

"I'm going to crack this, Kate. I just need some help."

"Well, Tallie should be easy to find. She keeps a low profile these days, but she's still around the eventing circuit somewhere."

"Who?" My insides freeze at the name.

"Tallie. Maggie Talmadge. That's what she went by in college, but after she graduated, she started introducing herself as Maggie."

Anna is googling on her phone. "Hi, Kate. This is Anna, Lauren's assistant. Do you know her full name?"

"Margaret S. Talmadge. I don't know what the S stands for. She'd never tell us. I used to tease her by calling her Shirley because she was always saying"—Kate changes her voice into a perfect imitation of Tallie's—" 'surely you don't mean that, Katie Parker.' "

"You were friends?"

"We ran in the same crowd in college, but we were never friends. She was always causing trouble and telling lies about other people. I steered clear of her mostly."

"I think I have her," Anna says. "Looks like she married a month before the horse was killed. Margaret Talmadge Bouling. Is this her?" She holds her phone out for Victoria and me to see.

"That's Maggie," Victoria says.

I want to throw up. It's the woman I know as Tallie. I've been set up and used. She pretended to be my friend, then fucked the woman I've fallen in love with. My shame turns to rage. "That fucking bitch. I'm going to drag her out of her house and through the mud." I meant that figuratively, of course, and I know these women in our conversation group will recognize the Southern expression.

"I guess she's also the woman you know as Tallie?" Anna's question is rhetorical, but I give a curt nod.

"If anybody has a photo of the security guard, can't you use some fancy facial-recognition software to check for an alias? That's what they do on *CSI*," Victoria says.

Normally, I'd dismiss anything from a television show, but facial-recognition software isn't a bad idea.

"We do!" Anna says. "I gave the guard's name to my girlfriend, Alisha. She's a research librarian and has access to several court and criminal databases. She found several police mug shots of him."

"We have a friend who has a friend in the FAA," Kate says. "I can ask if she'll run his picture through their database. If it won't get her in trouble, of course."

"Alisha turned up four different mug shots. He has a beard in one, and his hair has the tips bleached in another. They all look very different." Anna readies her pen and paper. "Give me an email address, and I'll send you all of them."

Finally. The dead end I've been looking at is opening up to several possibilities. "I'll leave tracking down the security guard to you guys. I'm going after Tallie-slash-Maggie. I've got a very personal bone to pick with her."

CHAPTER TWENTY-TWO

The bar in Cancun is a dive, a far cry from the fancy hotels and white beaches where tourists hang out. He's slouched in a straight-back chair at a small table in a dark corner. The FAA friend came through, and we've traced his alias to here. I immediately recognize him from the mug shot I've mentally labeled scruffy stubble.

"Robert Michael Swearington?"

He tenses and peers up at Skyler and me. "You got the wrong guy."

"No. We don't." I hold out my phone that displays the scruffy-stubble mug shot. "We're not cops. We just want to talk to you."

A tired-looking woman comes to our table. "Get you drink?" she asks in English, but I hold out my credit card and reply in Spanish.

"Two of your best local beers, unopened bottles, please. A bottle of the very best tequila you have, and a hundred-dollar tip for yourself."

Her face brightens, and with a nod, she heads back to the bar.

"Mind if we sit down?" It's clear Skyler intends to sit no matter how he answers.

He shrugs. "Not if you're going to share that tequila she just ordered." His bottle is empty, and the glass in front of him holds only a finger of liquor.

We sit. He stares at us, and we stare at him. Finally, he breaks the silence.

"You shouldn't have given her your credit card. Even with the hundred-dollar tip, her old man who owns this dive will steal the information from it."

"I've traveled extensively, Mr. Swearington, so I know the tricks. That's why I requested unopened bottles. I want nothing but beer in my bottle. And the card I gave her is preloaded. If she runs the number again, the most she can get is a couple hundred dollars. And judging from this place, she could use the money."

The woman reappears with two unopened bottles of beer and a bottle opener, then scurries back to the bar, where an older man is unlocking a cabinet built under the shelves that hold his liquor selection. While he digs around for the top-shelf tequila, she polishes two shot glasses with a clean cloth.

"So. What do you want to talk to Robert Swearington about?" He carefully avoids confirming his identity.

I want to smile. His impatience tells me that all those *Law & Order* episodes I binged while I was in my cups over Marsh's rejection are paying off. The detectives always let the suspect stew until he gets nervous and starts talking.

The woman appears again, placing the shot glasses before Skyler and me, then a bottle of Patrón Extra Añejo between the glasses. Robert straightens in his chair, his eyes never leaving the bottle as Skyler fills both shot glasses.

I activate my iPod-sized recorder and slide it to the middle of the table. "You can rot in this bar for all we care, but we want to know who killed that horse four years ago so we can finally clear our friend Marsh."

Skyler downs her shot of Patrón and plunks the glass back on table. She licks her lips. "Damn, that's smooth."

When Robert unconsciously licks his lips, Skyler moves my shot halfway toward him. He reaches for it, but she pulls it back an inch or two. "Not yet."

I prod him. "I want to know what happened the night Kate Parker's horse, Jakobi, was killed."

"How should I know? I was a temporary security guard, not a police detective."

Skyler slides the shot glass back toward us. "Try again."

His hand trembles as he withdraws it. "Ask that Talmadge bitch. She can give you all the details, including why her twisted mind thought it up."

Skyler slides the shot glass all the way to him this time. He snatches it and closes his eyes as he swallows. He hums, then shoves the glass back to Skyler. She refills it but doesn't push it back to him. "We want the details from you before we corner her."

Both his hands are trembling so bad, he hides them in his lap, under the table.

"I can't. She's got me by the balls." His eyes flick to me. "Sorry, ma'am."

I want to laugh. Skyler is about four inches taller than my five-nine, with broad shoulders. She's very slim but not as fine-boned as I am. Obviously, he's decided that she's my muscle for this interrogation. I decide to play a little good cop-bad cop. Or, I prefer, mafia boss and enforcer. I have to get out of my head, or I'll burst out laughing and blow the scene we've set.

"We don't want to hurt you, Robert. We want her. If she's blackmailing you, we can help protect you."

He looks from me to Skyler, then to the Patrón. I nod to Skyler, and she pushes the full shot glass to him. He downs it and pushes it back for her to refill.

"Tell us what happened that night, Robert. Help us clear Marsh. Let us help you. We need evidence to take the Talmadge bitch down." I keep my voice soft, and he leans forward in his chair, like a snake charmed by my words.

He closes his eyes briefly, then begins.

"She's a dominatrix, and I was one of her *students*. I'm not really into that stuff, but she's an expert. She singles out a teen, sometimes younger, and it doesn't seem to matter if they're male or female. She looks for a kid who either has no family or one with great ambition but no resources. That was me. I knew about Marsh because Maggie—she made me call her mistress when we weren't in public—would whip me if I couldn't get the horse to do what she wanted. And while she was whipping me, she'd tell me how good Marsh was. Marsh could ride any horse, she'd say. Marsh never misses a jump. Marsh is perfect at dressage and fearless on the cross-country route. So much better than me."

His hands are shaking again, so Skyler shoves a full shot to him, and he knocks it back. When he places it on the table, she refills it. He holds it with his fingertips but doesn't drink yet.

"I never actually met Marsh, though. Maggie has farms in the States and an estate in Germany. I think she married young and inherited that when her old geezer of a husband died. Hell, she probably figured out a way to kill him and get away with it."

He's drifting off course, so I pull him back in.

"What happened that night, Robert?"

He downs the shot in his hand. "She married Bouling. He isn't old but has the same kink she does. She wanted me to let him fuck me. That's when I left. I had nothing but a few thousand in cash and the phone number of another guy who escaped her. He'd gotten a job with a stable in South Carolina and sent a secret message to me. He said he could get me a job with the polo people down there." He raised his eyes to me. "I just wanted to be around horses, you know. They are beautiful and honest, not like people."

Skyler refills his glass again, and he drinks it. "How could you kill Jakobi, if you love horses so much?"

He shakes his head vigorously. "I didn't kill him. She wanted me to, but I couldn't do it, so she did."

Skyler fills his glass one more time. "Lay it out for us, Robert. What was her plan?"

He stares at the shot of Patrón but doesn't drink it. His tolerance for alcohol tells me he's a heavy drinker because he shows few signs of being drunk.

"I made it as far as North Carolina, and my truck broke down. I called my friend, and he said he could come pick me up in a few days when he was off work. In the meantime, he told me about the big international show near Southern Pines. Go there, he said, and you can probably pick up some work cleaning stalls or something to get some cash. So, I left my truck with a mechanic and hitched my way down there. They had an opening for two guards to keep an eye on the premium barns at night. All we had to do was watch the monitors and walk through to check on the horses every hour. If somebody came around who wasn't listed on our clipboard, we were told to turn them away and call the police if they gave us any trouble. The pay was good, and there was a really cheap hotel close by, where the other guard was staying. He said there were two beds in his room, and we could share if I would give him half the cost when they paid us off at the end of the show."

My beer is empty, and the bar is stifling. Our hostess returns with two fresh, cold beers. I tuck twenty dollars in her hand and point to Robert, but he shakes his head.

"Can't stand beer," he says.

"That night?" I prompt him again.

"Guess who I literally run into on my way to check out the barns? Maggie. She saw the ID badge they gave me clipped to my shirt and offered to take me to lunch. I'd been eating fast food for weeks, and I knew she wouldn't eat at any restaurant that has a drive-through. She was being all nice and begged me to forgive her for the Bouling thing. I knew better, but she'd had me under her thumb since I was fifteen, almost ten years. It was so easy to fall back under her sway. Maggie fed me, fucked me in her hotel room, and put two thousand in cash in my pocket. It was more than enough to hitch a ride back to the garage that had my truck and pay off the bill. But everything comes with a price."

He downs the shot in his hand and runs a shaky hand over his buzz cut. "Maggie said Marsh would check on Jakobi, because she always checks the legs of any horse the night before she rides them. Maggie told me to wait until Marsh came by, then she gave me a bag of rat shit…you know, the little pellets, and a small knife. She told me to make small cuts in the cable going to the security camera, like a rat chewed it, and sprinkle the turds around it. I knew she was up to something, but I didn't know what."

He closes his eyes and takes a deep breath.

"Marsh came by. We talked a bit while she checked Jakobi over good. She was really nice to me, but I didn't tell her I knew Maggie because they were still involved. So, I disabled the camera and texted Maggie like she said. She showed up minutes later with latex gloves on. She gave me the syringe and told me to inject Jakobi, but I wouldn't do it. I knew it must be something to hurt him. He was so beautiful."

Robert's eyes fill with tears. Maybe it's the Patrón opening him up, but he doesn't even try to hide them when they trickle down his cheek into his stubble.

"She snatched the syringe from me and injected it right into his vein. I was frozen for a few minutes. I couldn't believe she did it. Jakobi stumbled in his stall. I grabbed my phone to call the emergency-vet number they gave us if anything went wrong, like a horse going down with colic during the night, but she slapped it out of my hand. I told her I was going to call the police, but she said the only fingerprints on the syringe were mine because she was wearing gloves, so I better shut up and play it cool."

His shoulders shake with silent sobs now. "She told me what to say and made me repeat it back several times while she waited to make sure he'd die." Robert clamps his hands over his ears. "I could hear him struggling to stand up and grunting with pain."

Skyler pours him another shot and downs one herself while he drinks it. She pours again, and they drink.

"I don't know what was in that syringe, but I wished I had another one to stick her with. Then I wished for another one so I could stick it in my own vein. When she was sure he was dead, she told me to wait an hour and call the vet. I don't know how I handled the police. They wrote off my muddled account of what happened because I obviously was in shock."

I give him a minute to collect himself a little, but I have more questions. "How did you end up down here, Robert?"

"Maggie always kept several fake passports for me. I found out why when she put one in my hand and bought me a ticket on a plane to here. She told me to lay low for a while and paid for a small apartment on the better side of town that first year. She kept money in an account for me to live on. She'd fly down every month or so and fuck my brains out for a few days, then leave. But that night haunted me. I had nightmares and started to drink. I was drunk the last time I saw her. She said I was disgusting and told me to straighten up, or I'd be sorry. We had a huge fight. A couple of days later, I woke up in a hospital ward. They said I'd overdosed and that a woman brought me in, paid my bill, and left me. I think she drugged me but took me to the hospital knowing they'd save me. It was a warning. The next time she'd leave me to die."

I shudder. This is the same woman who befriended me, sucked me right in. She had to be a psychopath. Has my life been in danger? Will it be in danger if I can prove what Robert has told us?

"I'd been stashing the money she'd been sending me, so I walked away with my clothes and rented a crappy room on this side of town. She's probably already tracked down where I am, though. I figure I'm a dead man if I ever try to go back to the States, but I'm ready to risk it. I'm drinking myself to death here."

"I've recorded what you said, but if we get a lawyer here to transcribe it as an affidavit, will you come to his office and sign it?" I leave out that he'll need to be sober and cleaned up to do that.

He looks at us. His eyes and nose are red from crying, but I see a new spark in his eyes. "I can do better than that. If you'll take me back to my place, I'll put hard evidence in your hands."

Chapter Twenty-three

My heart leaps when I see her. Her new stallion, Crescendo, is in the crossties and her back to me as she feels along his front legs for any signs of soreness or heat indicating inflammation.

"Hello, Marsh." It's been nearly a month since I walked in on Marsh with Maggie-Tallie, and in the past two weeks, we've managed to put the final pieces of the sordid puzzle together. I've practiced what to say over and over during the past twenty-four hours but can't remember any of it now.

She stands slowly and turns around. I see something new in her eyes—longing, sadness, resignation. I smile and hold her gaze, hoping to convey all the love I have for this woman. For the young teen who was expertly wooed and manipulated by a psychopath. For the scarred adult who has survived but carries the weight of her past on her shoulders. She turns away and kneels again, but her hands rest on the stallion's legs without resuming the examination.

"You shouldn't be here, Lauren."

"I'm exactly where I should be, Marsh. I was wrong not to tell you that I was writing a fictional account loosely based on your unsolved mystery. I am so sorry for that."

"It doesn't matter."

"It does. I love you, and I'm here to fight for you."

Clapping sounds from the open door of the tack room, and Maggie steps out. "That's so touching. Isn't it, Marsh, dear?"

"Shut up, Maggie." Marsh stands again and glares at her. Then she unhooks Crescendo from the crossties and secures him in his stall. "I've warned you about going after Lauren. If you harm one hair on her head, I'll go to prison gladly after I break your neck."

My heart soars, and I step up to grab Marsh's hand in mine.

Her eyes are so full of sadness when she looks at me. "Leave, Lauren. I'm a virus that spreads to everyone around me as long as she's around."

I touch her cheek. "It's okay. You're not the one going to prison." I raise my voice. "Marshal." An armed man holding out his US Marshal's badge steps into the barn corridor, and I point at Maggie. "That's her."

He walks toward Maggie. "I'm US Marshal Trent Ford," he says. "Margaret Talmadge Bouling, you are under arrest for destruction of property, felony animal cruelty, and obstruction of justice, for starters."

Maggie's face grows red. "What's this about?" She whirls on Marsh. "What have you done?"

Skyler and Kate, who flew back a week early to be here for Maggie's arrest, step into the corridor behind the marshal.

"We found Robert Swearington, Maggie," Kate says.

"And you're arresting me because of some outlandish story he's told you?"

"Lauren and I intended to get an affidavit from him, but as it turns out, we didn't need it," Skyler says.

I squeeze Marsh's hand and pick up the story. "You see, Maggie-Tallie, Robert knew you were up to something bad, though he didn't know what. So he disabled the security camera like you instructed, but before he texted you, he planted a second camera in the rafters you didn't see. It recorded everything." I held up a thumb drive. "I brought you a copy so you can give it to your lawyer."

Marsh grabs it as Maggie lunges to get it. "What does this show?"

"Robert was one of the students she groomed from a teen, like you," I tell her. "She ordered Robert to inject Jakobi with an overdose of selenium. When he refused, she snatched the syringe from him and did it herself. You see, she was wearing latex gloves, but he wasn't. She pointed out that his fingerprints were the only ones on the syringe and threatened to turn it over to the police if he didn't go along with her. Then she shipped him out of the country under an alias. That's why Kate couldn't find him."

"I'll kill him." Maggie snarls the words. "Where is the little drunk?"

"He's in rehab at an undisclosed location," Kate says. "We think that, with therapy, he'll survive the damage you've done to him. I'll make sure he gets the help he needs and a job when he's able."

"And I can add communicating threats to the charges against you," the marshal says, pulling out his handcuffs.

Maggie spins and runs for the opposite entrance, and Marsh moves to chase her, but I hold her back as Harrison and Alex appear, blocking Maggie's escape. The marshal handcuffs her and recites her Miranda rights as he leads her away.

Marsh turns to Kate. "I'm so sorry. I was trying to get away from her and make my own way when I offered to ride Jakobi for you. If you hadn't hired me, she wouldn't have killed your horse."

"Not true, Marsh. She's mentally ill and would have gone after Jakobi anyway because he was going to take first place from her entry. She's the only one to blame, and I'm so sorry I didn't follow through and figure this out for you four years ago. Lauren is the one who insisted you'd never be free of it until we did find who did kill Jakobi. She never gave up on you."

Harrison comes to his sister and hugs her long and hard. "It's all okay now. We're going out to watch some of the show so you and Lauren can talk. She's a good woman, Marsh. You can trust her."

Kate and Skyler walk past us to follow the men, but Skyler pauses to squeeze Marsh's shoulder. "If you're not up for it, either Jules or I can show Crescendo for you today. You've got a couple of hours until your class, so you or Lauren just let us know if you need us. We've got your back."

I lead Marsh into the small office, and she sags against the door after I've closed it to give us privacy. "Maggie has Butter and says she'll shoot him if I don't ride for her again."

Her eyes fill, and she looks up at the rafters to collect herself. "That's what you saw, Lauren. She said she'd tell me where he is and let me buy him back if I'd fuck her one more time. I knew I couldn't trust her, but I was desperate." Her breath hitches. "He was my horse when I first tried out for the Olympic team, but he was too young then and not quite good enough. Maggie made me give him up and ride a better horse. I hunted him down and talked the owner into leasing him at my stables when he wouldn't sell him. I'll probably never find him again. She might have already killed him."

I hold her face in my hands. "I have him. It's a long story, but Alex and Harrison told me what Maggie was holding over your head, and we tracked him down, too. Kate Parker has a lot of connections. Turns out, Maggie's husband bought Butter for her, but the papers were still in his name. He was happy to sell him to me when we told him she was about to be arrested. Butter is safe, and I'm his new owner. I'm just waiting to see if you have a stall free for a new boarder. That is, if you'll let me come back to Langston Farms."

I'm caught off guard when Marsh falls into my arms and sobs. We slowly slide to the floor, and I hold her as tight as I can.

CHAPTER TWENTY-FOUR

"What do you need, Lauren?" Marsh's lips, her tongue taste my neck, and I close my eyes.

"I...I don't know." Truthfully, I do know, but I'm afraid to ask. She reads my hesitation. "Yes, you do." She fills my glass again with the potent mixture of Fireball and Apple Crown Royal, my favorite cocktail.

We've been a bit shy with each other since we reconnected a week ago. We made slow, sweet love the night of our reunion, and it was so deep, so emotional. A new Marsh has emerged since Maggie was arrested. She is kind and lighthearted, and I fall even more in love with her every day.

But I miss some of the old Marsh, the one kissing down my neck right now. I treasure our soft moments together, but sometimes I still hunger for the dominating Marsh willing to bend me over the dining-room table and take me. I struggle to explain that contradiction to her now, fearing it might drag out bad memories of Maggie's sexual demands.

I gulp down more of the truth-inducing liquor, but my fear is too great, and I deflect. "I'm never going to get the hang of posting a trot. I'm just too awkward."

"You are not." She emphasizes each word. "You are beautiful on horseback." She kisses her way up my neck and sucks my earlobe.

I only need to sway backward an inch, maybe less, to feel her breasts against my back. Are her nipples as hard and aching as mine? If I fall against her, will her arms come around me?

"I want to be beautiful for you. I just can't find the rhythm." I hope she can hear the plea in my tone, read the submission in my words.

"You have control issues, but I understand." Her lips are gentle as she moves to the other side of my neck, tasting and caressing. "When you finally win control of your life, it's hard to give up even a little to anyone else. I understand. And it's okay." The kisses stop, and I feel her arms relax and the pressure of her breasts against my back lessen. She's pulling back.

A shudder runs through me, and I tilt my head in invitation for more. "I don't know." I'm talking about posting a trot now, but she's talking about sex. "You make me want to. I need for you to help me."

"But you have to tell me what you want, what you really need."

I whimper as I stare into the fireplace. Haven't I told her before with my actions? If I spell it out for her, will my words burn us like the flames that are consuming the wood?

She turns me in her arms, and her mouth is on mine. Her lips, smooth and warm, taste of the cognac she's drinking. Her long fingers stroke my cheek and down my neck as her tongue asks entrance and I open to her. I hum as she explores my mouth, our tongues sliding and flicking and filling, an unconscious rehearsal of what we both hope will follow.

"I can help you, Lauren, if you'll tell me what you need, what you desire."

I tremble. Can I? I stare at the floor and whisper my fear. "I don't want to hurt you."

She freezes, still as a statue for several long seconds, an eternity while I drown in my fear. She lifts my chin with her finger, and her expression of confusion makes my eyes fill.

"I love you, Marsh. I'm so in love with you, I never want my desires to cause you pain."

"Oh, Lauren. Don't you know I'm in love with you, too? How

do you know your desires aren't also mine?" She brushes her lips against mine, then kisses the tears on my cheeks. "I've never been in a wholesome relationship, but I've spent a lot of time in therapy after getting away from Maggie. I've learned relationships don't survive without truth and communication. You have control issues, and I have trust issues. We're not going to last long if you aren't honest and open with me so I can trust that you won't keep things from me again."

I nod. She's right. I clear my throat and try to scrape up some courage, but my mouth opens and closes with no words forming. I'm so afraid we're both too damaged to be together.

"Talk to me, please. I have to know that if I do something you don't like, you'll tell me. If you don't, then I'll find it hard to tell you what I need, what I desire."

"You promise to be honest, too?"

She touches my lips with hers again. "I promise."

I swallow hard to loosen the tightness in my throat. "Because of my overbearing father, I do insist on having control of almost everything in my life." I shrug. "I don't mind advice, but I make my own decisions. Don't ever order in a restaurant for me unless I ask you to. It's a trigger."

"Noted. I don't like people whispering behind my back and keeping things from me. So, no matter how well-intentioned, never try to throw a surprise party for me."

I nod. This is getting easier. "Never accept a dinner invitation for us without checking with me first, even if you know I'll want to accept. That's another trigger."

For the first time, Marsh averts her eyes from mine. Her jaw works like she's chewing on the words she wants to say.

I touch her cheek to bring her gaze back to mine. "Tell me," I say softly.

She looks stormy. "I don't share."

Share? Food? Her closet? Her shower with another person? "Can you be more specific?"

"I don't want to share you with other lovers. I don't have a right to ask, but you're the only woman I want in my bed, and I want to be the only one in yours."

"You have every right, and that's what I want, too." I place my hands on her cheeks and draw her in for a heated kiss to seal the deal. We're both breathing hard when I finally release her. Her admission is the courage I need.

I clear my throat. "There's one exception to my control issues." My cheeks are burning. How do I say this?

"Tell me," Marsh says, turning my own soft words back on me.

I suck in a breath. "While I like to be in control..." I pause while she takes my hand and brings it to her lips for a soft kiss, "I...I like giving up that control in the bedroom."

Her eyes darken, and her voice lowers to a sexy tenor. "What about the dining room?"

My belly tightens at the memory of her bending me over my dining-room table and fucking me. I clarify. "Anywhere we choose to be intimate." Then the image of Maggie bent over Marsh's desk surfaces. My entire face and neck scorch now, but with anger rather than embarrassment. Anger at Maggie Talmadge Bouling.

"It's taken me a long time to admit that to myself, and even longer to find the woman I trust to give that control to." I hold her gaze so she can see the truth in them. "I love when we make gentle, sweet love together, but I also like when you take control." I force myself not to look away to speak my last truth. "I don't want it, though, if it hurts you. If it reminds you of what Maggie demanded from you."

Marsh's blue eyes blaze with desire and power. "It wasn't just that I was young when she seduced me. She culled me from a group of teens because she could see my natural desire to dominate, and she used that tendency to bind me to her."

I gasp as she spins me around and pulls me against her. My earlier questions are answered. I *can* feel her breasts through the thin silk of my shirt, and her nipples *are* as hard as mine. Her breath is on my neck again, hot and sweet from the cognac.

"I'm going to the kitchen to get a tray of something for us to eat. While I'm gone, I want you to go into the therapy room, strip, and get in the whirlpool." She touches my cheek. "Go now."

Yes, no. Can I trust that this is truly what she wants, what she needs, too? This is what I've wanted my entire adult life. A strong, handsome woman to whom I could trust my deepest secret desires.

❖

The water is hot and swirls sensuously around my naked body. The throbbing between my legs is growing along with my anticipation.

Marsh reappears as my hand is sliding down my belly for a little self-relief to take the edge off, and the whirlpool jets choose that moment to rest. I jerk my hand up, sure that she saw and read my intention as the water settled.

"I'll have to be more specific with my instructions," she says, setting a large tray at the pool's edge. Crackers, neat squares of cheese, and dark caviar are arranged next to two bottles of water and a black blindfold. Apparently, she has a thing for blindfolds.

She lowers her tall frame to the floor and pulls off her paddock boots. "Before I cover your eyes and accept the gift of your trust, I want to give you something."

Marsh stands and strips in a slow, deliberate tease.

She tugs her shirt from her jeans, then releases each button. My mouth is dry when the garment drops to the floor. No bra covers her small, high breasts. She is smooth yet sinewy like a cat, lean muscles gliding under golden skin as she moves. Her tan lines are faint, and I imagine her standing on a mountaintop—bare-chested, arms flung back—to soak in the sun where it isn't permitted to touch while she is clothed. She flicks open the buttons on the fly of her jeans and slides them and her underwear down smooth hips and impossibly long thighs to step out of them. She's a true blonde, neatly trimmed and glistening. Is that because of me? I force my gaze up to hers, and she smiles. "Maybe I'll allow you to taste me later."

She picks up the blindfold and slips into the pool. "Sight can be distracting, like static on an old speaker when you're trying to listen to music." She moves behind me, molding my naked body to hers. I close my eyes and moan at the slide of her breasts along my shoulders, the fit of her hips cupping my ass, the glide of her skin caressing mine. "Your desire to experience intimacy on a deeper level just triggered your natural reflex to shut down your sight and concentrate on your other senses."

I open my eyes. She's right. That's why we close our eyes when we kiss? When we orgasm?

She moves around to face me and holds up the blindfold. "We're going to use the blindfold to help you concentrate on what you're feeling."

Before I can respond, her mouth is on mine, soft and asking, then hot and demanding. I barely feel the blindfold slip over my closed eyes. I desperately wrap my legs around her lean torso and crush my breasts against hers to anchor myself in this darkness. She gently ends our kiss. My breath is loud and ragged in my sightless world, but I can feel her heart pounding along with mine.

"You're an eager student, but you have to learn to pace yourself," she says. She guides me over to an underwater ledge, where she sits and pulls me onto her lap. Then she takes my hand and wraps my fingers around a bottle.

"Hold on to this. We're going to taste some things, and you'll need to clear your palate in between with this water."

I take a long drink. What I really want is to taste her, all of her.

"Open," she says, dropping a morsel on my tongue.

Cheese. Creamy, yet sharp. "Brie?"

"Very good. Drink some water."

I do as she tells me.

"Open." Another morsel. Both sweet and buttery, melting instantly on my tongue.

I hum with pleasure. "Butter fudge. You didn't get that in Germany."

"No. I flew back through London and picked it up in the airport." This correct response earns me another long kiss, and I take advantage of our weightlessness in the water to turn and straddle her lap before the kiss ends.

I drink some water, pleased with myself. Ready for more, I flex my hips to rub my aching clit against her hard abdomen. Her arm encircling my ass tightens.

"Open." The earlier gentle request is now a curt command. A buttery cracker laden with something thick and salty, like how I know she'll taste. "Caviar. The expensive type."

"Drink the rest."

I drain the bottle as she rises and carries me from the pool to lay me on what I surmise is the massage table. Then she's drying me, a thick, heated towel caressing my skin, rubbing across my swollen nipples. She's careful to dry every inch of me—the plane of my collarbone, my armpits, every finger on my hand, inside my navel. She skips my crotch and diverts to my feet, where she dries both feet and each toe in a gentle massage. Then she sucks each toe into her mouth while I squirm and then dries them again. She rubs the towel up one leg, then down the other. I'm a boiling volcano aching to erupt.

"Marsh."

"You are so beautiful, Lauren. I could spend an entire night just touching you and worshipping your body."

"Please, I need you." I move my hand toward my crotch to indicate where I need her, but she grabs my hand and closes it around the table's edge.

"Don't let go of the table. And do not climax. You will come only when I give my permission."

That command alone is enough to make me come, and I squeeze my legs together to hold my climax off. I hear the small sound of something popping open, and then her hands are massaging something warm and oily into my calves. My focus narrows to her hands as they travel farther up my legs. Her probing fingers are past my knees now, and the pounding between my legs is excruciating. She digs into the quads of one leg, then the other. When she picks up each leg to flex my knees and then extend my hamstring, I wonder if she can see my arousal dripping onto the sheet under me. I can't bear it any longer.

"Marsh, please. For God's sake."

She growls and grabs both of my legs to jerk me toward the end of the table. I pull my knees up and open to her. Her fingers close on one nipple and twist hard.

I cry out at the pain but buck my hips at the pleasure it gives me. "I'm only allowing you to come to take your edge off so you can concentrate on your lesson." Her voice is tight, words fierce. Need, not anger. She wants this, too.

Then her mouth is on me, flicking and licking. She doesn't tease, and I am so ready that pressure builds almost immediately in my belly. "Yes, Marsh. Yes." She sucks hard and my clit swells tight, then explodes in waves of orgasmic pleasure.

As my climax fades, I feel suddenly dizzy and shove the blindfold up to orient myself. Her eyes are indigo pools as she looks up at me from between my legs. My juices wet her cheeks, and my legs still tremble from my release.

"You want to stop?"

Stop? I need more. I want her inside me. I want her on top of me. I want her under me. "No. I was a little dizzy. I needed to reorient my brain." I replace my blindfold, a little surprised that I'm instantly plunged back into the world of nothing but my spread legs and her hot breath. I like being temporarily blind. I shiver when her tongue bathes across my tender sex again.

"You taste like the finest caviar," she says.

I'm being lifted but this time settled on my feet. Her breasts press against my back, angling me forward, and her hands guide mine to the table.

"Keep your hands there and wait."

I listen to the slap of her bare feet as she leaves the room. Surprisingly, the waiting is as delicious as foreplay. Marsh is teaching me many things. The minutes seem endless before she's beside me again, roving my nakedness with her hands, massaging my breasts, tweaking my nipples, skating down my belly and finding my still-dripping sex. She strokes through my folds, kissing across my shoulders as she fingers my entrance. I am so ready for her.

"I need you inside me," I said. "Please, Marsh."

"I'll give you everything you need, Lauren, and more."

"Yes." My belly clenches as she thrusts a fat dildo between my legs and guides my hand to feel the length of it. "God, yes." I push against her hips, bending more to give her easy entrance, but her warm flesh moves away.

"Not now. You have a lesson to master."

She turns and lifts me. I wrap my arms around her neck, my legs around her hips, without thinking. I feel only the brush of her breasts against mine, the leather harness around her hips biting into my soft inner thighs, and the thick dildo bumping my belly as she walks. Then we are sitting, straddling a padded bench, and her mouth is on my neck, hot and sucking.

"I knew the day you walked into my stable that you would be an exquisite equestrian. Only you are holding yourself back. I don't want you to do that. You can touch me, too."

Afraid to unleash all that I feel, I hesitantly reach for her cheek, then trail my fingers down the strong curve of her shoulder. I palm the soft flesh of her breast and taste the rigid contour of her nipple, nipping it and smiling when she stiffens. She lifts my thighs to overlap hers and draws me closer, then slides her hand between my legs. I am stretched wide in my desire to press against her, and she easily thrusts two fingers inside. I gasp and cling to her.

She whispers in my ear as she pushes me back to lie on the bench. "Are you ready, Lauren?"

"So ready."

She pushes her way into me with a single smooth stroke, stretching me, filling me completely, just as she has filled my dreams since first I saw her. I clutch at her as she lifts me and reverses our positions. My blindness again threatens to disorient me, but the movement of the dildo and her soothing hands anchor me. She is lying on the bench, and I'm perched on top with my feet on the floor.

She draws me down and kisses me, her tongue exploring my mouth as her hips flex and her cock massages my ache. It is so delicious. I begin to move, sliding along her eight inches of pleasure, but we are out of sync. Marsh grasps my hips to stop me, and I whimper.

"You have to let go to flow with the rhythm, Lauren, rather than try to control it. Feel it."

She pushes my shoulders so that I'm sitting again. Is she stopping? I'm going to beg, plead. She can't stop now.

"Raise yourself a few inches."

I do as she asks, and she begins to pump into me. It isn't nearly enough, but I almost weep in relief.

"Feel the two-two beat. It's like a horse's trot."

My frustration is growing. I only want to feel the thrust of her cock, hard and fast.

"Concentrate. Master this, and I promise to give you a ride you won't forget."

Two-two beat. Two-two. Thrust, thrust. Thrust, thrust. Thrust, thrust.

"Now, on every second beat, you're going to rise and move your hips forward until my cock almost slips out. Then you'll sit back down on the next first beat." Her hands are on my hips. "Relax and let me guide you. Ready? Two-two-one."

My breath catches in my chest as the cock head scrapes across that spot inside that makes my clit swell and my body sing. One-two, one-two. Nothing exists but that long, shallow stroke, followed by a short, deep penetration. One-two. Long-short. Oh, ah.

I am so lost in our dance, the burst of orgasm catches me completely by surprise. I cry out and lose my stride, scrambling for the security of Marsh's embrace.

"That's how you post a trot," she says when I still. "You came without asking for permission. I'm going to let that slide and save that lesson for another time."

"I may need to practice it a few more times." I'm nowhere near sated and groan as she withdraws her cock slowly and smoothly.

I snatch off my blindfold and toss it away, then lick at the sweat coating her belly. I hold her eyes as I move lower, pulling the harness and dildo down her hips to expose her blond curls. "May I reward the teacher?"

Now she groans but nods her consent.

Her clit is long and fat. I suck it between my lips, then tongue the length of it. She is thick and salty, and she growls as I feed hungrily on what she offers. She tangles her long fingers in my hair and tugs painfully, and I clamp her tender tissues carefully in my teeth. Her hips surge upward, and my tongue finds the hard knot of nerves that makes her curl up from the bench with a shout and shudder.

Her grip on my hair relaxes as her climax releases her to fall back to the bench. "I think that was worth extra credit." I'm pleased that she sounds a bit breathless.

I sit up and pull the harness over her hips again, quickly tightening the straps.

"No. I have a different extra credit in mind." I stand and turn my back to her. Then I bend to place my hands on the bench, presenting myself to her at eye level. "Show me how a professional rider does it, Marsh. Show me everything." I close my eyes. I want to focus on the pleasure she promises.

I shiver at her fingertips caressing my sensitive buttocks, then her warm lips placing soft kisses in their wake.

"I like to gentle my rides, so I check them over before I mount."

Her fingers slide across my stiff clit, then into my slick entrance. I'm dripping halfway down my thighs after two orgasms, and she gathers my moisture to spread it upward. I've never been much for anal play, but I squirm at the surprising sensation when she circles my anus, pressing only lightly.

"Do you like that, Lauren?"

"I haven't…it does feel good, but I haven't—"

"It's okay." She presses a little more, then eases back.

More kisses along my buttocks. My belly, my sex clenches. I want her inside me, pushing, filling. The kisses move up my back, and her hard nipples rake across my butt cheeks, then press against my shoulders. Her teeth are sharp as she bites my shoulder. The bulbous head of her cock presses into me. I feel nothing but its slow, tortuous progress past that sweet spot of sensation as she stretches and fills me fuller than I'd ever felt before. Only then do I realize that while I concentrated on her cock stretching me, she's also pushed her finger into my ass.

Sweet Jesus, yes.

"Good girl," she croons. "You took that well. Now, let's put you through your paces."

She starts slow, too slow, easing her cock and finger out, then in. Out, then in. My fingernails bite into the padded bench, and I arch my back like a shameless whore in heat as she rides me.

"Faster, baby. I need you to fuck me, damn it."

She pauses, her breathing heavy. She must need it, too. She slowly withdraws her finger from my ass. I'm surprised to miss it and open my eyes to look over my shoulder at the sound of her fumbling with something.

"I need both my hands free," she says. "And you're open enough to handle this. Close your eyes again."

I do as she bids and jerk at the cool, smooth object pressed against my puckered hole. She flexes her hips, working her cock as she pushes the slim, oblong object into my ass. It goes easily, then begins to vibrate.

"Oh, my God. Oh, my God." My hips buck involuntarily, and then Marsh is bent over my back again, her arm encircling my waist, her hips thrusting into mine in a steady rhythm.

I want to hold on forever, but the vibration in my ass, the glide of her cock in and out of my pussy, and my clit stretched tight as I'm filled again and again are too much. All of it gathers low in my belly and bursts like an overfilled balloon, flooding through me in wave after wave.

Marsh rides out my climax in steady, smooth strokes until my screams die and I'm gasping for breath. I expect her to slow and withdraw, but still she rides me.

She rises and grips my hips. I gasp. Her change in angle hits something different. Her thrusts are deeper, more forceful. Yes. Sweet Jesus. Yes.

I give myself up, give her my control, feel her rhythm.

Her hips slap against my butt as she increases her pace. Out, IN, out, IN, out, IN. Her groans turn to growls. She jerks my hips back as she thrusts forward. IN, IN, IN. Slap, slap, slap. Her cock bores into me again and again. Slap, slap, slap.

I vibrate with each penetration. She takes me higher, closer with each stroke. My abused sex impossibly swells again, so full I think I'll die from the bolts of pleasure that radiate through me each time she pounds into me.

We are approaching the big jump and gathering to take it together.

"Lauren." Her call is hoarse and tight, and my heart and mind and body sing as I answer it.

"Marsh, yes."

"Touch yourself."

My hand flies to my clit, and we cry out together.

Epilogue

"A re you ready?"

Marsh leads Butter out to where I've tacked up Fancy for my lesson. Butter has been stabled most of the week since he was delivered to Langston Farms because Marsh wanted to make sure he wouldn't colic after his long trailer trip. Technically, he's my horse now, but I'm waiting for Marsh to give me her expert okay.

"Are you going to ride him?"

"Nope. You are," she says.

"Really?" I don't try to stop my grin.

"He's your horse, and he's perfect for you."

I glance around. The last class of kids has pretty much cleared out, and Alex is watching Jules ride Crescendo in the big ring. I steal a quick kiss. "You're perfect for me."

Marsh smiles and draws me to her for a longer kiss. "Let's see if those lessons pay off," she says when she ends our indulgence.

She gives me a leg up onto Butter. He's taller and not as round as Fancy. Marsh adjusts my stirrups and double-checks the girth. "How's he feel?"

I grin down at her. "Fantastic. He's tall."

"He has a longer stride than Fancy, so take him in the ring and walk him a bit until you feel comfortable. Then I want you to try a trot."

I make myself breathe and relax. Horses can feel your moods, and I am so nervous the reins would be slipping out of my hands if I wasn't wearing soft leather riding gloves. Halfway around the ring, I'm marveling at how smoothly Butter moves. Maybe that's where he got his registered name, Smooth as Butter.

We don't make it fully around the ring before I lift the reins and use my knees to urge him into a trot so smooth, I have no trouble sitting it. So, I press again with my knees, and he cleanly shifts into a faster trot. I ride nearly the length of the ring realizing that I'm posting his trot with no problem. We're in perfect sync.

"Oh my God, Marsh. He is so incredibly smooth." I urge him into a canter. It's like riding a rocking horse. I slow him again, curious to see if I can still post his trot. Several more times around the ring, and Marsh waves us in.

"If he doesn't feel right, Alex said he'd buy him, and we can find you another horse." The amusement in her eyes tells me she's teasing.

"He's perfect, and I'm never selling him."

"That's probably enough for him today. You'll need to ease him in before longer workouts." She mounts Fancy and waves for me to follow.

Butter and I ride alongside Marsh and Fancy on the wide, sandy tractor path that leads to the main pasture.

"I think I figured out your problem with posting," she says. "Over the years that you've been a runner, your body has developed a specific rhythm, and your brain locks it in. It's not that you were too tense to find Fancy's rhythm. When you relaxed, your brain wanted to settle into the more familiar rhythm of when you run. So, instead of insisting you learn to find the horse's rhythm, we needed to find a horse that matches you."

"And how did you know it would be Butter?"

"Seems that your lessons taught me something." Was that a blush creeping up her cheeks? "I rode Butter for several years, so after a few of our, uh, private riding lessons, I realized the two of you have the same rhythm."

Now my cheeks are burning. I'm about to tell her I may need frequent refresher lessons when Butter lifts his head and lets out a long, loud whinny.

Marsh laughs. "He's eager to see his old friends."

We reach the gate and dismount, then unsaddle both horses and check their feet for small stones that might be wedged in their hooves. Then Marsh opens the gate, and we lead them through. Butter whinnies to his friends again, and they raise their heads to scope out the newcomer. A mare calls to him, and part of the group abandons their grazing to walk toward us. Marsh releases Fancy, and Butter obediently lowers his head when I reach up to pull his bridle over his ears. As a reward, I'm careful not to let the bit clank against his teeth when I remove it.

It's a fairly brisk day and his workout was brief, so there's no sweat under his saddle. I pat his shoulder. "Go see your friends," I tell him.

Butter takes a few steps, then breaks into a beautiful prance as he nears the mare who answered his call. They put their heads together, nostrils flaring, and then Butter breaks away and stretches his long legs in a ground-eating trot, mane and tail flying, his greeting party right behind him. We watch as they chase each other, kick up their heels, and then pause to roll in the grass.

I nearly tear up at their joyous display. "That is unbridled joy."

Marsh places the saddle in her hands on the board fence and takes me in her arms.

"That's what you've done for me," she says. "Even after I left Maggie, I felt still bridled, with her holding the reins to jerk me back when she wanted. And she nearly did. I always suspected that she killed Jakobi, but I couldn't prove it. So, when she threatened to euthanize Butter, I believed she would if I didn't do what she wanted. I was so angry and ashamed when you walked in on that."

I smooth my hand over her cheek and touch my lips to hers. "Don't think about it. She can't hurt either of us, or Butter, any longer. I may have freed you, but you did the same for me. You are the only one I trust with my deepest desires. So, I'd say we've both been unbridled."

"I love you, Lauren Everhart."

"I'm glad, because I am so in love with you."

We pick up our saddles and start the walk back to the barn.

"Alex and Harrison want us to come over for dinner tonight. I told them I had to check with you."

I bump my shoulder against hers in a show of affection. "Only if we don't have to stay long after we eat. I'm hoping for a little unbridled joy myself tonight."

About the Author

D. Jackson Leigh grew up barefoot and happy, swimming in farm ponds and riding rude ponies in rural Georgia. She is a career journalist but has found her real passion in writing sultry lesbian romances laced with her trademark Southern humor and affection for horses.

She has published fourteen novels and one collection of short stories with Bold Strokes Books, winning four Golden Crown Literary Society awards in paranormal, romance, and fantasy categories. She was also a finalist in the romance category of the 2014 Lambda Literary Awards.

You can friend her at facebook.com/d.jackson.leigh.

Books Available From Bold Strokes Books

Flight SQA016 by Amanda Radley. Fastidious airline passenger Olivia Lewis is used to things being a certain way. When her routine is changed by a new, attractive member of the staff, sparks fly. (978-1-63679-045-9)

Home Is Where The Heart Is by Jenny Frame. Can Archie make the countryside her home and give Ash the fairytale romance she desires? Or will the countryside and small village life all be too much for her? (978-1-63555-922-4)

Moving Forward by PJ Trebelhorn. The last person Shelby Ryan expects to be attracted to Iris Calhoun, the sister of the man who killed her wife four years and three thousand miles ago. (978-1-63555-953-8)

Poison Pen by Jean Copeland. Debut author Kendra Blake is finally living her best life until a nasty book review and exposed secrets threaten her promising new romance with aspiring journalist Alison Chatterley. (978-1-63555-849-4)

Seasons for Change by KC Richardson. Love, laughter, and trust develop for Shawn and Morgan throughout the changing seasons of Lake Tahoe. (978-1-63555-882-1)

Summer Lovin' by Julie Cannon. Three different women, three exotic locations, one unforgettable summer. What do you think will happen? (978-1-63555-920-0)

Unbridled by D. Jackson Leigh. A visit to a local stable turns into more than riding lessons between a novel writer and an equestrian with a taste for power play. (978-1-63555-847-0)

VIP by Jackie D. In a town where relationships are forged and shattered by perception, sometimes even love can't change who you really are. (978-1-63555-908-8)

Yearning by Gun Brooke. The sleepy town of Dennamore has an irresistible pull on those who've moved away. The mystery Darian Benson and Samantha Pike uncover will change them forever, but the love they find along the way just might be the key to saving themselves. (978-1-63555-757-2)

A Turn of Fate by Ronica Black. Will Nev and Kinsley finally face their painful past and relent to their powerful, forbidden attraction? Or will facing their past be too much to fight through? (978-1-63555-930-9)

Desires After Dark by MJ Williamz. When her human lover falls deathly ill, Alex, a vampire, must decide which is worse, letting her go or condemning her to everlasting life. (978-1-63555-940-8)

Her Consigliere by Carsen Taite. FBI agent Royal Scott swore an oath to uphold the law, and criminal defense attorney Siobhan Collins pledged her loyalty to the only family she's ever known, but will their love be stronger than the bonds they've vowed to others, or will their competing allegiances tear them apart? (978-1-63555-924-8)

In Our Words: Queer Stories from Black, Indigenous, and People of Color Writers. Stories Selected by Anne Shade and Edited by Victoria Villaseñor. Comprising both the renowned and emerging voices of Black, Indigenous, and People of Color authors, this thoughtfully curated collection of short stories explores the intersection of racial and queer identity. (978-1-63555-936-1)

Measure of Devotion by CF Frizzell. Disguised as her late twin brother, Catherine Samson enters the Civil War to defend the Constitution as a Union soldier, never expecting her life to be altered by a Gettysburg farmer's daughter. (978-1-63555-951-4)

Not Guilty by Brit Ryder. Claire Weaver and Emery Pearson's day jobs clash, even as their desire for each other burns, and a discreet sex-only arrangement is the only option. (978-1-63555-896-8)

Opposites Attract: Butch/Femme Romances by Meghan O'Brien, Aurora Rey & Angie Williams. Sometimes opposites really do attract. Fall in love with these butch/femme romance novellas. (978-1-63555-784-8)

Under Her Influence by Amanda Radley. On their path to #truelove, will Beth and Jemma discover that reality is even better than illusion? (978-1-63555-963-7)

Swift Vengeance by Jean Copeland, Jackie D & Erin Zak. A journalist becomes the subject of her own investigation when sudden strange, violent visions summon her to a summer retreat and into the arms of a killer's possible next victim. (978-1-63555-880-7)

Wasteland by Kristin Keppler & Allisa Bahney. Danielle Clark is fighting against the National Armed Forces and finds peace as a scavenger, until the NAF general's daughter, Katelyn Turner, shows up on her doorstep and brings the fight right back to her. (978-1-63555-935-4)

When In Doubt by VK Powell. Police officer Jeri Wylder thinks she committed a crime in the line of duty but can't remember, until details emerge pointing to a cover-up by those close to her. (978-1-63555-955-2)

A Woman to Treasure by Ali Vali. An ancient scroll isn't the only treasure Levi Montbard finds as she starts her hunt for the truth—all she has to do is prove to Yasmine Hassani that there's more to her than an adventurous soul. (978-1-63555-890-6)

Before. After. Always. by Morgan Lee Miller. Still reeling from her tragic past, Eliza Walsh has sworn off taking risks, until Blake Navarro turns her world right-side up, making her question if falling in love again is worth it. (978-1-63555-845-6)

Bet the Farm by Fiona Riley. Lauren Calloway's luxury real estate sale of the century comes to a screeching halt when dairy farm heiress, and one-night stand, Thea Boudreaux calls her bluff. (978-1-63555-731-2)

Cowgirl by Nance Sparks. The last thing Aren expects is to fall for Carol. Sharing her home is one thing, but sharing her heart means sharing the demons in her past and risking everything to keep Carol safe. (978-1-63555-877-7)

Give In to Me by Elle Spencer. Gabriela Talbot never expected to sleep with her favorite author—certainly not after the scathing review she'd given Whitney Ainsworth's latest book. (978-1-63555-910-1)

Hidden Dreams by Shelley Thrasher. A lethal virus and its resulting vision send Texan Barbara Allan and her lovely guide, Dara, on a journey up Cambodia's Mekong River in search of Barbara's mother's mystifying past. (978-1-63555-856-2)

In the Spotlight by Lesley Davis. For actresses Cole Calder and Eris Whyte, their chance at love runs out fast when a fan's adoration turns to obsession. (978-1-63555-926-2)

Origins by Jen Jensen. Jamis Bachman is pulled into a dangerous mystery that becomes personal when she learns the truth of her origins as a ghost hunter. (978-1-63555-837-1)

Unrivaled by Radclyffe. Zoey Cohen will never accept second place in matters of the heart, even when her rival is a career, and Declan Black has nothing left to give of herself or her heart. (978-1-63679-013-8)

A Fae Tale by Genevieve McCluer. Dovana comes to terms with her changing feelings for her lifelong best friend and fae, Roze. (978-1-63555-918-7)

Accidental Desperados by Lee Lynch. Life is clobbering Berry, Jaudon, and their long romance. The arrival of directionless baby dyke MJ doesn't help. Can they find their passion again—and keep it? (978-1-63555-482-3)

Always Believe by Aimée. Greyson Walsden is pursuing ordination as an Anglican priest. Angela Arlingham doesn't believe in God. Do they follow their vocation or their hearts? (978-1-63555-912-5)

Courage by Jesse J. Thoma. No matter how often Natasha Parsons and Tommy Finch clash on the job, an undeniable attraction simmers just beneath the surface. Can they find the courage to change so love has room to grow? (978-1-63555-802-9)

I Am Chris by R Kent. There's one saving grace to losing everything and moving away. Nobody knows her as Chrissy Taylor. Now Chris can live who he truly is. (978-1-63555-904-0)